CHAPTER ONE

"I knew it was a bad idea to wear this thing."
The teenage boy in the tight-fitting costume was scratching at the material of the costume's neck. It was a black Lycra number with a fluorescent skeleton print on the front.

The boy underneath the costume was Darren Lewis and he and his girlfriend Lucy Smith were attending a Halloween party at Lucy's college. She had chosen a more comfortable outfit, and she was observing the father of her child through a werewolf mask.

"This feels strange," she said. "I think it's the first time we've had a proper night out together since Andrew was born."
The baby was over a year old now, and he was safely tucked up in bed upstairs in Lucy's adoptive parents' house.

The sixth-form college hall was packed to the brim. Half of the students were on the dancefloor. Vampires were dancing with teenagers dressed like Frankenstein's monster. A couple of witches were dancing like Egyptians to the music, and two ghosts were locked in an intimate embrace off to the side.

"Come with me to the Ladies?"
It was Jane Banks. Lucy's best friend was the only one at the party who was dressed as a zombie. She'd really gone to town with the costume and the ragged clothes and pieces of fake flesh hanging from her face really did lend her an undead look.

"Sure," Lucy said.
"Why do girls always have to have company when they go to the toilet?" Darren wondered.
"You wouldn't get it," Jane said.

"Of course I wouldn't get it," Darren said. "If two blokes went to the toilet together, people would start to talk."
"What are you supposed to be anyway?" Jane asked.
"What does it look like? It's a skeleton costume."
"I'm one of the undead."
"I can see that," Darren said.
"But I'm going to change that," Jane said. "You'll see."
Darren frowned at her. He couldn't see the equally puzzled expression on Lucy's face beneath her mask.

Lucy came back five minutes later. She was on her own.
"What's wrong with Jane?" Darren said. "She's acting really odd."
"Something's bothering her," Lucy said. "She wouldn't tell me what it was, but I know when something's up with her."

A Bruno Mars song came on through the speakers.
"Do you want to dance?" Darren asked.
"I hate this song," Lucy told him.
"It's a brilliant song."
"There are no brilliant songs out at the moment."
"Your taste in music is pretty suspect," Darren said.
"Blame my dad," Lucy said. "He's educated me in the fine art of proper music."
"What the fuck..."

Lucy looked in the direction that Darren was facing. A group of people had gathered around someone on the dancefloor. The song was reaching its climax now. The figure everyone was focusing their attention on was Jane Banks. She had her hands on her face and she was tearing away at the fake flesh.
"Why is she doing that?" Darren wondered.
"Let's go and see what's wrong," Lucy said.

They made their way over to the group of people. A girl dressed as Harley Quinn was trying to talk to Jane. Lucy's friend continued to tear at the rubber flesh. The song stopped and wasn't replaced with another one. The silence inside the hall was eerie. Lucy removed her werewolf mask.
"What's wrong?" she asked Jane.
Most of the zombie flesh had been ripped away from her face now. Lucy watched as she removed something from her jeans pocket.
"The Preacher has spoken."
"What are you going on about?" Darren said.
"He has foretold how it has to be," Jane carried on. "The Preacher knows everything."
Jane raised the razor to her neck and sliced her throat open in one continuous motion.

CHAPTER TWO

"I wonder how the Halloween party is going," Detective Sergeant Erica Whitton said.

"They're probably all rat-arsed by now," Detective Sergeant Jason Smith reckoned.

"It's a sixth-form college party," Whitton said. "There won't be any alcohol there."

"That's not going to stop them. I bet that by now there'll be students puking all over the place."

He didn't know then how right he was, but the college students weren't getting sick due to the effects of alcohol.

"Do you think we should go up and check on Andrew?" Whitton said. Smith nodded to the baby monitor on the table. "That's what those things are for. Besides, Laura and Fran have been taking good care of him."

"What are they up to?" Whitton said. "It's far too quiet up there."

"They're probably watching something on Laura's tablet."

"That's what I'm afraid of. I don't like the fact that kids their age can access pretty much anything they want on the Internet."

"The tablet has restricted access," Smith reminded her. "I'm going out for a smoke. Do you want me to bring you another beer on the way back?"

"I'd better not. What if something happens to Andrew?"

"You worry too much."

Smith got up and cast a glance at the dogs. Theakston and Fred were fast asleep on the two-seater sofa. Neither of them looked like they were planning on moving anytime soon. Smith headed for the kitchen and opened the door to the back garden. A blast of icy air came inside, and Smith shivered. It was late October, and he knew that York was gearing up to winter. His city wouldn't warm up again for at least another four months, and the thought made him shiver once more. There was a faint whiff of sulphur in the air – the aftermath of fireworks. There was still a week to go before Guy Fawkes Night, but a few impatient residents had been firing them off for a while already.

Smith lit a cigarette and took a long drag. He looked across to the house next door. He still found it strange to think that he and Whitton owned the property now. They'd bought the place when the Smith household had become rather crowded and now Lucy, Darren and Andrew were making a life for themselves a stones' throw away. It suited them all fine – Smith and Whitton now had plenty of room for Laura and Fran, and Lucy and Darren had a bit of privacy. Plus, they always had a babysitter on hand. Darren had quit college, and the teenage boy was always happy to help out when Smith and Whitton were called into work without warning.

That hadn't happened for a while. In the aftermath of the *Workshop* investigation things had got back to normal at work. Smith knew better than to allow himself to get lulled into a false sense of security, but he had to admit that he was starting to enjoy the peace and quiet.

"I'm getting old," he said to the sky.

There was a loud bang close by, followed by a flash of colour. A dog started to bark somewhere down the street. Smith was glad that his dogs weren't fazed by the explosions the fireworks made. Theakston and Fred barely flinched at the sound and Smith wondered if the aged Bull Terrier and the gruesome Pug were slightly deaf.

He finished his cigarette and was debating whether to smoke another one when he caught the sound of his mobile phone ringtone in the kitchen. It wasn't a ringtone he'd assigned to anyone at work, and he was relieved. He was feeling relaxed and the last thing he needed was to be called out for work.

The clock on the wall told him it was just after eight, and Smith wondered who could be calling at this time.

It was Frankie Lewis. "Sorry to bother you."

"Is something wrong?" Smith asked.

He couldn't remember Darren's father ever phoning him before.

"I need your advice," Frankie said. "Is now not a good time?"

"It's fine. What do you need to know?"

"It's about these cursed fireworks," Frankie said. "I know it's getting close to Bonfire Night and all that, but the blasted things have been going off for weeks now, and I was wondering if there was anything the police can do to stop it."

Smith really wasn't expecting this.

"I don't think it's really a police matter," he said.

"I thought as much," Frankie said. "If you ask me, the damn things should be banned altogether. Mrs Fowler next door has to medicate her poor dogs because of them. The poor critters are petrified."

"As far as I'm aware," Smith said. "It's not against the law to set off fireworks on a private property."

"Well, it should be."

"Do you know who the culprits are?" Smith said.

"I know exactly who it is."

"What if you asked them to show some consideration," Smith suggested. "Explain the situation with the dogs and ask them to stop setting them off."

"Mrs Fowler already tried that, and she got an earful of abuse for her efforts. Are you sure there's nothing the police can do?"

"I'm afraid not," Smith said. "If the fireworks are causing a problem, it's a matter for the council."

"Fat lot of use that lot are."

"Unfortunately, that's the law."

"I bet the police would get involved if I was to pay those scumbags a visit and fired some of their fireworks up their backsides."

"Don't do anything stupid," Smith warned. "Promise me you won't do anything you might regret."

"I don't have much choice, do I? What with my record. It just makes me mad as hell that there are innocent animals out there who are terrified because of a few selfish people. They should make all fireworks illegal."

"I'm on the same page as you, Frankie," Smith said. "I've never seen the attraction of fireworks, but my hands are tied as far as the law is concerned."

"Thanks for nothing," Frankie said.

The drone on the other end of the line told Smith that the conversation was over.

"Who was that?" Whitton had come into the kitchen.

Smith took a beer out of the fridge. "Darren's dad. He wanted to know if the police could do anything about people setting fireworks off."

"They are a curse," Whitton said.

"He's worried about the dogs next door," Smith said. "I never had Frankie Lewis pegged as an animal lover."

"Does he know who's responsible for setting them off?"

"He knows," Smith said. "But they're not interested in listening to reason. There's no point stressing about it – our hands are tied."

He took a long drink from the beer and his phone started to ring again. The screen told him it was Darren Lewis.

"This doesn't look good," Smith said. "The only reason Darren would be calling right now is if something has happened to my car."

"You don't know that," Whitton said.

"What else could it be about? If the little prick has had an accident, he can kiss borrowing my Sierra goodbye once and for all."

"Perhaps if you answer it, you'll find out," Whitton said.

Smith did just that. He waited to see what the teenager had to say. Whitton couldn't hear the words that were being spoken but she knew from the rapid change in Smith's facial expression that it was something much more serious than a car accident.

CHAPTER THREE

Vincent Allen downed his pint and caught the attention of the barman at the Lamb's Arms.

"I'm off."

"So early?" John, the barman said. "It's not yet nine. You're not working tomorrow, are you?"

Vincent shook his head. "I'm not back on shift until Tuesday. I'm just not in the mood."

With that, he got up from the bar stool and left the pub. The explanation he'd given was not strictly true. Something was bothering him – he couldn't quite translate it into words, but there was an uneasy feeling in his stomach. He'd had the sensation before, and experience had taught him it wasn't something to dismiss.

The first time his insides had stirred like this was when he was in his early teens. He'd been away on a school camping trip and he'd been overcome by a sudden, unexplained agitation. He'd never felt anything like it before and he couldn't figure out what had caused it. It stayed with him throughout his time at the camp, and when it was time to leave it still wouldn't budge.

The campsite was isolated, and communication with the outside world was non-existent. The uneasiness remained on the bus ride back to the city, and Vincent recalled that it had intensified as he got closer to home. He knew something was wrong when he looked at the faces of his mother and father when he stepped off the bus. Nothing was said until they were halfway home. Then his father told him the news - his dog Harvey had run into the road and been hit by a car. The poor brute was killed instantly. When Vincent went through the series of events in his head, he realised that his best friend had breathed his final breath the exact moment the uneasy feeling had invaded his being. Vincent didn't understand what that meant.

There were more similar episodes throughout his life, and Vincent knew better than to ignore the sensation when it materialised. That's why he was now on his way back from the pub long before closing time. The heaviness in his stomach was something he could not overlook.

He took out his phone and called his wife as he walked home. Perhaps the ominous feeling was telling him that something bad had happened at home. Maggie's phone rang a few times and then a voice told Vincent that the subscriber he had dialled was not available at present. He tried his son's phone, and the engaged tone told him that Robert was busy on a call. Vincent sighed – he shouldn't have been surprised. Robert was fifteen and he spent most of his waking life on his phone.

Vincent quickened his pace and flinched when a firework went off somewhere close by. The explosion was followed by a display of lights above the house three doors down from his. The Jenkins family were clearly celebrating Bonfire Night early.

The door to his house was unlocked, and Vincent made a mental note to bring this up with Maggie and Robert. He'd always drummed it into them to keep the door locked when they were at home. Crime in Heworth wasn't really much of a problem but there had been a few incidents of opportunists trying their luck and some of those burglaries had occurred while the occupants were at home.

Vincent closed the door behind him and locked it. He could hear the sound of his son's voice in the living room. Robert was talking to someone on his phone – probably his girlfriend. Vincent took off his coat and hung it on the rack in the hallway. Robert was perched on the three-seater with his legs over the arm of the sofa. He removed them as soon as he sensed his father's presence in the room. Maggie was nowhere to be seen.

"Where's your mother?" Vincent asked.

"I'll call you back," Robert told the person on the other end of the line and turned to face his dad. "What?"

"Where's your mum?" Vincent said.

"How should I know?"

"Because you live in the same house as her. I tried phoning her but the call went straight to voicemail."

"What are you doing home so early?" Robert said.

The bad feeling was stronger somehow.

Vincent knew he wasn't going to get anything useful out of his teenage son so he left the room, and after checking the kitchen he made his way upstairs. He wondered if Maggie had been hit with one of her migraines and gone for a lie down. She'd been getting them more and more recently, and that would explain why she'd switched her phone off.

After checking the room that Maggie used as her art studio, Vincent headed for the bedroom. The lights were off, and the curtains were drawn, but there was still sufficient light coming from the landing to see if anyone was lying on the bed. It was made and it was empty. Vincent switched on the light and his eyes came to rest on something on the bedside table. What he was looking at made no sense whatsoever. It was unmistakably his wife's mobile phone – the fluorescent green cover was hard to miss, but the screen of the phone had been smashed to smithereens. Pieces of the broken screen had landed on the bed and there was more shattered metal and plastic on the table. Vincent didn't know how to interpret what he was looking at.

He left the room and headed back downstairs. He stopped next to the bathroom when he noticed that the door was closed.

"Maggie," he said. "Are you in there?"

If she was, she didn't tell him so.

Vincent tried the door. It was locked.

"Maggie," he called again. "Are you alright?"

Nothing.

Robert came upstairs. "What's up?"

"I think your mum's in there," Vincent said. "And I found her phone smashed to pieces in the bedroom."

"What?"

"When did you last see her?"

A shrug of the shoulders followed.

"Emma wants to know if I want to go round to her house?" Robert said.

"It's late," Vincent said.

"It's Saturday, and it'll only be for a few hours."

Vincent wasn't listening. His thoughts were focused on the situation with the locked bathroom door. Maggie never locked the door.

"It'll only be for a few hours." Robert repeated.

"Alright," Vincent said.

"Cool."

Robert went back downstairs, and soon afterwards the front door slammed.

Vincent tried the door again, but it still wouldn't open. The lock on the other side of the door was a flimsy slide latch. Vincent had fitted it himself and he knew it wouldn't be difficult to break. He called Maggie's name again and aimed a kick at the part of the door where he knew the latch was located. There was a crunch as the lock broke and the door flew open.

Maggie Allen was curled up in the shower cubicle. She was fully clothed and there was something in the cubicle next to her. Vincent knew exactly what it was. He ought to – he'd collected the prescription for the fast-acting sleeping tablets himself. An overdose of Zopiclone isn't necessarily life-threatening, but when Vincent's eyes came to rest on the empty vodka bottle next to the shower cubicle, his heart stopped beating for a moment. It was now quite clear what the agitation he'd experienced in the pub meant. It was telling him about the plight of his wife, but it had materialised far too late to change a damn thing.

CHAPTER FOUR

The scene that met Smith and Whitton in the car park of the sixth form college where Lucy attended was like something from a surreal horror movie. Car headlights were shining on wailing vampires and sobbing ghouls. A group of girls dressed as witches were engaged in a group hug, and a solitary figure with a *Scream* mask around its neck was sitting on the kerb puffing away on a vape. Parents were consoling their costumed offspring, but they didn't appear to be doing a very good job of it.

Smith spotted Lucy and Darren next to his Ford Sierra and he and Whitton walked over to them. The expression on Lucy's face was deeply concerning. There was no emotion in her eyes – they were dead eyes, and Smith deduced that she was in shock. He'd seen it many times before at the scene of a brutal murder and he wasn't sure how to handle it now that it was pasted onto the face of his adopted daughter. Smith noticed that Lucy had blood on her face too.
"Are you OK?" he asked her.
She remained silent.

Whitton didn't speak either. Instead, she wrapped her arms around the teenage girl and held her tightly. Lucy didn't reciprocate. Her arms hung by her side and the blankness in her eyes didn't change. Darren Lewis looked equally stunned. He'd removed the skeleton mask and the luminous bones that clung to his skinny frame would have been mildly amusing under any other circumstances.

Darren wasn't laughing now. Smith placed an arm on his shoulder and led him away from the car.
"What happened?"
Darren didn't reply. Instead, he shook his head.
"We should get you both to hospital," Smith said.

Right on cue an ambulance pulled into the car park. Another one arrived shortly afterwards.

"Is Lucy hurt?" Smith asked Darren. "She has blood on her face."

Another shake of the head. "It's Jane's blood."

His eyes closed, and Smith caught him just in time as his legs gave way and he became a dead weight. Smith helped him to the ground, took off his jacket and wrapped it around his shoulders.

"I'm going to get some help," he told Whitton.

She was still holding onto Lucy.

"And I'm going to see if I can make some sense out of what the fuck happened here," Smith added.

He walked towards the main entrance of the college. When Darren had phoned him the only information he'd been given was that Jane Banks was dead. Darren hadn't been able to elaborate on that and Smith wanted some answers. This was supposed to be a college Halloween party – it was meant to be a fun event, and Smith wanted to know why Lucy's best friend had died during the course of it.

"Nobody is allowed inside."

It was a woman Smith vaguely recognised. He remembered her from some parents' evening or other. A spark of recognition flashed in her eyes too.

"Oh, it's you."

She introduced herself as Flora Newton, and she told him she taught English at the college.

"What happened?" Smith asked.

"Nobody seems to know. I was called upon to man the refreshment stand, and all hell broke loose. There was screaming and students running around like headless chicken. The music had stopped for some unexplained reason, and that made the whole scene much more pronounced. It was chaos in there."

"Did you not see what happened?"

"I..." Flora said. "I'm sorry."

"It's OK," Smith said.

"I only saw her afterwards."

"Are you referring to Jane Banks?"

Flora nodded.

"One of the students I did manage to get any semblance of sense out of – a strange boy for whom nothing appears to strike any emotional chord, told me that Jane killed herself. Right there on the dance floor."

"Where is this boy now?" Smith said.

He realised he'd switched to detective mode without thinking. Technically speaking, a suicide isn't a matter for CID, but this was personal, and he felt like he was involved whether he wanted to be or not.

"I don't know," Flora said. "As I said, chaos ensued and students ran amok."

"A name will do," Smith said.

"Brian Illman. What's going to happen now?"

"Is there anyone still inside the building?"

"I thought it best to get everyone outside."

"You did the right thing. Was it you who contacted the parents of the students?"

"The majority of them took care of that themselves. Mobile phones are a curse, but they do have their uses, don't they?"

"I suppose they do."

"Is this a police matter? I phoned the police because I didn't know what else to do. Where are they, by the way? They should have been here by now."

"Until we know exactly what happened," Smith said. "It's impossible to say whether it's a matter for the police. Unfortunately, it's Saturday night, and we have a lot to deal with over the weekends. Are you the only teacher here?"

"Mr Grigg was also roped in. He's the head of Maths."

A solitary police car arrived, and Smith watched as the PCs Miller and Griffin got out. PC Miller spotted him and walked over.

"What took you so long?" Flora Newton asked.

"Sorry, Ma'am," PC Miller said. "We got held up at an altercation at a new pub in the city centre. What happened?"

"We don't know the details yet," Smith replied for her. "I want you and PC Griffin to see if you can get any sense out of any of the students. Some of them will need medical attention, but we have paramedics on hand."

"What are you doing here, Sarge?"

"Our daughter is a student here," Smith said. "The dead girl was her best friend."

CHAPTER FIVE

Two hours later, Smith was ready to leave. He'd done everything he could. Lucy and Darren had been attended to by the paramedics on the scene. It had taken quite a while – they weren't the only people at the party suffering from the effects of what they'd borne witness to. Some of them had been taken to hospital but most were allowed to go home. Jane Banks' body had been examined, and she too had been taken away. According to one of the paramedics, Jane had died from the single laceration to her neck. The wound was deep and both carotid arteries had been severed. Death would have been extremely quick.

Smith was still somewhat in the dark about what had actually happened. Lucy hadn't spoken a word since they got there, and Smith didn't press her. The student Flora Newton had spoken about couldn't be located, and Smith decided he would track down Brian Illman tomorrow. It had been a stressful few hours for everybody who attended the Halloween party and Smith didn't think he was going to get any more answers tonight.

Whitton told him she would take Lucy home in her car and Smith offered to drive with Darren. They were halfway to the car when PC Simon Miller intercepted them.
"What is it?" Smith said.
"We've just had a call about another suspected suicide, Sarge."
"*Suspected*?"
"PC Baldwin said the bloke wasn't making much sense," PC Miller said. "He came home from the pub early because he felt that something was wrong. Found his wife locked in the bathroom. You can only lock it from the inside. She was in the shower cubicle with a vodka bottle and an empty pack of sleeping pills next to her. We're on our way there now, and I thought you should know."

"Why?" Smith said. "Sounds like a cut and dry suicide. It happens. I have to get this kid home."

Darren remained silent for the first half of the journey. Then he suddenly shot up in the seat as though he'd been given an electric shock.
"Where's Andy?"
"Relax," Smith said. "After I got off the phone to you, I called Whitton's mother. She's at our house now with the girls and Andrew. They're probably getting spoilt rotten. Are you alright?"
"Not really," Darren said. "I can't make any sense out of what happened tonight."
"Don't dwell on it now."
"I can't get it out of my head. One minute she was asking Lucy to go with her to the Ladies and then she totally lost it."
"Do you feel like talking about what happened?" Smith said.
"We were messing around like we always do," Darren said. "I said I couldn't understand why women always have to have company to go to the toilets, and Jane asked me what my costume was supposed to be. Then she told me that she was one of the undead, and that's when she started acting weird."
"In what way?"
"She said she was undead, but she was going to change that."
"What do you think she meant by that?" Smith said.
"There's only one thing to think. She was planning on killing herself. But why do it like that?"
"We'll talk about it in the morning," Smith decided.
"I don't get why she did that," Darren carried on anyway. "She was ripping the zombie flesh from her face – she said something about a preacher, the music stopped, and she sliced her throat open. Lucy was standing right in front of her."
He stopped there, and Smith wondered if he was going to cry.

He didn't, and Smith wished he had done. He knew for a fact that both Darren and Lucy had an extremely difficult road ahead of them. They didn't say anything else on the drive home. Smith parked outside his house, Darren got out and headed straight for the house next door. Smith let him go. What he and Lucy had seen at the party was something they needed to process in their own time.

Whitton's mother was still there. She and her daughter were drinking coffee in the kitchen.

"Where's Lucy?" Smith asked.

"She went straight back to their house with Andrew," Whitton said. "She held onto him like she was afraid he was going to break. I'm really worried about her."

Smith got a beer out of the fridge. "I don't know how to handle this."

"Can I say something?" It was Jane, Whitton's mum.

"Of course," Smith said.

"That young lass has seen so much horror. She's seen more than anyone should have to see in a lifetime, and she's bounced back. This time will be no different."

Smith took a long swig of beer. "I don't know, Jane. Everybody has a breaking point. Everyone has a limit and when that limit is reached they just snap."

"You don't."

Smith found himself smiling, and he knew it was highly inappropriate under the circumstances.

"Thanks, Jane," he said. "And thanks for stepping in to look after the kids."

"That's what me and Harold are here for, love. That poor girl must have been terribly troubled to want to end it all. Did Lucy say anything about what might have been bothering her?"

"Lucy hasn't spoken a word since it happened, Mum," Whitton said.

"I suppose I'd better be off," Jane said.

"You don't have to go," Smith said. "You can always stay the night – the girls won't mind bunking up together for one night."

"I wouldn't want to impose," Jane said. "Besides, his Lordship will only moan if I'm not there to make his breakfast in the morning."

"How is Dad?" Whitton said. "Is his arthritis still playing up?"

"He's got used to that. No, he's been like a bear with a sore head ever since he was told he needed to take pills for his blood pressure. He's seventy-five for Pete's sake. I'd say he's done well to get this far without them. I'll see myself out."

"Do you think Lucy will really be alright?" Smith said when Jane had gone.

"I don't know," Whitton said. "She's still a kid. She might have given birth, but she's still no more than a child herself. She's already watched one of her friends die, and I don't think she's going to bounce back from this."

"Why do you think she did it?" Smith asked. "Jane, I mean."

"Let's not dwell on that tonight. It's late, and I could do with some sleep."

"I'll be up in a bit," Smith said. "I'm just going outside for a quick smoke."

Smith couldn't help dwelling on it. He was no stranger to suicide. The image of his father swinging from a tree in the back garden was one he would never be able to erase, and it was one of the defining points in his life, and he'd seen the aftermath of a suicide attempt many times since, so he was somewhat hardened to the concept of self-termination, but it was the way Jane Banks had carried it out that was puzzling him now. She'd had an audience for her final act by all accounts, and Smith couldn't find a logical explanation for that.

He went outside and lit a cigarette. Jane Banks' chosen method of killing herself was truly baffling. This was a girl who Smith had spent time with. Jane had been to his house many times – she'd eaten at his dinner table, and he never would have suspected that she was capable of something like this in a million years.

He finished the cigarette, stubbed it out and was about to go back inside the house when he heard a noise coming from the house next door. A window was open in one of the rooms upstairs and Smith could feel his heart breaking a little bit when he realised that he recognised the noise. It was the sound of Lucy sobbing as though her own life had ended.

CHAPTER SIX

The first item on the agenda in the morning briefing the next day was the suspected suicide in Heworth. Smith could do without it in light of what had happened at Lucy's college, but there were a number of suspicious circumstances surrounding the death of Maggie Allen and it was their job to look into them in more detail.

"Uniforms were alerted to the death of a thirty-six-year-old woman just after nine last night," DI Smyth began. "Vincent Allen arrived home to find his wife Maggie dead in the shower cubicle in the bathroom. According to Mr Allen the bathroom door was locked, and he had to break it open to gain access."

"Why is this considered suspicious?" Smith asked. "PC Miller told me the husband found a vodka bottle and an empty packet of sleeping pills next to the shower."

"Let me finish. The husband also showed the uniforms what was left of Mrs Allen's mobile phone. It was in pieces in the bedroom. It had been smashed to smithereens. Mr Allen couldn't give any reason as to why his wife had done that, and that leads me to believe that it may not have been Maggie who broke the phone."

"I hate to interrupt again," Smith said. "But let me get this straight. You're suggesting there is something more to Mrs Allen's suicide than a woman who locks herself in the bathroom and OD's on pills and booze based on a knackered phone? How else could it be interpreted? Unless we have some kind of *locked room* mystery to solve, there isn't any other explanation. The door can only be locked from the inside – the windows in most of the bathrooms in that part of town are too small to climb in or out of, so how can this be anything other than a woman taking her own life? To be honest, I could really do without this right now."

DI Smyth nodded his head.

"I heard what happened last night at Lucy's college," he said after a moment had passed. "Everybody on the team will understand if you and Whitton need to take some time off."

"I don't need any time off," Smith said. "I'm telling you that this is an open and shut case of suicide. Why are we even discussing it?"

"Because something the husband told Baldwin when he reported it sounded some warning bells inside her head," DI Smyth said. "You've always said yourself that Baldwin's intuition is rarely wrong. I've got a recording of the call. Harry."

DC Moore tapped the keypad of his laptop, inserted a memory stick and soon afterwards a man's voice came over the speakers.

My wife is dead.
Could you please repeat that, sir? It was Baldwin.
The man repeated it.
I knew there was something gravely wrong. I could feel it.
Where are you?
At home. I sensed it so I came home early. She's dead. I think she might have killed herself, but Maggie had absolutely no reason to do that.

The next part of the recording didn't make much sense. Baldwin was trying to get the relevant information out of the man, but he kept telling her about his ultra sensitivity to dark events. She finally managed to extract an address out of him, she asked him not to touch anything and she assured him that some officers would be there shortly.

"The man's clearly in shock," Smith said when the recording was finished. "He's just found his wife dead – he's going to behave out of character."

"It needs checking out," DI Smyth said.

"Was Mr Allen alone in the house?" DC King asked.

"They have a fifteen-year-old son," DI Smyth said. "He was at his girlfriend's place when our officers arrived at the house. I've arranged for a door-to-door in the surrounding area, but I want to talk to the husband and the son this morning. Smith, you and Kerry can take Mr Allen and Whitton, I'd like you and DC Moore to speak to the teenage boy."

"Why can't me and Kerry speak to both of them?" Smith wondered.

"Because the boy refused to leave his girlfriend's place," DI Smyth said. "When he heard the news about his mother, he refused to come home. Baldwin has both addresses. Bridge, I have another job for you."

"Sir?" Bridge said.

"It's rather delicate," DI Smyth said. "We can talk in my office."

* * *

"What do you think that was about?" DC King asked.

She and Smith were on their way to Heworth.

"What was what all about?"

"The thing with Bridge and the DI."

"God knows," Smith said. "This is a waste of time. The woman overdosed on pills and booze and locked herself in the bathroom. It's as cut and dry as any suicide I've ever seen."

"The DI seems to think otherwise," DC King said. "I heard about what happened at your daughter's college. How is she?"

"Destroyed," Smith said. "Utterly destroyed. She watched her best friend slice her throat open. She was standing right in front of her when she did it."

"That must have been awful. Does she know why she did it?"

"She hasn't spoken a word since it happened, and I'm not going to press her. I don't understand it myself. People kill themselves – it's a sad fact of life, but why do it like that? You want to end it all, you don't do it with an audience. A final act of desperation is a deeply personal moment – it's intimate, and you don't share that moment with a hall full of people."

"She must have had her reasons," DC King said.

"I suppose we'll never know, will we? And this is the last thing I need right now – wasting time on another poor bastard left behind after a suicide. I know exactly what it feels like, and I can tell you it is the emptiest feeling in the world."

CHAPTER SEVEN

Vincent Allen opened the door so quickly that Smith wondered if he'd been watching from the window. After introducing himself and DC King they were invited into the living room. Vincent didn't offer them anything to drink. The walls inside the room were covered with framed paintings. The majority of them were landscapes, with a few portraits dotted between them. Smith didn't know much about art, but he had to admit that these paintings were really good.

"What exactly are you doing here?" Vincent asked.
"We're very sorry for your loss, Mr Allen," DC King offered. "Is there anything we can do for you?"
"What can you possibly do now?"
"We could arrange for a family liaison officer to pop by," DC King said. "To offer you help and support."
"I'll ask you the question again," Vincent said. "What can you possibly do now? Maggie is gone. She's not coming back. What exactly has my wife's suicide got to do with York CID?"
"We're just following up on a few things," Smith said.
Vincent started to laugh, and it caught Smith off guard. It lasted a few seconds and stopped as abruptly as it had started.

"I'm sorry," he said. "I don't know where that came from. Something just occurred to me, and it tickled me. I wondered if you were here to perhaps arrest my dead wife for killing herself. Suicide was once against the law, wasn't it?"
"A long time ago," Smith confirmed. "We won't take up too much of your time. When you phoned the switchboard, you told the PC that you left the pub early because you had a bad feeling. Can you explain what you meant by that?"

"What's to explain?" Vincent said. "I left the Lamb's Arms early because I felt agitated."

"What brought on this agitation?" DC King asked.

"Maggie's suicide of course."

"You knew she was planning on taking her own life?" Smith said.

"Of course not. My wife had shown no indication that she planned to do that. If she was suicidal or even depressed, I would have picked up on it."

"Then why didn't you?" Smith said.

"I just told you that I did."

"I'm really not following you, Mr Allen. You claim to have had a bad feeling when you were at the pub and that's what made you leave early, but this feeling didn't materialise early enough to warn you about your wife's planned suicide. Is that correct?"

"Correct," Vincent said. "Perhaps I'm not making myself clear enough. It's happened before, you see."

"What has happened before?" Smith said.

"The feeling of foreboding. The first time was when I was on a camp with school. I got this sense of dread. It consumed me, and I didn't know what it meant. When I got home, I was told that my dog had been hit by a car and killed. The sense of dread appeared the exact same moment he was hit by the car. I knew when my grandmother had passed away too."

"You sensed it?" Smith said.

"You probably think I'm mad."

"Not at all," Smith said. "I believe that there is more on heaven and earth than we can possibly perceive."

"Close," Vincent said. "But very true. In Hamlet, the man himself actually said *there are more things on heaven and earth, Horatio than are dreamt of in your philosophy*."

"I've never been a big fan of Shakespeare," Smith said. "And we're getting side-tracked. Talk us through the events of last night. What time did you leave the house to go to the pub?"

"Half-seven. I'm a creature of habit. I always go to the Lamb at half-seven on a Saturday night and I leave after last orders."

"Can anyone confirm this?"

"Why would you ask that?"

"It's just routine," Smith said. "Can someone confirm that you were at the pub? Did you perhaps meet with someone?"

"I always drink alone," Vincent said. "I'm a bit of a loner, but John, the barman will corroborate my story."

"And you left the pub at nine?"

"That's right," Vincent said.

"And Maggie seemed fine? She wasn't acting strange at all?"

"She was as she always is. She had a book she was keen to read – we kissed our goodbyes, and I set off for the pub."

"At half-seven?"

"Correct."

"And you usually stay until closing time?" Smith said.

"Also correct."

"But last night you didn't?"

"No," Vincent said. "I didn't. I came home as soon as I knew something was wrong. Excuse me."

He left the room without offering any explanation.

He returned a few minutes later with a tray of coffee.

"I didn't even think to offer. Help yourselves."

Neither Smith nor DC King did. Smith's attention was drawn to the artwork on the walls, especially one particular painting. It depicted a colourful boomerang with an upside-down map of Australia painted in the middle of it.

"Who is the artist?" he asked.

"Maggie," Vincent said. "She's quite a talented amateur painter."

"She certainly is. They're very good. I love that boomerang."

"That was during Maggie's abstract phase," Vincent said. "That period didn't last long. Did you come here to talk about art?"

"No. Can you talk us through the events after you left the pub?"

"What do you need to know?"

"You left the pub and came straight home?" Smith said.

"The door was unlocked," Vincent said.

"Is that unusual?" DC King said.

"Unfortunately, not. I've explained to Maggie and Robert how important security is, but it often falls on deaf ears."

"What did you do then?" Smith said.

"I asked Robert where his mother was. He was on the phone to his girlfriend – he ended the call and told me he didn't know where she was."

"Did you think that was odd?" Smith said.

"Not at all. I ceased to try to understand the mind of a teenager a long time ago. I left him in the living room and went upstairs. I checked the rooms and that's when I saw the phone in the bedroom. It was smashed to pieces, and the feeling inside me intensified."

"Why do you think that is?"

"Because there was no logical explanation for it," Vincent said. "What possible reason would there be for someone to destroy a perfectly good phone?"

"You told the officer on the switchboard that you kicked in the bathroom door," Smith said.

"It was locked."

"And it only locks from the inside?" DC King said.

"It has a simple slide latch," Vincent said. "I fitted it at Robert's insistence. It's useless from a security perspective, but it offers some privacy. You know what teenagers are like."

"So, you kicked in the door," Smith said. "And you found your wife in the shower cubicle."

"I knew she was dead when I saw the sleeping pill packet and the empty bottle of vodka."

"Where did she get the pills?" DC King asked.

"They're mine," Vincent said. "I've got a prescription. They're not especially dangerous but mixed with vodka…"

He stopped there and rubbed his eyes.

"You haven't touched your coffee."

"It's fine," Smith said. "I think we're finished here."

He stood up. DC King did the same.

"Could I take a look at the bathroom?" Smith said.

"What for?" Vincent said.

"I just want to check something, and I wouldn't mind relieving myself while I'm there. I really must stop drinking so much coffee. Occupational hazard, I suppose."

"If you must. Upstairs, second door on the right."

Smith left the room and headed upstairs. He made a slight detour on the way to the bathroom. He pushed open the door to the main bedroom and took a look inside. The first thing he noticed was the mobile phone on the bedside table. Vincent had left the broken phone there, and Smith wondered why he hadn't disposed of it. It had been smashed to pieces, and it was doubtful whether it would ever work again.

Smith left the bedroom and went inside the bathroom. There was no indication that a woman had taken her last breath in here recently. Maggie Allen's body had been taken away hours ago, and the pill packet and empty vodka bottle were also gone. Smith didn't need to use the toilet – he wanted to take a look at the window. It was bigger than he expected and, even though it was chilly outside it had been left slightly ajar. Smith opened it wider and looked outside. There was a drainpipe right next to the window and Smith decided that it would be possible to exit the window and climb down the drainpipe without too much effort. It wasn't a long drop, and anyone with a reasonable level of fitness would be able to manage it. He still didn't believe that was what had happened. Murdering someone by forcing sleeping pills and vodka down their throat is not only tricky, but there would be evidence of it. Smith had made up his mind – Maggie Allen took her own life.

CHAPTER EIGHT

"What is it you want me to do, sir?"

Bridge was sitting opposite DI Smyth in his office.

"It's not strictly work related," DI Smyth said.

"I see."

"I believe you have a friend who is something of an IT wizard."

"Barry Stone," Bridge said. "We've used his talents a couple of times in the past."

"Like I said, this is rather delicate, and I don't want it broadcast."

"I can live with that."

DI Smyth smiled. "I was hoping you might say that. I'm not sure whether you're aware that I've been in a relationship with Porter Klaus for a while."

"I am," Bridge confirmed.

"I try to keep my personal life separate from work," DI Smyth said. "I'm sure you'll understand. This is 2021, but attitudes in the force still seem to be somewhat stuck in the past."

"What is it you need Barry to do for you, sir?" Bridge asked, mainly to urge DI Smyth to get to the point.

"Porter has a number of instructional videos on YouTube," DI Smyth said. "Elementary hypnotism and the like, and the videos are open to comments. The majority of these comments are positive, but recently one particular subscriber seems determined to ruin Porter's reputation. The comments posted are verging on the defamatory."

"If you're asking whether Barry can trace the person posting the comments," Bridge said. "I don't think that will be possible. YouTube subscribers can post anonymously, and the company itself is notoriously secretive about the identities of its subscribers. We're talking court orders and all sorts of red tape. You must know that."

"I do. But the malicious comments have not stopped with YouTube. Porter has received a number of emails he believes are from the same troll. That's what I need your friend's help with."

"What kind of emails are we talking about?"

"Let me give you a bit of background," DI Smyth said. "Porter Klaus isn't his real name. He was born Dieter Bergman but he changed it when he was prohibited from practicing psychology. He made a terrible mistake and unfortunately, it cost him dearly. The psychology community isn't a very big one and when mud like that sticks, it tends to stick fast. This troll is threatening to expose every sordid detail, and he's threatening to do it on a huge scale. For some reason, he wants to destroy Porter's life."

"Does he have any idea who it could be?" Bridge said.

"He doesn't. We don't even know if it's a man or a woman, but they seem adamant to make him pay."

"Are we talking blackmail here?"

"Not yet," DI Smyth said. "But it's possible that things might go in that direction. Porter is reasonably financially comfortable, but this is more about his reputation. Somebody wants to obliterate that reputation and it's killing him. He's not sleeping, and his health is taking a turn for the worse. Do you think your friend can help? I don't want anybody at work to know about this."

"I'll see what he thinks," Bridge said. "And I'll put him in touch with Porter. Email addresses can be tricky to trace too, especially if you take VPNs into account, but if anyone can sort this out it's Barry."

"I appreciate it."

"You do realise that none of the people on the team give a rat's arse about your sexual orientation?" Bridge said.

DI Smyth smiled. "Eloquently put, but yes, I do understand that. But it's not the men and women on the team I'm concerned about. I was in the armed

forces for over a decade, and I have first-hand experience of prejudice and harassment. It stinks, but that's just the way it is in some professions."
"I'll give Barry a call now," Bridge said. "We'll figure this out, sir."
"Thank you. I really appreciate it."
Bridge got to his feet. "We're a team – what's the point of being part of a team if we don't have each other's backs?"

* * *

Whitton wasn't quite sure what she was looking at when the door of Robert Allen's girlfriend's house opened. The creature standing there resembled an extra from a vampire film. He was dressed all in black – his long hair was black, and he was wearing black eyeliner. The nails on the hand holding the door had also been painted black.
"Can I help you?" he asked.
"Is this Emma Illman's house?" Whitton said.
"It might be."
"Is it her house or not?" DC Moore said. "We don't have time for games."
"What do you want with Emma?"
Whitton took out her ID. "We're actually here to talk to her boyfriend. Is Robert still here?"
"Last time I looked."
"Brian." A woman's voice was heard from inside the house. "Who's at the door?"
"Cops," he shouted back.
Shortly afterwards, a tall woman with pink hair appeared in the doorway. "What's going on?"
"We'd like to talk to Robert," Whitton said. "Robert Allen."
"The poor love. He's been in a proper state since, you know."
"Could we just have a quick chat?" DC Moore said. "We won't keep him for

long."

"I suppose you ought to come in then."

She introduced herself as Shelly Illman and told them to take a seat in the living room while she went to fetch Robert. He came in soon afterwards with a pretty girl who looked to be in her mid-teens. She was dressed in a pair of jeans and a T-Shirt with a huge ladybird on the front. Robert's eyes were rimmed with red and Whitton guessed he hadn't slept much.

"We're very sorry about your mother," she said.
Robert looked at her but remained silent. Smith had phoned Whitton as soon as he and DC King had left the Allen household. Vincent had told him something interesting. Moments before making the grisly discovery in the bathroom, Robert had asked if he could go round to Emma's house. He'd also mentioned that Robert was with him outside the locked bathroom, and he didn't seem particularly fazed by it. This struck Smith as suspicious, and he wanted to bring it to Whitton's attention before she talked to the boy.

"I know this is hard," she said. "But we need to ask you a few questions about last night, OK?"
Robert didn't get the chance to reply. The figure dressed in black came into the room and made himself comfortable on the single seater. He looked at Whitton and grinned. She noticed that his teeth were unusually pointy, and she wondered if he'd had them sharpened on purpose.
"We're in the middle of something here," DC Moore told him.
The creature of the night got to his feet. He walked past Emma Illman and slapped her on the shoulder.
"Loser."

"Who is that?" DC Moore said.
"My brother," Emma said. "Brian."
"He seems like quite a character," Whitton said.

"He's full of himself at the moment," Emma said. "He was at the sixth-form party last night. He saw that girl kill herself."

"He was at the Halloween party?" Whitton said.

Emma nodded.

"Did he not get changed out of his costume?"

Emma frowned. "No, he always dresses like that. He's a proper Emo and he thinks he's immortal."

Whitton didn't know how to interpret this.

"Can you tell us the last time you saw your mum, Robert?" she said.

"I can't remember," he said.

"Your dad came back from the pub at around nine," DC Moore said. "Is that about right?"

"I suppose so."

"The bathroom door was locked," Whitton said. "And you asked if you could come here. Didn't you want to know why your mother had locked herself in the bathroom?"

"What for?"

"Perhaps you were curious?" DC Moore said. "Your mum had locked herself in the bathroom and she wasn't answering when your dad called to her. I would have found that a bit odd."

"You don't know my parents."

"What do you mean by that?" Whitton said.

"Nothing."

"Can you remember whether your mum was acting strange at all?" Whitton said. "Was she behaving out of character?"

"How should I know?" Robert said.

"Maybe because you live in the same house as her," DC Moore suggested.

"They're a pair of losers," Robert said. "I avoid them most of the time."

"I like them." It was Emma.

Robert rolled his eyes. "You don't have to live with them."

"You don't have to live with a brother who thinks he's going to live forever."

"Robert," Whitton said. "I need you to think very carefully. What were you doing when your father arrived home?"

"I was on the phone," he said.

"Who were you talking to?" DC Moore said.

"Emma."

"And before that?" Whitton said. "What did you do before that?"

"I checked out a few things on Instagram."

"Do you remember where your mum was?"

"Upstairs, I think."

"Did you hear anything strange while she was upstairs?"

"Strange?" Robert repeated.

"Any odd noises," Whitton said. "Anything that struck you as unusual?"

Robert shook his head. "No. I was looking at Insta with my air pods in."

"Is the window usually open in your bathroom?" Whitton said.

"What?" Robert said.

"The window," DC Moore said. "Is it usually kept open in the bathroom?"

"How am I supposed to know?"

DC Moore opened his mouth to say something, but Whitton got in first.

"I think we've covered everything here. We won't keep you any longer."

She stood up. DC Moore did the same.

"I'm not going back there," Robert said when they were in the doorway.

"You're not going back where?" Whitton said.

"Home."

"You can stay here," Emma said.

"That's none of our business," Whitton said. "We really are sorry about your mum."

CHAPTER NINE

"You don't mind waiting in the car, do you?" Smith said.
"It'll be better if you go in by yourself," DC King said. "I don't know the woman."
Smith walked up the path to the house. He'd only ever been here a few times, and on those occasions, he'd found Jane Banks' mother to be a pleasant woman. He got the impression that she was one of those *what you see, is what you get* people, and Smith liked those kinds of people.

He wasn't quite sure why he suddenly got the urge to come here. The house was on the way back to the station and it occurred to him that it was the right thing to do. He wasn't sure how Kelly Banks would be feeling right now, but he guessed she would be in the worst place of her life. He wasn't even sure if she would let him in or not.

He certainly wasn't expecting what she did when she opened the door to him. The embrace was tight, and it lasted a very long time. Smith could feel her entire body shaking, but she didn't cry. Kelly broke the embrace first.
"Do you want to come in?"
"Only if you want me to," Smith said.
She didn't say anything about this, but when she walked down the hallway, Smith took it as an invitation.

They sat in the kitchen. There was an overflowing ashtray on the table and the room was thick with cigarette smoke. Kelly opened the back door and lit another cigarette.
"I don't normally smoke in the house."
"I think you can make an exception," Smith said. "I'm not going to ask how you're feeling because I can't imagine what you must be going through, but I felt that I needed to come and see you."
Kelly took a long drag of her cigarette. "My sister threatened to come round.

But we don't really speak much these days, and she wanted to bring me some of her knockout pills, so I told her I was fine. She means well, but she can be a bit overbearing. She thinks that because she's six minutes older than me, she has to be overprotective."

"Six minutes?" Smith said.

"She's my twin sister."

"You don't have to talk about this," Smith said. "And you can kick me out at any time, but can you think of any reason why Jane would want to do what she did?"

"I've thought about nothing else since they told me," Kelly said. "I stayed up all night thinking about it, and I'm still none the wiser. We weren't particularly close – we didn't have that mother/daughter relationship you see with some families, but I'd like to think I would know if something was bothering her so much that she had to..."

"It's OK," Smith said. "You don't need to talk about it now. Do you mind if I smoke?"

Kelly started to laugh, and Smith laughed too. It wasn't really appropriate, given the circumstances, but it felt right.

Smith took out his cigarettes and lit one.

"I nearly lost her once before, you know," Kelly said. "When she was a baby. She developed a raging fever one night, and we just managed to get her to hospital in time. Another few minutes and she wouldn't have made it. We walk a fine line between life and death, don't we?"

Smith couldn't agree more.

"We certainly do. Jane's dad is no longer on the scene, is he?"

"He left us when Jane was six. Good riddance to the bastard – left me for a tart he met in Blackpool. I heard they got married and they have three kids now. I suppose I ought to tell him."

"That's up to you."

"I'm not doing it because I think he'll give two hoots," Kelly said. "I'm doing it because it's the right thing to do. Do you want something to drink? Coffee, perhaps or maybe something a bit stronger?"

"I'm supposed to be on duty," Smith said. "So I'll pass, thanks."

"You don't mind if I help myself to a drop of something?"

"Not at all."

"I know alcohol isn't recommended for shock," Kelly said. "But what do the experts know?"

"Next to nothing," Smith said. "Alcohol was used to alleviate shock centuries before the so-called experts decided otherwise."

Kelly opened one of the cupboards and took out a bottle of vodka. She poured herself a decent measure, took a long drink and topped up the glass. "I really don't want to know why she did it. I was up all night, wondering but the truth is – I don't want to know."

Smith didn't know how to react to this.

"I know it probably sounds crazy," Kelly said. "Most people would want to know, wouldn't they – to get some kind of closure, but I don't. What good would it do?"

"It's your decision," Smith said. "I'm not going to argue with you."

Kelly drained the vodka in the glass and poured herself another. "How is Lucy coping?"

"She's in a bad way," Smith said. "She was standing in front of Jane when it happened. She's been through so much, and I'm not sure how we're going to help her through this."

"Do you want me to talk to her?"

"You don't have to do that," Smith said. "You've got enough on your mind."

"I'd like to," Kelly said. "It might do us both good. You probably think I'm a terrible mother."

"I promise you, I don't."

"Sitting here drinking vodka before noon," Kelly said. "Right after my daughter has ended her life."

"It's not my place to comment," Smith said. "People cope with situations like these in different ways, and I have no right to judge. I'd better be getting back to work. If there's anything you need, give me a call."

He took out one of his cards and placed it on the table.

"Anything at all."

"There is something you can do for me," Kelly said.

"Of course," Smith said.

"Come upstairs with me."

Smith looked like he'd been hit in the face with a brick. "What?"

Kelly started to laugh. "I didn't mean it like that. I haven't been able to bring myself to go into Jane's bedroom, and I'd like to do that now. Will you come with me?"

"OK," Smith said.

He followed Kelly out of the room, and they went upstairs. The door to Jane's bedroom was closed. Kelly hesitated before pushing it open and they both went inside. The room was neater than Smith expected it to be, and he realised that Jane was a teenager who liked everything in its correct place. The bed was made, and the books on the bedside table were stacked neatly. Smith studied the titles. He was no expert in literature but even he knew that these books were definitely not on the syllabus at the sixth-form college. Sandwiched between *Lolita* and *The Catcher in the Rye* was William Burroughs' *Naked Lunch*.

"Interesting reading material," Smith commented.

Kelly wasn't listening. Her focus was taken by something on the desk against the wall. The laptop was closed and there was something next to it – something damaged beyond repair. That's what Kelly was looking at. The mobile phone had been smashed to pieces.

Smith took out his own phone and made two calls in quick succession.

CHAPTER TEN

"Two suicides," Smith said. "And two obliterated mobile phones." As soon as he'd seen what had been done to Jane Banks' phone, he was instantly awake. The first call he'd made was to Vincent Allen, telling him not to touch his wife's broken phone. The second call had been to Grant Webber. He'd asked the Head of Forensics to see if he could get anything from the phones. Smith didn't know exactly what the condition of the two mobile phones meant, but he sensed it was extremely important.

"Are you suggesting that the suicides are connected?" DC Moore said.
"I don't know," Smith said. "But the phones can't be discounted. Both Maggie Allen and Jane Banks ended their own lives at roughly the same time, and both their phones were destroyed. We can't ignore it."
"Do we know if they were acquainted?" DC King asked.
"Not yet. According to Kelly Banks, she'd never heard her daughter mention anyone called Maggie Allen but that doesn't mean anything. Teenagers rarely tell their parents everything. Webber has retrieved both phones and hopefully he'll be able to tell us something."
"Even though they were destroyed," Bridge said. "The tech team might still be able to get some info from them. What kind of phones are they?"
"How should I know?" Smith said. "I'm knocking on for forty – I'm not a teenager."
"If the sims and SD cards are still intact," DI Smyth said. "We ought to be able to access the history. For what it's worth."
"What's that supposed to mean?" Smith said.
"You said yourself that these were suicides. Two tragic events but suicides nevertheless. What exactly are we hoping to achieve by going through the phones?"
"They were both smashed to pieces, boss," Smith said. "Surely you can see

that's suspicious. Why destroy a phone before ending your life? It doesn't make any sense."

"Perhaps there's something on them the women didn't want anyone to find," DC King suggested.

"That's understandable in one instance, Kerry," Smith said. "But two phones smashed up by two women who kill themselves at the same time is more than coincidence. I know it is."

"What are you suggesting here?" DI Smyth said.

"We do some digging, boss," Smith said.

"Can I say something?" It was DC Moore.

"Harry," DI Smyth said. "How many times do I have to tell you, you do not have to put up your hand when you want to speak."

"Sorry, sir. I appreciate that it does seem suspicious that two women smash up their phones before killing themselves at roughly the same time, but where do we even start from a legal perspective? It's pretty clear that these women acted alone when they ended their own lives. Suicide isn't illegal so what do we hope to gain by even investigating it? As far as I can see, nobody can be held accountable apart from the women who carried out the suicides."

"Do you not comprehend the concept of *digging*, Harry?" Smith said. "Something stinks here, and if I'm the only one who can smell it, I reckon it's time the rest of you considered a change of career."

"That's enough," DI Smyth said. "I appreciate that you're upset. The suicide at the college was a bit too close to home, but Harry has a point. What exactly do we hope to achieve by investigating a couple of self-terminations?"

"Peace of mind?" Smith suggested. "Aren't you even curious? And it's not like we're snowed under with other work right now."

"What were you even doing at Jane's house?" Whitton asked.

"I don't know," Smith admitted. "It seemed like the right thing to do."
"How is Kelly?"
"Still in shock. I don't think it's quite sunk in yet, but it will, and that's why I want to find some answers. Something doesn't feel right about this, and I want to know why that is."
"OK," DI Smyth said. "You win. Take a closer look at the lives of these women. Smith, you and Whitton are too personally involved in the death of Jane Banks, so I want you to focus on Maggie Allen."
"I disagree."
"I don't give a damn if you disagree," DI Smyth said. "That's how it's going to be. I want you and Whitton to find out everything you can about Maggie Allen. Speak to her family and friends. It's possible that she'd been planning this for a while, and she might have spoken about it to someone close to her. Bridge, you and Harry can take a closer look at the life of Jane Banks. Talk to her teachers and speak to her friends, for what it's worth. Teenagers are notoriously secretive, but we might get lucky."
"I need some coffee," Smith said.
He got up and left the room.

"Do you think he's onto something?" Bridge said.
"Unfortunately," DI Smyth said. "When Smith gets a bee in his bonnet, it's dangerous to ignore it. He's never been wrong in the past."
"There's always a first time for everything," DC Moore pointed out.
"I think he might have a point," DC King joined in. "The broken phones can't be ignored."
"How long will it take to find out if there's anything incriminating on the phones?" Whitton said.
"If the IT team are able to access them," DI Smyth said. "We ought to know something by the end of the day, but it's a long shot. It's possible the sims were destroyed along with the rest of the phones."

Smith came back inside the room.

"Coffee machine not working?" Bridge asked.

"I didn't get as far as the canteen," Smith told him. "I was interrupted by a phone call – a very interesting phone call. Vincent Allen managed to pry something out of his son."

"I thought Robert was refusing to come home," Whitton said.

"Vincent went round to the girlfriend's house. He wanted to try and reason with the boy – Robert refused to budge, but he did mention something extremely interesting in the process. Just after Vincent left for the pub last night Robert remembered his mother acting strange. He didn't pay much attention to it at the time – teenagers rarely notice much, but he did tell his father about something his mum said. He recalled her saying *The Preacher has spoken*."

"Why is that interesting?" DC Moore said.

"Because a few seconds before Jane Banks sliced her throat open, she spoke of something similar. Darren Lewis was standing next to her, and he told me that she also mentioned someone called *The Preacher*."

CHAPTER ELEVEN

"What do you think it means?" Whitton asked.
She and Smith were in the car on the way to Robert Allen's girlfriend's house.
"I have no idea," Smith said. "But now we have two suicides, two broken phones and two preachers. We have to take this seriously now."
"Can Darren remember exactly what it was that Jane said?"
"I asked him," Smith said. "And he said Jane told them that *The Preacher has spoken*, and *The Preacher knows everything*."
"Why would she say that? Why say that before killing herself?"
"I really don't know. I've never heard of anyone called *The Preacher*, but I'm hoping young Robert Allen can help us."

Smith turned right onto Tang Hall Lane and increased his speed.
"Do you suspect that there's more to these suicides than meets the eye?" Whitton said.
"I think there is," Smith said. "Two women kill themselves at almost exactly the same time – both of them leave smashed phones behind and now we have this preacher to look into. There's more going on here than we're aware of."
"Are you thinking coercion? Do you believe these women were forced into committing suicide?"
"It's not unheard of," Smith said. "But it's extremely tricky to pull off, and it's even more difficult to prove. I've got a sinking feeling that we're going to have our work cut out with this one."
"When don't we have our work cut out for us?"
"Fair enough. What did you make of Robert Allen when you spoke to him earlier?"

"I got a weird feeling about him. His answers were all rather vague."
"He's a teenager," Smith said.
"No," Whitton said. "It was something more than that. It was almost like he's somehow detached from reality. He didn't have a reply for any of the questions posed to him, and I got a really strange vibe from him."

"We're lucky with Lucy and Darren, aren't we?" Smith said.
Whitton turned to face him. "Where did that come from?"
"They're good kids really. Teenage pregnancy aside, they've turned into responsible adults just when they needed to."
"Lucy has always been a responsible teenager."
"It's actually a miracle when you think about it," Smith said. "Considering their family backgrounds. A clan of criminals and a family of police detectives. You couldn't make shit like that up. What's the address again?"

Shelly Illman looked like she'd been roused from her bed when she answered the door. Her eyes were puffy, and her pink hair was in dire need of a brush.
"What do you want now?"
"We'd like to ask Robert some more questions," Whitton said.
She introduced Smith and asked if they could come inside.
"It's been like bloody Picadilly Circus since that kid came here," Shelly said. "Robert's dad was here earlier."
"So we believe," Smith said. "Can we come inside?"
"I suppose I don't have much choice, do I?"

She told them to take a seat in the living room.
"Feels like bloody déjà vu," she added.
Robert Allen also looked like he needed a few extra hours in bed. The teenage boy looked even worse than he did earlier. His eyelids were red and swollen, and his lips were cracked. Smith didn't need to ask him how he was feeling.

"Can we have a quick word?" he asked instead.

"I suppose so," Robert said.

"When your father was here earlier," Smith said. "You mentioned something your mum said yesterday evening. It was when your dad was at the pub."

"She said something about a preacher," Whitton said. "Can you remember that?"

Robert nodded.

"What did she say?" Smith said. "Can you recall her exact words?"

"She said The Preacher has spoken. And The Preacher knows everything."

"Do you know what she meant by that?"

Robert shrugged his shoulders.

"Have you heard her mention The Preacher before?" Smith said.

"I don't think so."

"Could you think harder? This is important."

"Why?"

"Is there something you're not telling us?" Smith said.

"No."

"Because it looks to me like you're either incredibly unobservant, or you know more than you're letting on. Which one is it?"

"I don't know what you're talking about."

    The conversation was cut short by an ungodly wail coming from upstairs. This was followed by the sound of violent guitars. Smith listened carefully and he had to admit that the raw music was rather melodic.

"What's that?" he asked Robert.

"That will be Brian. I'll give him five seconds before his mum makes him turn it off."

He was wrong. The intro to the song ended and a man started screaming. Twenty seconds into the song everything went quiet.

The door to the living room opened and Brian Illman came in. He grinned his vampire grin at Whitton and his eyes met Smith's.

"Interesting music," Smith said.

Brian made himself comfortable on the single seater. "You like it?"

"I didn't say I liked it."

"It's The Four Horsemen of the Acropolis."

"Clever play on words," Smith said. "You must be Brian."

"Guilty as charged. What's Robert done now? Let me guess – you must be from the fashion police."

"If we were," Smith said. "You would be in the back of a police car already."

"Funny guy."

"Don't you have something better to do?" Whitton said.

"Nope," Brian said. "And the last time I looked, this was my house."

"Could you give us some privacy please?" Smith said. "We're in the middle of something here."

"He won't tell you anything," Brian said.

"What makes you say that?" Smith said.

Brian got to his feet. "That's just how it is."

CHAPTER TWELVE

Brian Illman hadn't been exaggerating. The peculiar teenager was right when he told Smith that Robert Allen wouldn't tell them anything. After another twenty minutes of questions, Smith and Whitton were still as much in the dark as they had been when they first went inside the house, and Smith realised they were wasting their time with Robert Allen.

"He knows something," Smith said in the car park of the station. He lit a cigarette, took a long drag and exhaled a cloud of smoke.
"I got that impression too," Whitton said. "But we're not going to get anything out of him."
"We could always haul him in and interrogate him."
Whitton shook her head. "On what grounds? The DI will never authorise it."
"He was in the house when his mother killed herself," Smith said. "And he just happened to make himself scarce just before his dad found her. If that's not suspicious, I don't know what is. I saw the window in the bathroom, and it would be quite possible for someone of Robert's age and size to climb out and shimmy down the drainpipe."
"Do you really think he killed his own mother?" Whitton said. "And where does Jane Banks fit into the equation? The broken phones and the mysterious preacher link the two together, but we know for a fact that Robert couldn't have been involved in Jane's suicide."
"His girlfriend's brother was at the Halloween party," Smith pointed out.
"You're clutching at straws," Whitton said. "You of all people should know how fruitless speculation is. And where is Robert's motive? Why would he want to kill his mother?"
"God knows," Smith said and sighed deeply.
   A car raced up and screeched to a halt.
"Someone's in a hurry," Smith said.

He watched as a man and a woman got out of the shiny black Land Rover. Both of them were dressed in similar tracksuits and both tracksuits were at least three sizes too small. Their excess flab was threatening to burst out of the flimsy material. The man opened the boot and took out a large box.

"Has Walmart finally arrived in York?" Smith wondered.

Whitton laughed. "You're terrible."

"Look at the state of them. That is some serious inbreeding on display right there."

"You can't say things like that these days."

Whitton was trying very hard to keep a straight face and she was failing miserably.

"Fuck," Smith said. "They're coming over."

"Do you work here?" It was the man.

Up close, Smith saw that the tracksuits were identical, and both the man and the woman were sporting similar haircuts. *Mullets* – Smith recalled.

"We work here, yes," he said.

"What are you going to do about these?"

The man nodded to the box he was holding.

"What's in there?" Smith asked.

"Two-hundred quid's worth of fireworks."

"I'm not a big fan of fireworks," Smith said.

"These ones are useless now," the man said.

"Someone set the hosepipe on them," the woman joined in. "Flooded the shed, and we know exactly who it was. We want to report them."

"I'm sure someone will be able to help you inside," Whitton said. "Speak to someone at the front desk."

"Do you work here or not?" the man said. "We've got proof. Got the whole thing on camera. Frankie Lewis isn't going to get away with this."

This got Smith's attention.

"You caught it on CCTV?"

"Clear as day," the woman said. "He'll go down for this, what with his record. Once a criminal, always a criminal."

"Speak to the officer manning the front desk," Whitton said.

She placed an arm on Smith's shoulder and urged him to walk with her towards the entrance of the station.

"What a hideous couple," she said inside.

"Frankie said he was going to do something about the fireworks," Smith said. "I never thought he would. He could get into shit for this."

"It's not our problem," Whitton said. "And it'll probably come to nothing. It's not exactly a serious offence."

"I'm going to get that coffee I missed out on earlier," Smith said.

He headed upstairs to the canteen. He took out his phone and called Frankie Lewis on the way. Smith and Darren's dad hadn't got off to the best of starts but Smith had grown to like the ex-convict, and he wanted to give him a heads-up about the fireworks. The call went to voicemail and Smith left a short message asking Frankie to phone him back as soon as he could.

Bridge and DI Smyth were deep in discussion at one of the tables. Smith selected a strong coffee from the space-age machine and joined them.

"Why the serious faces?"

"Nothing for you to worry about," DI Smyth said. "Did you have any luck with Robert Allen?"

"He's not talking," Smith said. "Something is going on there, but I have no idea what it is."

"Does he have any idea about the *Preacher* character?" Bridge said.

"He reckons he doesn't, but I don't believe him. I find it hard to believe that a boy's mother kills herself the same night as a girl who attends the same college as the boy's girlfriend's brother."

"That is quite a coincidence," DI Smyth agreed. "But perhaps that's all it is.

We've had word back from the tech team. They found nothing on either of the phones. And when I say nothing, I mean absolutely nothing at all."

"I thought they could retrieve stuff that had been deleted," Smith said.

"Those phones were clean," DI Smyth said. "And the report from the IT guys went so far as to suggest that both phones had never been used."

"How is that possible?" Smith said. "Surely there has to be something on them."

"There wasn't. Both of those phones were brand new – straight out of the box."

CHAPTER THIRTEEN

"This just gets weirder and weirder."

Smith was the first to speak in the afternoon briefing. A couple of phone calls had cleared some things up but in doing so they had thrown even more confusion into the mix.

"According to Vincent Allen," Smith said. "Maggie had an iPhone 12. The phone Webber retrieved from the bedroom was an iPhone 6. The broken phone wasn't Maggie's."

"Why didn't the husband spot that?" DC Moore said.

"It was smashed to pieces, Harry," Smith said. "And Vincent just focused on the cover. Maggie had a luminous green phone cover, and the one that had been smashed had an identical one."

"Do we know where her phone is?" DC King said. "The iPhone 12, I mean."

"It's missing," Smith said. "Which leads me to believe that there is definitely something suspicious happening here."

"What about the phone found in Jane Banks' bedroom?" Bridge said.

"Same thing," Smith said. "Jane's mother confirmed that Jane had a contract for a Samsung Galaxy S21."

"That's a fancy phone for a teenager," DC Moore pointed out.

"It's a phone, Harry," Smith said. "And it's not the phone that we found in Jane's bedroom. The one that had been obliterated was a cheaper model – a Samsung A15. The S21 is also unaccounted for. Why make it look like you've smashed your phone? It makes no sense whatsoever. We need to locate those missing phones."

Smith's own phone started to ring. The screen told him it was Frankie Lewis, and he rejected the call. He would phone back later.

"Any thoughts?" he asked the team around the table.

"What about the service providers?" DC Moore said. "We might be able to see when the genuine phones were last used, and we should be able to check the call history without having the actual phones."

"I'm still finding it hard to understand why they would destroy brand new phones," Bridge said. "What's the point?"

"We don't know," DI Smyth said. "And we won't waste time on guesswork. Our priority now is finding out where the other phones ended up."

"Are we conducting an actual investigation now?" Smith asked.

"I thought that's what we'd been doing right from the start," DI Smyth said.

"I just needed it confirmed."

His phone started to ring again. It was Frankie Lewis.

"Excuse me," he said. "I need to take this."

He left the room and took the call outside.

"I've just had a visit from your lot." Frankie didn't beat about the bush.

"What did you do, Frankie?" Smith said.

"I made sure their fireworks couldn't traumatise any more poor animals."

"I had the pleasure of meeting the couple who own the fireworks," Smith said. "They seem like lovely people."

"They're not."

"I was being sarcastic. What did the police officers say?"

"I've been warned that charges might be brought against me for wilful damage to property," Frankie said.

"Is that all?"

"I was told that the Jenkins' are demanding a full investigation into the matter," Frankie said. "Are your lot really going to waste time on a few fireworks?"

"If the Jenkins' want a case opened, and they have enough evidence to support it, the police are obliged to take it seriously. I'm a bit busy right now. Will there be anything else?"

"I could do without this right now," Frankie said. "I was wondering if you might have a word with the Jenkins'. Persuade them that it will be in their best interests to drop it."

"How am I supposed to do that?"

Frankie told him, and it wasn't what Smith was expecting to hear.

* * *

While Darren's dad was explaining to Smith how he might be able to help with his firework predicament, a young man was glued to the screen of his phone in the city library. Keith Peters scrolled down and listened to the words carefully. Then he listened to them again, even though the instructions were quite clear.

Keith removed his air pods and stood up. He smiled at the librarian clearing the books from the same table. Later, when questioned by the detectives of York CID she would describe the smile as somewhat strained. She would say that she thought the man had a lot on his mind, and she would regret not asking him if there was anything she could do to help. She didn't know then, but she was going to recall that smile for a very long time afterwards.

Keith picked up his rucksack, left the table and made his way towards the exit. Once outside, he looked left and right, took out his phone and deposited it in a rubbish bin. He didn't need it anymore – the instructions were quite clear, and he was able to remember every word.

Keith went inside a mobile phone shop and selected a mid-priced phone. "It works out much cheaper on contract," the salesman informed him. "In fact, we've got a special on right now with that particular model. You get the usual minutes and data, and you get two phones into the bargain."

"I only need one," Keith told him. "And I don't need a contract. It would be pointless."

The salesman thought this was a strange thing to say, but he processed the sale and accepted Keith's credit card. Keith left the receipt on the counter and exited the shop.

He turned right onto Gillygate and continued north. He was fifty feet from the York St John University when he stopped and checked his watch. According to the timetable, the bus would be along in less than two minutes. Keith wasn't going to wait for it at the designated bus stop – that wouldn't work at all.

It was Sunday afternoon and the streets were quiet. Across the road, a man walked by with two toddlers in an oversized pushchair. Keith waved at him and the man quickened his pace. There was a bench just up ahead and Keith headed for it. He sat down, removed the new phone from the plastic cover and placed it on the bench next to him. Then he took out a rock from his rucksack and smashed the phone into a hundred pieces.

Leaving the destroyed phone and the rucksack on the bench Keith stood up, crossed the road and started to walk back in the direction he'd just come from. The number 42 bus had stopped to let passengers off further back down the road. Keith picked up his pace and he'd almost caught up to the man with the pushchair when he heard the sound of the engine behind him. When he was sure the bus was close enough, he stepped into the road and prepared himself for what was to come.

CHAPTER FOURTEEN

Smith wondered if he'd made a big mistake as he pressed the bell on the door of the house at the end of the street where Darren's parents lived. Frankie's idea had taken him by surprise, and Smith wondered if it was going to work, but in the end, he decided that whether he liked it or not, Frankie Lewis was family now and families were supposed to look out for each other.

Lenny Jenkins answered the door dressed in the same tracksuit as before. Frankie had told Smith their names. Lenny and his wife, Sheila lived with their seventeen-year-old son Wayne.
"You're that policeman."
Smith showed him his ID. "Can I have a word inside? It's about the fireworks."
Lenny studied the warrant card for quite some time.
"Detective Sergeant? You're taking it seriously then?"
"We take all cases of criminal damage seriously, Mr Jenkins."
"Come in," Lenny said. "Do you want something to drink? Tea or coffee?"
Smith declined.
Lenny looked down at Smith's feet. "Would you mind taking off your shoes?"
"What?" Smith said.
"Your shoes," Lenny said. "I have a thing about shoes in the house. It stems from my childhood. It's not quite a phobia, but it's pretty close."
Smith obliged. He left the shoes by the front door. He realised that he was wearing odd socks.

He couldn't understand why he'd been asked to take off his shoes when he ventured further into the house. The place looked like it hadn't seen a vacuum cleaner in years. Lenny led him to a kitchen that should probably be condemned. Smith's feet stuck to the ancient linoleum as he walked, and he didn't dare to guess what the mystery sticky substance was. He decided he would buy some new socks before he went back to the station. He would dispose of the odd pair he was wearing. The kitchen was somewhat of a paradox. The overall filth and squalor aside, Smith couldn't help but notice the expensive appliances dotted around the room. The six-burner gas stove looked like it was brand new and the name on the front told him it was not cheap. A double door fridge took up far too much space against one of the walls.

Lenny caught Smith staring at it.
"It's a Bosch. Top of the range with a water dispenser and ice maker."
Smith wondered why someone would want an ice maker in Yorkshire, but he didn't comment on it.
"It didn't come cheap," Lenny told him. "But then, money is no issue anymore after the big win."
Smith didn't bother to ask about this either.
"Take a seat," Lenny said. "What do you need to know? I imagine you'll want us to fill in some paperwork. The woman at the station didn't seem too bothered."
"I just need to get some details," Smith said and sat down at the kitchen table.
"We got it all on camera."
"So you said."

The woman Smith now knew was Sheila Jenkins came into the room and a strange smell came in with her. It was something sickly sweet and it made Smith feel slightly ill.
"They're taking it seriously, pet," Lenny said to her. "Frankie Lewis will think twice about pulling a stunt like that again.
"Proper thing too," Sheila said. "People like him need to learn they can't go around terrorizing decent people like us."

"There are a few formalities I need to get out of the way," Smith said. "For the record. Could you state your name please."

"Lenny Jenkins. Aren't you going to write this down?"

Smith tapped his head. "I have an exceptional memory. I'll fill in the forms later. What do you do for a living, Mr Jenkins?"

"I work at the Tesco on Hull Road. I know you must be wondering why I'm still working after the big win, but money doesn't have to change you, does it?"

Smith couldn't care less.

"Are you employed full time?"

"That's right."

"What hours do you work?" Smith asked.

"Eight to four," Lenny said. "Tuesday to Saturday. I get Sundays and Mondays off."

Smith turned to Sheila. "What do you do, Mrs Jenkins?"

"Cleaner," she said. "I work for a company that has contracts to clean schools in the city."

"And is that also full time?"

"Why do you need to know all this?" Sheila said. "What's it got to do with the damaged fireworks."

"He's just getting all our details for the record, pet," Lenny said.

"That's right," Smith lied.

"Do you want to see the camera footage?" Lenny said.

"Not just now," Smith said.

"It's high-quality footage. You can't argue with it."

"We'll come back to that," Smith said. "Where did you get the fireworks from?"

"What?"

"Where did you buy the fireworks?"

"The newsagents on Gordon Avenue."

"I know the place," Smith said. "What would you estimate the value of the damaged goods to be?"

"Over two hundred quid."

"I'm going to need to see some proof of that."

"What for?" Sheila said. "Don't you believe him?"

"It's not what I believe that matters," Smith said. "In cases like these it's important to establish what has actually been damaged. For compensation purposes, I mean. If the charges against Mr Lewis are successful a court will award you compensation and that compensation needs to be commensurate with the actual value of the property that was damaged. Do you understand that?"

Smith was finding it a real struggle to suppress the smile that was trying to form on his face.

"Do you understand?" he asked again.

"Not really," Shelia said.

"We're going to get the money back for the fireworks," Lenny explained.

"But in order to do that," Smith said. "We're going to need proof of the value of the damaged goods. Do you perhaps have a receipt? Maybe you paid by credit card."

"Go and have a look will you, pet," Lenny said.

Sheila nodded and wobbled out of the room.

She returned shortly afterwards with a triumphant grin on her face. She placed the receipt on the table in front of Smith.

"That's great," he said. "It says here that you paid in cash."

"Cash is king," Lenny said.

"True," Smith said. "Did either of you take any time off work last week?"

"What?" Lenny said.

"Were you and your wife both at work the entire week?"

"I think so," Sheila said.

"We were," Lenny confirmed.

"All week?"

"All week. What's that got to do with anything?"

"Who purchased the fireworks?" Smith said.

"I did," Lenny replied straight away.

"Are you sure?"

"Of course I am. I think I'd remember buying fireworks."

"I don't know if you're aware of the laws pertaining to the sale of fireworks," Smith said.

"You can get them in loads of shops," Sheila said.

"That's not what I'm referring to," Smith said. "Fireworks can only be sold to persons over the age of 18."

"I'm definitely over 18," Lenny joked.

"The penalties for anyone breaking that law are severe, Mr Jenkins. Both for the seller and the purchaser."

"What's your point?"

"You didn't buy the fireworks, Mr Jenkins," Smith said. "According to that receipt the transaction was carried out on Wednesday last week, at 11:23. You've just confirmed that both you and Mrs Jenkins were at work at that time. Let's move on to CCTV footage, shall we?"

"I can show it to you on my phone," Sheila offered.

"That's not the CCTV footage I'm referring to. Like I said, I know the newsagents on Gordon Avenue, and I know they have cameras inside the shop. I reckon that if I were to ask to see the footage from Wednesday morning, we'll see that it wasn't you who purchased those fireworks."

"What is this?" Sheila said.

"I'm just doing my job, Mrs Jenkins," Smith said.

He realised that he needed to finish this now. The smile was bubbling below the surface, and he wasn't sure how long he would be able to keep it at bay.

"It was your son who purchased the fireworks," he said. "Wayne is seventeen, isn't he?"

"I bought them," Lenny insisted.

"No," Smith said. "Wayne did. CCTV cameras do not lie. They're a godsend for us in the police."

"What exactly are you telling us?" Lenny said. "Is this some kind of threat?"

"Not at all. I'm just bringing to your attention what will happen if you pursue the charges against Mr Lewis. Everything will need to be investigated and that will include the initial purchase of the fireworks. Our officers are extremely meticulous."

"Are you forcing us to drop the charges?" Sheila said.

"Of course not," Smith said. "I wouldn't dream of it - I'm just giving you a heads-up on what the consequences could be. In all likelihood Wayne will get away with a fine of a few hundred pounds. I could be wrong of course."

Lenny and Sheila exchanged glances. Smith was sure he could hear cogs turning in both of their heads.

"Can I be brutally honest with you?" he said.

Mr and Mrs Jenkins nodded.

"You didn't hear this from me," Smith said. "But York Police could really do without the criminal damage thing and the underage purchasing of fireworks. It'll involve a mountain of paperwork we really don't need, and you have the power to make it all go away. I would appreciate it if you would do that."

"We drop the charges against Frankie Lewis," Lenny said. "And you forget about the underage sale of fireworks?"

"I'm glad we're on the same page. You're clearly smarter than I originally thought."

Lenny grinned. "Just because I work at a supermarket, doesn't make me a moron."

"I can see that now," Smith said. "What do you say?"

"Thank you, I suppose," Lenny said.

Smith was close to breaking point now. He needed to make a sharp exit before the laughter that was brewing came to the surface.

"I'm glad we've got that cleared up," he said. "I'll keep hold of this, if that's OK."

He picked up the receipt and put it in his pocket.

"I suppose there's no harm done really," Sheila said.

"Just one more thing," Smith said. "I would advise against setting off any more fireworks. I suggest you keep a low profile for a while."

"We can do that," Sheila said.

"I'll see myself out," Smith said.

He couldn't get out of there quickly enough. He picked up his shoes, but he didn't put them on. No sooner had he closed the door behind him, the belly laugh he'd kept buried exploded with a vengeance. The fit lasted for quite some time and when it was over, Smith realised that a young girl was taking a keen interest in him. She was sitting on the wall of the house opposite, and she too was giggling. Smith managed to compose himself enough to wave at her. She gave him a wide grin and waved back.

CHAPTER FIFTEEN

"What have I missed?" Smith said before he sat down in the small conference room.
The visit to Mr and Mrs *Mullet* had gone better than he could have hoped. They'd fallen for the bluff of the CCTV cameras in the newsagents, hook, line, and sinker. Frankie Lewis had told him that his son Gary had been in the shop the morning Wayne Jenkins had bought the fireworks, but he made no mention of CCTV cameras. Smith had winged it with that part, and it had played out beautifully. He'd driven straight to the station once he was sure he'd got the laughter out of his system. He'd forgotten to buy some new socks.

"Where have you been?" DI Smyth said.
"You don't want to know, boss."
"Actually, I do. You've been missing in action for over an hour. Let me remind you who pays your salary."
"I'll consider myself reminded. It won't happen again."
DI Smyth reacted to this with a raised eyebrow.
"What have I missed?" Smith asked again.
"We were just discussing the events surrounding Jane Banks' suicide at the Halloween party," DI Smyth said.
"Me and Harry have spoken to the teachers who were supervising the students at the party," Bridge said. "There were two of them. Mr Grigg the Head of Maths didn't witness the suicide – he was dealing with a minor altercation in the Gents, and he wasn't there when Jane killed herself."
"I spoke to the other teacher last night," Smith said. "Flora Newton."
"She teaches English," Bridge said. "She couldn't tell us much. She was manning the refreshment stand when she heard the screaming."
Something occurred to Smith.

"The music had been turned off. There was no music playing when Jane killed herself."

"I'm coming to that," Bridge said. "We also spoke to the bloke who'd been hired to DJ at the party."

"Young bloke," DC Moore said. "He hasn't been out of school long himself. When we asked him why the music had stopped, he said it was nothing to do with him."

"He was the DJ," Smith said. "Of course it had something to do with him."

"He didn't turn it off," Bridge said. "It went off by itself."

"And when we spoke to the college caretaker," DC Moore said. "And asked him to check the distribution board he confirmed that something or someone had caused the isolation switch for the plugs the DJ's decks were plugged into to trip."

"The lights are on a different circuit," Bridge said. "That's why they stayed on."

"Someone flipped the power to stop the music," DC King said.

"What does that actually tell us though?" Whitton asked.

"The power to the music was cut off just before Jane killed herself," Smith said. "Someone did that on purpose."

"Someone knew what she was planning on doing," DC King said. "And they cut the music to make it more dramatic."

"I wouldn't go that far," DI Smyth said.

"I think Kerry's right, boss," Smith said. "Jane wasn't alone in this. I'm not buying that she just happened to kill herself when the power to the plugs for the music was tripped. This was planned. And if I'm right it means that the other person involved was at the Halloween Party last night. Someone had to physically flip that switch."

"We've got a list," DC Moore told him. "And it's quite a long one."

"We'll prioritise," Smith said. "We can tick two names off straight away."

"Lucy and Darren," Whitton guessed.

"We will go through that list in its entirety," DI Smyth said.

Smith glared at him. "You can't be serious?"

"Lucy and Darren were not involved," Whitton said.

"We will interview everybody who attended that Halloween Party," DI Smyth said. "Lucy and Darren included.

"They don't know anything," Smith said.

"Then they have nothing to hide."

"If they knew anything about Jane's suicide they would have told us," Smith said.

"I am not having this debate."

"I'm not starting a debate," Smith said. "I'm stating a fact, and I would appreciate it if you'd have some faith in my instincts."

DI Smyth's phone started to ring and he was glad of the distraction. The tension inside the room was building, and he was worried that things were about to be said that couldn't be unsaid. He answered the call and the room fell silent.

"Thank you for bringing it to my attention," he said after a while.

"Is everything alright, sir?" DC King said.

"A man has jumped in front of a bus close to the Minster. A witness claims he waited for it to come close, and he jumped into its path. The officers first on the scene found a rucksack and a mobile phone on a bench close by. The phone had been smashed to pieces, and according to PC Hill, plastic packaging was found on the ground below the bench."

"A brand new phone?" DC Moore said.

"It looks like it."

"What the fuck is going on in this city?" Smith said.

"There's more," DI Smyth said. "The driver of the bus reacted quickly. He spotted the man and slammed on the brakes. He's badly injured, but he's still alive."

Smith was on his feet in a flash.

"Hold your horses," DI Smyth said.

"We need to speak to him."

"Not going to happen. He's in an induced coma. According to Baldwin it's highly unlikely he'll regain consciousness, and if he does there's a strong possibility, he'll have suffered some brain damage. I'm going to organise some uniforms to see if they can retrace his steps."

"Do we have a name?" Smith said.

"There was a wallet in the rucksack that PC Hill found on the bench," DI Smyth said. "The name on the credit card inside was Keith Peters."

Bridge and DC Moore turned to look at one another.

"Is something wrong?" DI Smyth said.

"We spoke to him earlier," Bridge said. "Keith Peters was the DJ at the Halloween party."

CHAPTER SIXTEEN

The Preacher couldn't see much through the window, but he could see enough. The activity on the monitor in the hospital room told him everything he needed to know – Keith Peters' heart was still beating, and that wasn't supposed to be the case.

The Preacher smiled at a nurse walking past and followed the signs for the exit. He made his way to his car and gazed up at the sky.

Jesus died for our sins. He recited the words in his head. *And you were supposed to die to atone for the sins of the person closest to you.*

He got into the car and slammed his hands on the dashboard.

"But you fucking didn't, did you?"

He started the engine, engaged first gear and drove out of the car park. The sky outside was tinged with orange, and The Preacher decided that it was a sign. It was a sign from the man upstairs that he was on the right track. In fact, the orange hue was due to the chemicals from all the fireworks that had been set off recently, but The Preacher didn't think of this – in his mind, there was fire and brimstone up there, and it was there for a reason.

He parked his car outside a house in Holgate and turned off the engine. After checking his appearance in the rearview mirror, he got out and walked down the path to the front door. The doorbell had two pieces of tape stuck over it so The Preacher rapped on the door three times.

Sarah Peters opened up soon afterwards and smiled at him. The Preacher had always thought she had a friendly smile.

"Keith isn't home."

"I'm aware of that. It's actually you I came to see. Can I come in?"

"Is everything alright?" Sarah asked.

"Everything's going to be fine."

Sarah invited him inside the house. The Preacher looked up and down the street before going in and closing the door behind him.

* * *

"Uniforms have managed to track some of Keith Peters' movements this afternoon," DI Smyth said. "According to his girlfriend, he was planning on visiting the city library, and CCTV inside the library confirmed that he was indeed inside from 13:00 to 13:23."

"Why does a library need cameras?" DC Moore wondered.

"Who cares?" Smith said. "Let's stick to relevant questions, shall we?"

"I was just…"

"Shut up, Harry."

"Like I said," DI Smyth said. "Mr Peters left the library at 13:23 and the camera outside caught him placing something inside the rubbish bin there. PC Miller searched the bin and came up trumps. He found a mobile phone. Unfortunately, it was switched off, and without Mr Peters' password it's going to be tricky to gain access to it."

"But it can be done?" DC King said.

"It can," DI Smyth said. "But it will take time."

"Who was the witness?" Smith said. "You said a witness saw Keith jump in front of the bus."

"A man out with his two children remembered seeing a man acting strangely," DI Smyth said. "He was on the opposite side of the road and the witness claims that he waved at him."

"Why would he do that?" DC Moore said.

"It's not important," Smith said.

"The witness went on his way," DI Smyth said. "And he didn't see what happened at the bench with the new phone. The next thing he was aware of was Mr Peters behind him and then he heard the screech of brakes and the bus slamming into the man. It was the witness who called for the ambulance."

"That phone is important," Smith said. "The fact that a brand-new phone is smashed to pieces can only mean one thing."

"You've lost me there, Sarge," DC Moore said.

"It's a diversion tactic."

"Misdirection?" DC King dared.

Smith smiled. "Dead right, Kerry. They destroy a phone they've never used because there's some kind of clue on their regular phone. We need to speed up getting into that phone."

"It'll take as long as it takes," DI Smyth said.

"What do we know about Keith Peters?" Smith said.

"He's a DJ," DC Moore offered.

"About that," Smith said. "The bloke worked as a DJ at a party where a teenage girl killed herself and the next day, he tries to top himself too. It can't be just me who thinks the two events have to be connected."

"We'll be trawling through the details of Mr Peters' life during the course of the day," DI Smyth said.

"How did he get the college gig?" Smith said.

"That's one of the questions we'll be asking. We do know that he lives with his sister in Holgate."

"He lives with his sister?" DC Moore said. "That's a bit weird, isn't it?"

"Not particularly. His girlfriend didn't give the uniforms who questioned her much more information than that, but we'll be speaking to her again in more detail."

"We need to know whether he's come across The Preacher," Smith said.

"I agree," DI Smyth said. "We've had three suicide attempts in the past twenty-four-hours – two of those attempts were successful and a preacher has been mentioned twice. What is the significance of this preacher?"

"Has the sister been informed of Keith's suicide attempt?" Smith said.
"Not yet," DI Smyth said. "She's not answering her phone, but I'll arrange for some uniforms to go round to see her later today."
"I'll do it," Smith offered. "We need to ask her some questions about her brother anyway, so we can kill two birds with one stone."

CHAPTER SEVENTEEN

Smith and DC King walked up the path to number 16 Grantham Drive and stopped outside the front door.

"Nice place," DC King said. "DJs must do alright for themselves."

"According to Keith Peters' girlfriend," Smith said. "Him and his sister inherited the house when the parents died. I don't think either of them could afford to buy the other out and that's probably why they both live here now."

"It doesn't look like the doorbell is working," DC King said.

The bell had been covered with two strips of duct tape. Smith knocked and waited.

"Perhaps she's not home," DC King said. "Do we know what she does for a living?"

"I have no idea," Smith said and knocked again.

He went to see if he could see anything through the downstairs window, but the curtains were closed in there.

"Why would someone close the curtains at this time?" he said.

He knocked again with the same result. He tried the handle and pushed the door open.

"Are we allowed to just barge in?" DC King asked.

"Not really," Smith said. "But that's never stopped me before."

He went inside the house and called Sarah's name. The house remained silent.

"I don't like this."

"Sarge?"

"Something's not right," Smith said.

He checked the living room. The curtains were thick and there wasn't much light to see by. Smith flicked on the light and saw that there was nobody inside the room.

There was a decent sized dining room next to the living room, and after a quick scan they found that one to be empty too. The kitchen was at the end of the hallway and the door was closed. Smith pushed it open, and the smell hit him immediately.

"Call it in," he said to DC King.

"Call what in?"

"I don't know yet, but I do know that smell. That's blood – a lot of blood."

Sarah Peters was face down behind the island in the middle of the room. The back of her head was a mess of blood and some kind of pulpy mash. More blood had pooled around her head. It had formed an almost perfect circle and the sheer quantity of it told Smith that Sarah Peters was definitely deceased.

He surveyed the room. On the kitchen island were two coffee mugs. One of them was half full. Smith stuck a finger into the liquid inside the mug. "It's still lukewarm. I think this happened very recently, and I think she knew the person who did this to her."

* * *

It didn't take Grant Webber long to figure out how Sarah Peters had met her end. The Head of Forensics picked up the cast iron pan by the end of the handle and was surprised by how heavy it was. Blood had stuck to the bottom of the pan and there were strands of hair glued to the edges.

"One good smack would be enough to do the trick with this thing," he commented.

"The kettle has recently boiled," Billie Jones said.

Webber's assistant found a glass in a cupboard, half-filled it with water from the kettle and dipped her little finger in.

Webber raised an eyebrow. "Is that some new forensic technique I'm unaware of?"

"You should really try to keep up with modern forensics," Billie said. "We need a door-to-door now. The person who did this isn't long gone. Smith reckons she knew her killer."

"As loath as I am to admit it, Smith is rarely wrong."

Webber crouched down over Sarah Peters. The blood on the back of her head was beginning to dry. From the position of her body Webber guessed that she'd fallen face forwards after the blow to the head.

"She was standing here when she was attacked," he said and stood back up. "Her attacker hits her on the back of the head – she loses consciousness and hits the deck. She didn't stand a chance."

"I don't think her killer came here with the intention of ending her life," Billie said.

"That's not our department," Webber said. "But I'm inclined to agree with you. The killer is invited in because they're acquainted – she makes coffee, and they have an argument. The cast iron pan is at hand and seconds later, it's all over."

"If we're correct," Billie said. "There's a strong chance he'll have been sloppy. We should be able to pull prints from the frying pan and the coffee mug."

"Indeed," Webber said.

"Can I come in?"

Webber didn't even turn around to look at Smith.

"Since when did you require an invitation?"

"This is the all-new Smith."

"God help us all," Webber said.

"I've organised a door-to-door," Smith told him. "This happened recently and it's possible one of the neighbours saw something. It's Sunday afternoon

so most of them should be at home. He didn't come here to kill her, did he?"
"It's funny you should say that," Webber said. "Billie and I were just coming to that conclusion."
"You might get lucky with the pan and the coffee mug."
"We've also had that discussion. Do you have any idea who could have done this?"

Smith wasn't listening. He was looking at something on the fridge. It was a photograph of Sarah Peters, and it was the uniform she was wearing that had caught his attention.
"Do either of you recognise this uniform?"
Webber and Billie had a look. Sarah was wearing a blue shirt with some kind of logo on the collar. Over the shirt was a high vis vest.
"I think that's what the drivers of East Yorkshire Buses wear," Billie said. "I could be wrong - it's been a while since I took the bus."

CHAPTER EIGHTEEN

"Sarah Peters was a bus driver," DI Smyth said.
It was getting late, but he decided to have one final briefing to discuss the murder of Keith Peters' sister.
"It's been confirmed. She's worked for East Yorkshire Buses for three years."
"And her brother just happened to try and kill himself by throwing himself in front of a bus," Smith said. "That is one connection we cannot ignore."
"It is," DI Smyth agreed. "It's yet to be confirmed but it's highly likely that Miss Peters died due to a blow to the back of the head. A heavy cast-iron frying pan was retrieved at the scene and there was a lot of blood on the surface as well as a number of hairs which are similar to Miss Peters' hair."

"I think she knew her killer," Smith said. "The two coffee mugs suggest this, and I also believe the killer didn't go there with the intention of ending her life. The pan was part of a set that was stacked on the counter in the kitchen, and it looks to me that this was a spur of the moment killing."
"Are you suggesting that they had some kind of altercation?" Bridge said.
"I don't know," Smith said. "But it looks like it started out very amicable. You don't make coffee for someone you're angry with. I think they drank their coffee - an argument broke out and it ended badly for one of them."

"The door-to-door didn't produce anything useful," DI Smyth said. "A man returning home from walking his dog thinks he saw a car he hadn't seen before parked close to Sarah's house."
"Did this dogwalker remember what kind of car it was?" Smith said. "The colour perhaps?"
"He thinks it could be blue or black," DI Smyth said. "It was a dark colour."
"Dead end then," Smith decided. "Sarah was killed not long before me and Kerry got there. If we'd been thirty minutes earlier we could have prevented

it."

"Don't dwell on it," DI Smyth said.

"I'm not dwelling on it out of guilt, boss," Smith said. "I'm finding it difficult to figure out how it's possible for a woman to be murdered so soon after her brother tried to kill himself. My brain can't process it properly. And if her killer is connected to Keith's attempted suicide, he was taking a massive risk going round there today."

"We have no proof that the two are actually connected," DC Moore said.

"Come on, Harry," Smith said. "They have to be linked. She was a bus driver for fucks sake."

"We're not going to get any news on Keith Peters' mobile phone any time soon," DI Smyth said. "And we're not going to hear anything from Forensics until tomorrow, so I don't see any reason not to wrap things up for today. Is there anything any of you want to bring up before we do that?"

The silence that followed told him that nobody had anything to discuss.

"Get lost then. I'll see you all bright and early in the morning."

There was a scraping of chairs as everyone got to their feet.

"Not you, Smith," DI Smyth said. "A quick word please."

"What is it?" Smith said when he was alone with the DI.

"Are you going to tell me where you disappeared to today?"

"I just had to sort out a bit of family stuff," Smith said.

"Is there anything I need to be aware of?"

"Nope. It's all sorted out now."

"How's your daughter bearing up?"

"She's not," Smith said. "We haven't had much chance to talk to her about what happened, but I know she's got a long road ahead of her. She watched her best friend kill herself. She was standing in front of Jane when she sliced her throat open – she ended up with Jane's blood all over her face, so I don't think she's going to get over it in a hurry. That's why I want to save her the stress of a police interrogation."

"I hear what you're saying, but you have to separate work from your personal life here. In reality you and Whitton ought to take a step back from this investigation. Protocol dictates it."

"You know me, boss," Smith said. "I've never really given a fuck about reality or protocol, so if it's alright with you I'll carry on doing what I do best."

"I can live with that."

"Good to hear it. I'm going to hit the road. There's a six-pack of beer in the fridge with my name on it, and I may even be tempted to get reacquainted with an old friend who goes by the name of Jack."

"Don't overdo it."

"Wouldn't dream of it, boss," Smith said. "Who knows – maybe the old bluesman will be tempted to show his ugly face again. I haven't played in ages."

His phone started to ring before he was even out of the door of the station. The screen told him it was Frankie Lewis.

"It worked then."

"I presume you're talking about the Walmart couple's sodden fireworks?" Smith said.

"I owe you one."

"Don't worry about it."

"No," Frankie said. "I really do owe you one. What have you got planned for this evening?"

"I was looking forward to a few beers at home."

"Then we're on the same page. Do you know the Green Man on Michael Street?"

"It's a complete dive," Smith remembered.

"You're thinking of the Green Man on the Tang Hall Estate," Frankie said. "This Green Man is close to where I live. It's a pretty decent pub."
"I'm really not in the mood, Frankie."
"Come on. A few pints – I'm buying, and I won't take no for an answer."
Smith found himself agreeing and he hoped he wasn't going to regret it.

CHAPTER NINETEEN

The exterior of the Green Man looked nothing like the rundown façade of its namesake in Tang Hall, and Smith had to admit that it did look like a half-decent pub. The car park was almost full, and Smith reckoned that this was a good sign too. He got out of his car and made his way to the entrance.

The interior of the pub was bright, and the décor was modern. The back of the room was dominated by a huge bar that looked like it was made of teak. Behind it were rows and rows of beer pumps. Smith had never seen so many different beers on offer. He scanned the pumps, and he was relieved when he saw that they sold Theakstons. He was a creature of habit, and he wasn't about to break the habit of a lifetime anytime soon. Frankie Lewis was nowhere to be seen.

He appeared from the side of the bar just as Smith had ordered a pint of Theakstons.
"That's on me, Bill," Frankie told the middle-aged barman.
Smith deduced that he was a regular here.
"Cheers," he said.
"I'll have a pint of my usual," Frankie said.
Definitely a regular, Smith thought.
They took the drinks to one of the tables.
"Cheers," Frankie said and raised his glass. "I appreciate your help."
"People like the Jenkins' shouldn't be allowed to buy fireworks anyway," Smith said. "They look like they live in a trailer park."
"This city is full of people like them. They're not short of a few quid, and they're not shy to advertise it."
"Lenny mentioned something about a big win."
"Lotto money. I don't play myself – it's a mug's game."
"What exactly did you do to their fireworks?" Smith asked.

"Are you sure you really want to know?"

"I wouldn't have asked otherwise," Smith said.

"I overheard Lenny bragging to a bloke in here a few nights ago. Mouthing off about how he conscientious he is with the storage of his fireworks. I heard him mention something about keeping them in the shed at the bottom of the garden and I went and had a look."

"You broke into their property?"

"Not really," Frankie said. "Not that time, anyway. You can see the shed from the alley that runs down the back of the road. That's when I saw the outside tap and the hosepipe. The idea came to me when I got home. I waited for it to get dark, and I went back and hopped over the fence. The window in the shed was easy enough to open – I've had quite a bit of experience in that department, so all I had to do was feed the hose into the shed and turn on the tap."

"You could have got into serious trouble for that," Smith said. "That's breaking and entering and wilful damage to property. You could have gone back inside. Didn't you see the CCTV camera?"

"I must be getting rusty in my old age. In the old days it would have been the first thing I looked out for. Anyway, it's done and dusted now, and I have you to thank for that."

"Please don't do anything like that again," Smith said.

"I can't promise anything. I hate fireworks and I hate how they traumatise the poor animals."

"That's the only reason I stuck my neck out for you," Smith told him.

"I'd hate to see what their water bill is going to be like. That hosepipe must have been running all night."

"What's the food like here?" Smith asked.
He was halfway through his second pint.

"Pretty good," Frankie said.

"I don't suppose they do a steak and ale pie."

It was his favourite meal at the Hog's Head, but the last time he'd eaten one there it had been a huge disappointment. The manager had changed the recipe and made the pie much worse. Smith vowed never to eat another one until the pub reverted back to the old recipe. He wouldn't be touching another steak and ale pie unless it had been made by his old friend, Marge.

"I can't say I've seen that on the menu," Frankie said.

"Probably for the best," Smith said. "Nothing can beat one of Marge's pies. I'll go and see what's on the board. I need the Gents anyway."

He headed towards the bar and scanned the specials board. He decided on the scampi and chips and followed the sign for the toilets.

It was the tracksuit that caught his eye first. The shiny green material caused Smith to shield his eyes. The second thing he registered was the ridiculous *mullet* hairstyle, and he wondered why people would actually pay to have their hair styled like that. Lenny Jenkins finished drying his hands and turned around.

"You?"

"Lenny," Smith said.

He went inside one of the cubicles and locked the door. He did what he needed to do, opened the door and went to wash his hands.

Lenny Jenkins was still there. He was admiring himself in the mirror. Smith watched as he wet his hands and ran them through his hair. It was rather amusing to witness. He repeated the process with his eyebrows and his porn star moustache. He was clearly deeply in love with himself, and he had absolutely no reason to be. Smith left him to his grooming and went back to the table.

Frankie called a waiter over and they ordered their food.

"How's your Lucy bearing up?" Frankie asked.

"Not great," Smith said. "Jane was her best friend."
"I heard she did it right in front of her."
"It's not something any teenager should have to witness," Smith said.
"Does she know why she did it?"
"I don't think she does," Smith said. "Lucy has always been open with us, and she would have told us if she knew anything."
Smith wasn't happy with the direction the conversation was heading.

"How's Gary doing?" he asked to change the subject.
"Busy," Frankie said. "He's getting a name for himself, and the work is coming in thick and fast. He's thinking about getting bigger premises."
"Where is he working out of now?"
"You don't want to know. It's not exactly above board."
"I don't want to know," Smith agreed. "Shit…"

Mr and Mrs Jenkins appeared at the table. Sheila was wearing an identical tracksuit to her husbands'. Her hair was styled exactly the same too. In fact, the only difference between them was the ugly sprout of growth over Lenny's top lip, and when Smith looked up at Sheila's face, he reckoned she would probably grow a moustache if she was able to.

"This is all very cosy," she said.
"It bloody well isn't," Frankie said.
"I knew there was something dodgy about you," Lenny said to Smith.
"Is there something you want?" Smith said.
"We should report you for this," Lenny said.
"Having a few pints after work is not against the law."
"Fraternising with the criminal fraternity must be though," Lenny said.
Smith really wasn't in the mood for this. The couple on the table next to theirs were taking a keen interest in them.

"Let me give you some advice," he said. "It's been a few years since I did the law degree, so my knowledge is a bit rusty, but I do remember most of it. The laws on slander are quite clear."

"You don't scare us," Sheila said.

"I suggest you stop talking," Smith told her. "Before the hole you're digging for yourselves becomes too deep to climb out of. Slander is defined as the action of making a false statement in public – a statement that is damaging to a person's reputation. The penalties for slander are harsh. Depending on the severity and the damage caused, you could be looking at a fine of up to fifty-thousand pounds or a maximum of five years in prison. Or both. Is there anything else you want to get off your chest?"

"You haven't heard the last of this," Lenny said.

"I still have that receipt for the sale of the fireworks," Smith reminded him. "Perhaps you could arrange for a family suite in prison. You can leave now." Sheila opened her mouth to speak but Lenny shook his head and led her away from the table.

"Good on you, mate," the man on the next table said. "That told them." Smith didn't comment. The food arrived and he was glad for the distraction. The scampi looked delicious, and Smith dug in. He didn't know then that a middle-aged man was minutes away from ending his life in the most horrific manner possible.

CHAPTER TWENTY

The first day of November dawned grey and wet. It was one of those autumn days that promised nothing but rain and dark skies. As Smith drove to work, he was sure that the miserable weather was reflected on the faces of the drivers of the other cars on the roads. This was Yorkshire and they had nothing but dark days and cold weather to look forward to for at least another four months.

The mood inside the station was equally bleak. Baldwin's usual cheery demeanour was absent this morning.
"Is everything OK?" Smith asked her.
"Dreary Monday blues, I suppose," she said.
"It seems to be contagious," Smith said and headed up to the canteen to get some coffee.

DI Smyth was sitting on his own at the table by the window. Smith selected his usual coffee and joined him.
"We've got good news and bad news from the tech team," the DI said. "With regards to Keith Peters' phone."
"Give me the good news," Smith said.
"They managed to access pretty much everything. Call history, all recent messages, including those that were deleted, and browser history."
"That's brilliant," Smith said. "What's the bad news?"
"The content," DI Smyth said. "According to the IT report some of the voice messages are deeply disturbing. At least one of the people who was forced to listen to it has taken time off because of it."
"It can't be that bad."
"It is," DI Smyth said. "I haven't listened to the messages yet, but we'll be going through them first thing in the morning briefing. I've been warned to

brace myself and my team."

"I'll look forward to it," Smith said.

"There's something seriously wrong with your brain."

"Thank you. Anything else to report?"

"Not a sausage. We should have the forensic report for the Sarah Peters murder sometime this morning."

"Webber will have found something we can use," Smith said.

"You seem very convinced."

"I don't think it was planned, boss," Smith said. "And in spontaneous killings the murderer doesn't have time to think ahead. They almost always leave something behind to incriminate themselves."

"Let's hope so."

Bridge and DC Moore came in together. Neither of them looked happy.

"Have you two had a lover's tiff?" Smith said.

"Not funny, Sarge," DC Moore said.

"It's this weather," Bridge said. "It gets you down."

"I thought you were a Yorkshireman," Smith said. "You should be used to the shit weather."

"I don't mind the cold," Bridge explained. "It's when we don't see the sun for days on end that gets to me."

"It's never bothered me, and there's fuck all you can do about the weather. The IT team have got something nasty for us from Keith Peters' phone."

"Great," DC Moore said. "That's all we need."

"Lighten up," Smith said and turned to DI Smyth. "What time is the briefing?"

"In ten minutes."

"Time for a quick smoke then," Smith said. "Perhaps the sun will be out when I get outside."

It was wishful thinking. If anything, the sky seemed to be even darker, and an ominous bank of clouds was drifting in from the east. It was definitely going to pour down soon. Smith lit a cigarette and savoured the nicotine rush as it entered his system. The first drops of rain began to fall, Smith closed his eyes and faced the sky, so the rain fell onto his face. He closed his eyes and opened them again when he heard the sound of a car door slamming close by.

It was a car he recognised. The black Land Rover was parked badly across two of the bays. Lenny Jenkins pressed the key fob to activate the car alarm and he and his wife made a beeline for Smith. They were wearing matching orange puffer jackets over their tracksuits today and it put Smith in mind of a couple of cartoon characters he couldn't recall the names of.

"Good morning," he said.
"It's not good for you," Sheila said.
"Lovely weather."
"You won't be smiling for long," Lenny said. "We're going ahead with the charges against your mate."
"I would advise against doing that."
"I don't care what you would advise. There's no cameras in the newsagents where we bought the fireworks. I checked. You were bluffing."
"What exactly do you hope to achieve by doing this?" Smith said. "You're clearly not short of money – what are you hoping to get out of it?"
"We don't have to talk to you," Sheila said. "And you've got nothing on us anymore. You can't prove that it was our Wayne who bought the fireworks."

Smith's cigarette had gone out and he didn't relight it.
"I don't have time for this. I have more important things to do."
"Not for much longer," Lenny said. "We're going to lodge a complaint against you too. It's our right as tax-paying citizens – I googled it."
"That's correct," Smith said.

"You think you're so clever," Sheila said. "Let's see how clever you are when you lose your job."

"Good luck," Smith said and walked back towards the station.

CHAPTER TWENTY ONE

Smith pushed all thoughts of Lenny and Sheila Jenkins out of his head as soon as he set foot inside the small conference room. He was more interested in what the tech team had found on Keith Peters' phone. DI Smyth's words of warning had intrigued him, and he was keen to listen to the messages, however disturbing they may be. He didn't know then that by the end of the briefing everyone on the team would be feeling sick to the stomach. Men and woman who had come face to face with the most depraved monsters humanity had to offer, would be utterly disgusted by the latest in a long line of sick individuals.

"Before we begin," DI Smyth said. "I've been told to warn you all to brace yourself. The material stored on Keith Peters' mobile phone is something, the likes of which none of you have ever had to deal with before."

"Have you listened to it?" Smith said.

"I haven't yet had that pleasure," DI Smyth said. "Shall we make a start? The IT guys have chronicled the phone history, so we have a sense of the timing involved."

The first voice message was from almost a month ago, and Smith thought it sounded innocent enough. The person who sent the message was speaking through a voice synthesizer and it was impossible to tell if it was a man or a woman.

Jesus died for our sins. Not everybody appreciates that.

"The sender of the message wasn't someone in Keith's contacts list," DI Smyth said. "And Keith blocked the number almost immediately."

"How did they manage to keep sending the messages?" DC Moore said.

"Different phone numbers," DI Smyth said. "In fact, each individual message was sent from a different number."

"Probably burners," DC Moore said.

"I wish you'd stop calling them that," Bridge said.

The tone of the messages grew darker a week or so later.

I know everything, Keith. I see everything, and I am the only one who can pass judgement.

Keith Peters replied to this message with three-word message of his own.

Who is this?

The reply came quickly. The creepy disguised voice was heard thirty seconds later.

I am The Preacher. I know everything and when I speak, you will heed my words.

"It sounds like a real nut-job," DC Moore said.

"Why did the tech team get so freaked out by this crap?" Bridge wondered.

DI Smyth resumed the messages.

I know what Sarah did. She is a murderer and yet she still walks free.

"What the hell?" Smith said. "What is he talking about?"

An eye for an eye, Keith. You will listen to what I say, and you will heed my words. Jesus died for our sins, and you will sacrifice yourself to atone for the sins of the one closest to you.

Once again, Keith replied to this.

I don't know what you're talking about.

The Preacher was quiet for a few days and then on the 25th of October a new voice message was received.

I hope you've had time to think, Keith. I pray that you've begun to understand what it is you need to do.

Keith's response was not what any of the team expected.

Fuck off.

"He's got balls," DC Moore said.

"Why didn't he take this to the police?" DC King said.

The next couple of messages answered her question.

I'm going to the police. This was Keith. *If you don't stop harassing me, I'm going to the police.*

You won't do that. You will do exactly what I say, and nothing else. On Sunday 31 October you are to visit the city library. You will remain there for twenty minutes and then you will leave. There's a rubbish bin outside. You will dump your phone in there after switching it off. You will then go to the mobile phone shop on Blake Street where you'll purchase another phone. You'll walk to the bench on Gillygate and sit down. After destroying the phone and leaving it on the bench, you'll cross over the road. The number 42 bus is scheduled to arrive at the stop there at 13:44. It may be late – it often is, but it doesn't matter. When it's close enough and has enough speed, you'll step out in front of it. It will be a quick and painless death.

DI Smyth stopped the recording there. None of the people on the team seemed to be able to speak. The voice message really was disturbing. It was about to get worse – much, much worse. Keith Peters' replied with a number of threatening messages, and he even went so far as to imply that the person sending the messages needed help.

This didn't seem to deter The Preacher.

Before you face the wrath of the bus you are to acknowledge me. You will own your actions and you and your murderer sister will receive retribution. You will then be welcome into the kingdom of heaven. It will be quick, Keith.

"I can't believe he actually went through with it," Whitton said. "What sane individual would fall for something like this?"

"I think he was threatened with something," Smith said. "It's the only logical explanation."

He'd hit the nail on the head. The final message explained everything, and it was something he would never forget.

Sarah likes to listen to music at high volumes when you're at work. She's particularly fond of 80s rock. She likes to dance along. I've watched her from the spare bedroom you're currently using as an office. There is a poster of Humphrey Bogart on the wall. I've been inside that room many times. I could be in there right now. I could be observing your sister as we speak. You have a DJ job at the Grand on Cotton Street on Friday. You're also booked to play at a 60th on Saturday night. Sarah will be home alone – I've checked her work schedule.

Keith's tone turned more serious.

What do you want?

You will do what I say. On 31st October you will take your own life to atone for the sins of the one closest to you.

What if I tell you to go to hell?

Your sister is already halfway there. You will give yourself to the Lord because the alternative is far worse. I will take Sarah. I will violate her in ways you cannot comprehend. When she thinks it can't get any worse, I will rape her some more. I'll flay her flesh, and I'll poke out her eyes. She will beg me to kill her, but I won't. When she's near death I'll violate her again. I will show her pain like no pain she's ever known. Her path to hell will be paved with immense torture and suffering. Do not doubt me. I will drag her by the hair and violate her in every room in your house, and you will not spend one more day there without thinking about this. I am The Preacher and I know everything. You will do as I say.

That was it. There were no more messages.

"He went through with it," Smith said. "It doesn't make any sense."

"The Preacher's threats were pretty awful," DC King said.

"And he seemed to know a hell of a lot about their lives," Bridge said. "What kind of sick fuck are we dealing with here?"

"Is there any way we can trace where the messages were sent from?" Whitton said.

"Unfortunately, not," DI Smyth said. "Every message was sent from a different phone – probably prepaid."

"He probably dumped the sim each time," DC Moore said.

"What did she do?" Smith said.

"What did who do?" Bridge said.

"Sarah Peters. What did she do that made The Preacher so pissed off? We still don't know what lies at the heart of all this. We discover what that is, and we get a step closer to The Preacher."

CHAPTER TWENTY TWO

"Sarah Peters was responsible for the death of a little boy," DI Smyth said. It hadn't been difficult to get hold of this information. The incident was on file.

"It was two years ago," DI Smyth continued. "She was behind the wheel of a bus and the child ran across the road and straight into her path."

"Was she charged with anything?" Smith asked.

"She was cleared of all culpability. There was a full inquiry, and it was ruled to be an accident. The boy's mother wasn't paying attention, and she didn't realise the boy was missing. There was nothing Sarah could have done to avoid it. It was a tragic accident, nothing more."

"And she kept her job?" Bridge said.

"She did."

"I find it harder to believe that she still wanted the job," DC King said. "After killing a child you'd think driving a bus would be the last thing she'd want to do."

"That's not important," Smith said. "We now have an inkling of a motive."

"How do you figure that out?" DC Moore said.

"Retribution, Harry. Once again, we appear to have an avenger on our hands. A clearly delusional one, but an avenger nevertheless."

"Was Sarah Peters sexually assaulted?" Whitton said.

"There was no evidence of it," Smith said. "Fuck..."

"What is it?" DI Smyth asked.

"He was interrupted. The bastard was interrupted by me and Kerry. He was inside the house while we were standing outside."

"How did he manage to escape?" DC Moore said.

"Damn it," Smith said. "We've been here before, haven't we?"

He took out his mobile phone and dialled Grant Webber's number.

The Head of Forensics picked up straight away.

"What is it?"

"When you were at Sarah Peters' house," Smith said. "Did you check all of the rooms?"

"There wasn't much point," Webber said. "The crime scene was downstairs, and that's what we focused on."

"Shit. I think The Preacher was there the whole time. We've just listened to the messages he sent Sarah's brother and the stuff he threatened to do to her is disgusting. But he didn't get the chance to carry it out because he was interrupted by me and Kerry. I think he hid somewhere upstairs."

"The house has been sealed off," Webber told him.

"But we don't have officers outside," Smith said. "He'll be long gone by now. Thanks, Webber."

"We managed to pull some prints from the coffee mug and the frying pan. Identical prints, and they didn't come from the victim."

"And?" Smith said.

"Not in the system."

"I thought as much," Smith said. "Damn it – we really should have checked the other rooms in the house."

With that, he ended the call.

"What's done is done," DI Smyth said.

"We dropped the ball big time there," Smith said.

"We still don't know if The Preacher did remain in the house," DI Smyth said. "But if he did there's more chance of him leaving something of himself behind. That's something at least."

"We already know that he isn't on file," Smith said. "The prints Webber got aren't known to us."

"He might have left something behind," DI Smyth said. "It's still early days."

"Sarah Peters was killed because her brother didn't succeed in killing himself," Smith said. "In the eyes of The Preacher she had sinned by committing murder, and that's why Keith needed to do what he did – to atone for her sin."

"She was cleared, Sarge," DC Moore said. "It wasn't murder."

"What part of *in the eyes of The Preacher* didn't you comprehend, Harry?"

"Sorry. I wasn't paying attention."

"Why not just punish Sarah?" Bridge put forward. "If he believes her to be a murderer, why get Keith to kill himself?"

"Making him commit suicide is a much worse punishment than death," Smith said. "Especially if she believes it was her fault that he did what he did. Living with that kind of guilt is infinitely worse than dying."

"There have actually been debates about it," DC King said. "I watched a documentary where there was a discussion about the death penalty. Some people argued that being put to death isn't actually a punishment."

"You can't be serious?" DC Moore said.

"I am. The argument stated that ending someone's life is final. The criminals who are executed will no longer be conscious of anything once the deed is done. A life behind bars is a miserable existence, and when you look at it from that perspective it is a more fitting sentence."

"This is all very interesting," DI Smyth said. "But it's hardly relevant to the investigation."

"I disagree, boss," Smith said. "It's highly relevant. This is precisely what The Preacher is doing. He's ensuring that the people he believes have sinned are punished by taking away the people closest to them. He's leaving them with such extreme guilt, and that is possibly the worst punishment he can dole out."

"We're not going to get into a lengthy discussion about justice and retribution," DI Smyth said. "We need to press on. We've had three suicide attempts – two of those proved fatal, and Keith Peters is by no means out of the woods yet. Are we in agreement that the three suicides are linked?"

"It's looking that way," Smith said.

"We still haven't managed to locate the phones belonging to Jane Banks and Maggie Allen," DI Smyth said. "But I don't believe we should spend time on a wild goose chase. The information on those phones will probably get us no closer to this Preacher."

"If he's using burner phones," DC Moore said. "There's no way to trace them back to him."

"How many times?" It was Bridge.

"Sorry, Sarge," DC Moore said with a grin on his face.

"Any thoughts about how we should proceed?" DI Smyth said. "Smith?"

Smith wasn't paying attention. His eyes were focussed on something in the corner of the room.

"Smith," DI Smyth said once more. "Are you still with us?"

"No," Smith replied. "I need to go."

He stood up without any explanation.

"What is it?" Whitton said.

"Keith Peters was forced to commit suicide because of what his sister did," Smith said. "And when he failed, Sarah was killed."

"We already know that," Bridge said.

"Sarah was the person closest to him," Smith said. "We haven't even begun to consider that with the other two suicides."

"Jane Banks and Maggie Allen," DC Moore said.

"Why were they forced to kill themselves?" Smith said. "What did the people closest to them do that was so bad?"

"I think we can probably assume that Maggie's husband, Vincent was the person closest to her," DC King said.

"What about Jane?" Whitton said.

Smith looked her in the eye. "I think we need to ask some unpleasant questions to our daughter. Lucy was the person closest to Jane, and the whole thing is making me feel sick to the stomach."

CHAPTER TWENTY THREE

"What have we here?"

Lloyd French was observing the chest freezer as if it were a briefcase loaded with banknotes.

"It looks brand new," his friend David Old commented.

The freezer didn't have a scratch on it, and the two men wondered why someone had disposed of it.

What was even more puzzling was the location chosen to dump it. Stockton Forest was a patch of woodland a few miles northeast of the city. The woods were a popular spot for hikers and dogwalkers but this section was rarely used. The only access road was via Sandy Lane and the freezer had been left on the side of one of the many gravel roads that trickled off it.

"It's a Samsung," Lloyd noticed. "Probably worth a few quid."

"I'll go and fetch the van," David said. "Even if it's knackered, I've got a mate who can fix anything."

"Good plan. It's not like we're nicking it, is it?"

"We're actually doing our bit as law abiding citizens," David said. "Dumping freezers is against the law. *Fly-tipping* – that's what they call it, isn't it?"

He set off back to where he'd parked the van. Lloyd remained behind with the freezer and carried out a closer inspection. He placed a hand on the handle and when he tried to open the lid, it didn't budge. The explanation for this was the peculiar lock on the front. Lloyd had never seen such a device before. It was a deadbolt system with a hasp attached to the lower part of the lock and a bolt on the top. Lloyd knew a thing or two about locking mechanisms but this one was completely new to him.

He soon figured out how it worked. As a security measure, it was rather pointless. The bolt had notches carved into it, and these were designed to catch in the slots in the hasp. In essence, it meant that when the lid of the freezer was closed the only means of opening it again was a mechanism that released the teeth in the bolt.

Lloyd clicked the lever, opened the lid wide and gasped. The freezer hadn't been switched on for quite some time, yet the man curled up inside looked like he'd frozen to death. His eyes looked up at Lloyd from a bluish grey face. The mouth was open wide as if trying to take in as much air as possible, and the skin around it had started to peel off.

Lloyd wasn't aware of the sound of the van's engine. It was getting closer, but his attention was solely focused on the wretched soul inside the chest freezer. There was blood on his hands. More blood was dotted around the side of the freezer. Lloyd couldn't see it, but there was a mobile phone by the man's feet. It had been smashed to pieces. He was also unaware that on the side of the freezer were two smudged words written in blood:
The Preacher.

* * *

"Out of the question," DI Smyth said. "How many times do I have to say it for it to register in that thick skull of yours?"

"Lucy is more likely to open up to me or Whitton than anybody else," Smith argued. "She won't talk to anyone else."

"You're too personally involved."

"Isn't that the whole point?"

"It's unethical for you or DS Whitton to interview a member of your family."

"I can get through to her, boss," Smith said.

"You will do as I say," DI Smyth said. "Or do I have to remind you that I can quite easily extract you from the investigation."

"You won't do that. You need me."

"I can feel the aging process speeding up as we speak," DI Smyth said. "You're going to be the death of me before I even reach retirement age."

"Probably for the best. Who wants to retire, anyway? It doesn't have to be a formal interview. I can have a chat with Lucy, and if she gives me anything I think is relevant to the investigation, she can come in and do it on record with someone else asking the questions."

"Have you always been like this?"

"Like what?" Smith asked.

"As stubborn as a mule."

"It's one of my greatest assets."

DI Smyth ran his hair through his hair. "OK, you win. But I want to know everything that is said in your little chat."

"No worries. I'll go and see her now."

DI Smyth's phone started to ring. It was Bridge.

"What are you waiting for?" he said.

"Aren't you going to answer that?" Smith said.

"Get out of here."

Smith was halfway out the door when he was stopped in his tracks.

"Hold on," DI Smyth said.

Smith turned around. "What is it?"

"A man has been found dead in a chest freezer up in Stockton Woods."

"You're kidding me?"

"I'm not. Two men found him. A couple of uniforms were sent out to investigate and it looks like we've got another victim of The Preacher. A mobile phone was retrieved from the freezer."

"Was it damaged?"

"It was smashed to bits," DI Smyth confirmed. "And that's not all – it appears that the man deliberately cut himself and used the blood to write on the side of the freezer."

"The Preacher has spoken?" Smith guessed.

"Close," DI Smyth said. "He only managed to write the first two words."

"Do we know if he died from the wound," Smith said. "Or the lack of oxygen in the freezer?"

"According to the officers first on the scene," DI Smyth said. "The laceration appeared to be superficial – definitely not life threatening. What are you thinking?"

"It's an unusual way to kill yourself," Smith said. "Jumping in a chest freezer and waiting for the air to run out. He must have had some will power."

"We don't know much at this stage. Webber is on his way there, and we'll get a precise cause of death after the post-mortem."

"I don't buy it," Smith said. "Modern chest freezers can be opened from the inside. It's a safety requirement. Surely, he would have cracked when the oxygen started to run out and opened the lid. It doesn't add up."

"Murder seldom does. I don't think it's necessary for you to attend. Go and speak to your daughter and see if she can shed any light on the reason her best friend chose to end her life."

CHAPTER TWENTY FOUR

It was Darren Lewis who opened the door. They'd come to an understanding. Even though Smith was the owner of number 18 Greenway Avenue they'd agreed that he would ring the bell before going into the house. It had taken a while to get used to, but Smith had got the hang of it in the end. Darren and Lucy deserved some privacy.

"Is everything alright?" Darren asked.
"Is Lucy home?" Smith said.
"She's upstairs. The college has closed for a couple of days, after what happened at the Halloween party. Probably for the best."
"Can I come in? I need to talk to her."
"Good luck with that," Darren said. "I haven't been able to get more than a few words out of her since the party."
"I have to try."
Darren opened the door wider, and Smith went inside.

Music was playing from Lucy and Darren's room. Smith stopped outside and listened. It was something he hadn't heard before, yet it sounded vaguely familiar. A woman with a soulful voice was singing over a background of hypnotic guitars. Smith thought it was rather depressing, and it didn't bode well for what he'd come to talk about.

"Can I come in?" he asked from the doorway.
He took Lucy's silence as an invitation.
"Interesting music."
The haunting guitars had now been joined by a meandering bass line. Smith had definitely heard something similar before, and when the carnival keyboards sounded, he knew exactly where he'd heard it.

"This is a rip-off of *The Doors*."

Lucy looked right at him. Her eyes were lifeless, and Smith didn't know what to do about it.

"It's pretty cool though," he said.

"It's Mazzy Star," Lucy managed.

"Mazzy Star? Weird name for a woman."

"The band is called Mazzy Star. The singer's name is Hope."

"I like that much better. And the song is growing on me, even if it is a bit morose."

"It's called *She Hangs Brightly*," Lucy told him.

Smith wondered if this was really suitable music to listen to after the suicide of a friend, but he reckoned that it was probably the sort of thing he would have chosen too.

"I need to talk to you," he said. "It's really important."

Lucy didn't comment.

"Can I sit down?"

Lucy nodded.

Smith sat at the end of the bed. The woman's voice really was dreamlike, and the bassline was speeding up as the song moved towards its crescendo.

"I need to ask you some questions that might be difficult to answer," Smith said. "I'm going to tell you something I shouldn't, and I want you to promise that none of this is to go any further. Can you do that for me?"

"Sounds intriguing."

For a brief moment Smith thought he detected a glint in Lucy's eyes. The old Lucy was back for a short while. It didn't last long before the dullness returned.

"We're investigating a murderer," Smith said. "The likes of which none of us have ever come across before. We believe he's appointed himself judge, juror and executioner and we also believe his rationale are somewhat delusional. He's punishing the people he believes to have sinned by forcing those closest to them to commit suicide."

The spark was back in Lucy's eyes, and Smith was half expecting what came next.

"Are you telling me that Jane was forced to kill herself?"

"I think she was," Smith said. "Three people have attempted suicide in the past couple of days. Two of those attempts were successful and the other man is fighting for his life. There are a number of similarities between the suicides and there is little doubt that the person we're investigating is behind all three."

"How?" Lucy said. "How could someone make a person do that?"

"Extreme measures," Smith said. "We're dealing with a ruthless individual with zero moral code. We have proof of what he threatened to do to one of the victim's loved ones if he didn't comply, and it's the stuff of nightmares."

The song finished and another, more upbeat track came on. This one was about sailing.

"What I need to ask you is this," Smith said. "The person we're interested in is under the impression that someone very close to Jane committed a crime. It was a crime so terrible that it warranted a threat to the perpetrator and the subsequent suicide."

Lucy's blank expression told Smith that she hadn't fully comprehended his implication.

"You know you can tell me anything," he said.

"I know that."

The light that had been switched on inside Lucy's head was now quite obvious in her eyes. She now wore an expression of utter disbelief.

"Get out."

"Just hear me out," Smith said.

"Get out of my fucking room."

"I understand that you're upset," Smith said. "But this is important. And whatever you tell me will not leave this room."

"You really think I've done something that terrible?" "Lucy said. "Something that made Jane kill herself. Do you really believe I'm capable of something like that?"

"I'm just following the logic that this madman follows. You're the person closest to Jane."

"I'm not."

"What?"

"I'm not," Lucy repeated. "We haven't been that close since Andrew was born. We're in different classes at college and we're no more than casual mates."

"But I thought..."

"You thought wrong," Lucy interrupted. "And I can't believe you'd think I could do something so terrible and keep it quiet. You're a fine one to talk. I know some things about you, remember. You can leave now."

This wasn't going according to plan, and Smith couldn't think of a way to make things better.

"I'm sorry," he said. "My intention wasn't to upset you. One more question and I'll leave you alone with your weird music."

His attempt to lighten the mood failed miserably. Lucy remained quiet.

"Who was Jane closest to?" Smith asked. "If you were to think about it, who would you say she was closest to?"

"Her mum," Lucy said without hesitating. "They've always had a special bond. Definitely her mum."

CHAPTER TWENTY FIVE

"Can you tell me what you were doing here?" Bridge asked.
He and DC Moore were talking to the two men who'd stumbled across the body in the chest freezer.
"We were just out for a walk," Lloyd French said.
"On a Monday?" DC Moore said. "Don't you have jobs to go to?"
"We're in between jobs right now," David Old said. "It's not easy these days."
"So," Bridge said. "You fancied a walk in the woods, and you came across the freezer. Can you tell us what you did then?"
"I stayed with the freezer," Lloyd said. "While David went to fetch the van."
"I'd parked it half a mile up the road," David elaborated.
"We were going to take it away," Lloyd said. "It seemed like the right thing to do. Fly-tipping is illegal, isn't it?"
　"Why did you open it?" Bridge said.
"Why not?" Lloyd said.
"Perhaps you thought there was something inside," DC Moore said.
"What are you saying?" Lloyd said. "I thought the locking mechanism was odd, that's all. Not to mention downright dangerous."
"What do you mean?" Bridge said.
"It's got a hasp and bolt that's designed to lock when the lid is down. You can open it from the outside by flicking the lever, but if you get stuck inside, you're history. Ask that poor bastard in there."
"A kid could have got trapped in there," David joined in. "What then?"
　"What's going to happen to the freezer?" Lloyd asked. "We found it, and that makes it ours, doesn't it?"
"The freezer will be taken into evidence," Bridge informed him.
"What about after that?"

"What about it?" DC Moore said.

"It's brand new," David said. "We could get a few quid for it."

"Are you having a laugh?" DC Moore said. "A man died inside that freezer, and you're asking if you can keep it."

"What about some kind of reward?" Lloyd said. "We didn't have to phone the police."

"Actually, you did," Bridge educated him. "It's your obligation as a law-abiding citizen to inform the authorities when a crime has been committed. We're going to need your fingerprints."

"What for?" Lloyd said.

"Because your prints will be all over the freezer," DC Moore said. "It's for elimination purposes."

"Will they be kept on file?" David said.

"Is that a problem?" DC Moore said.

"It's a violation of our civil rights," Lloyd said.

"I couldn't give a hoot about your civils rights, Mr French," Bridge said. "But, no – fingerprints taken for elimination purposes are not kept on file. Happy now?"

"Can we go?" David said.

"We're going to need a statement from you," DC Moore said. "As well as your fingerprints, so if you could present yourself at the station at your earliest convenience, we'd appreciate it."

"You can go," Bridge said. "We've got your details."

"What do you reckon?" DC Moore said when the two men had gone.

"What a way to die," Bridge said. "Suffocation isn't a method I would choose if I wanted to end it all."

"There are more peaceful ways to do it," DC Moore said.

"Shit," Bridge said. "This is all I need."

Billie Jones was on her way over to them. Webber's assistant and Bridge had been in a relationship for a while, but she'd ended it recently without warning. Bridge accepted the fact that he had no choice but to work with her, but he didn't have to like it. He was still bitter about the rejection. It didn't happen often, and it had severely bruised his ego.

"Hey there," she said.

"Billie," Bridge said. "Is there something you want?"

"The locking mechanism is an unusual one. In fact, I've never seen anything like it, and it might be worth checking out the manufacturers of those particular locks."

"Thanks for the tip," Bridge said. "Anything else."

"Don't be like that."

"I'm going to check that the uniforms have secured the area properly," DC Moore said.

"He's not very subtle, is he?" Billie said.

"He's a southerner," Bridge said.

"I miss you."

Bridge really wasn't expecting this.

"You were the one that dumped me," he reminded her.

"I wasn't in a great place, and I wasn't thinking straight."

"What are you trying to tell me, Billie?" Bridge said. "I don't do cryptic clues."

Billie looked behind her. Webber and Pete Richards were still busy examining the chest freezer. DC Moore was talking to someone on his mobile phone, and the uniformed officers were taping off the area.

"I hope this isn't too cryptic for you," Billie said.

She leaned forward and kissed Bridge on the lips. He froze for a while and then his lips parted without him realising it. He pulled Billie closer and closed his eyes. The embrace lasted some time and Bridge was the one to break it.

"Where did that come from?" he asked.

Billie smiled. "I'm sorry."

"I'm not."

"I didn't mean about the kiss, you idiot," Billie said. "I'm sorry I messed up with us."

"We shouldn't really be discussing this here," Bridge said. "There's a dead bloke in a freezer a few metres away."

"Since when has stuff like that bothered you?"

"Does this mean what I think it means?"

"Now who's being cryptic?" Billie said. "Can we talk later?"

"I think that's a bloody good idea," Bridge said.

DC Moore returned. "Have you two finished?"

"For now," Bridge said.

"I'll call you later," Billie said.

She left them to it. Bridge watched her go.

"God, I've missed that arse."

"You're a proper dinosaur, Sarge," DC Moore said. "And I have to say, that grin on your face is rather unsettling."

"Shut up," Bridge said. "We've got work to do."

CHAPTER TWENTY SIX

"The chest freezer the mystery man was found inside was locked with a very distinctive locking mechanism," DI Smyth began the afternoon briefing.
"I did a quick check on the net," DC Moore said. "And I came up empty handed. I couldn't find anything remotely similar to it on any of the hardware sites."
"Perhaps it was made especially for the purpose it was used for," Smith suggested.
"A home-made job?" Bridge said.
"You would need specialist tools to make something like that," DC King said.
"I don't think you would," DC Moore argued. "A spot welder and a grinder would do the job."
"Wherever the lock came from," DI Smyth said. "It was designed specifically to prevent the lid from being opened once the bolt was slotted into the hasp. The teeth face one way and only the lever attached to the hasp enables it to open again. As soon as the lid is closed the freezer can only be opened from the outside."
"What a way to kill yourself," Whitton said. "It must have been a slow and agonising death. I'm finding it hard to comprehend that someone would choose to end it all like that."

Smith's eyes opened wide. He looked at his wife.
"What?" she said.
"The suicides are commensurate with the crimes The Preacher believes have been committed."
"Could you say that once more in English, Sarge?" DC Moore said.
"The methods of self-termination correspond to the alleged crimes, Harry. Sarah Peters was responsible for the death of a young boy. It was ruled an accident, but we can't ignore the fact that she was the one driving the bus.

Her brother was forced to jump in front of a bus. There's method in this bastard's madness."

"Let's go back to the start," DI Smyth said. "Taking Smith's suspicions into consideration. Maggie Allen swallowed a load of sleeping pills and washed them down with vodka."

"The person closest to her killed someone in a similar manner," DC King put forward.

"Jane Banks sliced her throat open," DI Smyth continued.

"Are you suggesting that someone Jane knows well did that to someone?" DC Moore said. "Because I find that hard to believe."

"We're just going by this madman's logic," Smith said. "When I spoke to Lucy, she told me Jane was closest to her mother. She didn't hesitate before telling me this, and I thought it was odd because when I spoke to Kelly Banks, she claimed that she and Jane didn't have a very close relationship."

"Perhaps she wasn't aware of it," DC King said. "Maybe she just thought it was normal for a mother and daughter to be like that, and she didn't think much of it."

"And then we have the mystery freezer man," DI Smyth said. "We don't know who he is yet – there was nothing to ID him on his person, but if we follow the logic, it means we're looking for someone connected to a person who has perished inside a chest freezer. We have four victims, and three victims we're not aware of."

"I'm not following you, sir," DC Moore said.

"We know about the kid who was killed by the bus that Sarah Peters was driving," Smith explained. "But we don't yet have the connections to the other three suicides."

"And that's what we're going to focus on this morning," DI Smyth said. "We'll push Keith Peters to the back burner for the time being. Mr Peters' method of suicide has been explained, so we'll concentrate on the others.

Smith, I appreciate that you were the one to extract the information about Jane's mother, but you're to stay away from that one. I've already pushed the boundaries of what is considered acceptable too far already. According to the guidelines, you and Whitton should have been removed from this investigation as soon as Jane Banks' heart stopped beating, but we can't afford to lose you both."

"No worries, boss," Smith said. "I'll take the freezer bloke if that's OK with you."

"Could we please stop calling him that?" Whitton said. "It's not very respectful."

"Find out who he is," DI Smyth said. "And do some digging into similar deaths."

The door to the small conference room opened and Baldwin came in. "Sorry to interrupt," she said. "But I need a word with DS Smith."

"What is it?" he said.

"Can we talk in private?"

Smith got to his feet. "Sounds serious. I won't be long."

"What's that all about?" Bridge asked when Smith had gone.

"Probably nothing," DI Smyth said. "Bridge, I want you and Harry to focus on Maggie Allen. See if there are any skeletons in her husband's closet that can be linked to her suicide. Vincent Allen might be able to shed some light on why she chose that particular method to kill herself. Kerry, you can go and speak to Jane Banks' mother."

"Her name is Kelly," Whitton said. "We don't know her very well, but she's always come across as a down to earth sort of woman."

"Whitton, in Smith's absence, you can make a start on freezer man," DI Smyth said and instantly held his hands up in apology. "I mean the man found in Stockton Woods."

Smith returned and his facial expression told everyone that the conversation with Baldwin hadn't been a pleasant one.

"Can I have a word in private, boss?" he asked DI Smyth.

"What's with all the cloak and dagger crap these days?" Bridge said. "I thought we were supposed to be a team."

"You all know what to do," DI Smyth said. "Get onto it."

Bridge wasn't finished yet. "We shouldn't be keeping secrets from each other."

"This has fuck all to do with you," Smith informed him.

"On you go," DI Smyth said.

"I'm in a bit of shit," Smith told him.

DI Smyth sighed. "What have you done now?"

"You make it sound like it's a common occurrence."

DI Smyth raised an eyebrow. "Talk to me."

"It's about Frankie Lewis," Smith said.

"Your daughter's boyfriend's dad?" DI Smyth said.

"I might have bent the rules a bit for him."

"I was under the impression that Frankie Lewis was a career criminal."

"Not anymore. He's given up that life – he promised me, and I believe him."

"I'm listening," DI Smyth said.

Smith ran his hands through his hair.

"There's a family who live on the same street as Frankie. The Jenkins family. Apparently, they had a win on the lotto, and they believe they're superior to everyone else because of it. They've been setting off fireworks for the past week or so, and it's traumatising the animals in the street. Frankie's a big animal lover, and he couldn't let it go on."

"What did he do, Smith?"

"He heard Lenny Jenkins bragging in the pub about how he keeps his fireworks in the shed for safety reasons and he went to check it out. There was a hosepipe in the garden next to the shed and he turned on the water and flooded the shed, fireworks and all."

"So, we've got trespassing and wilful damage to property," DI Smyth said.

"And that's just for starters."

"The problem is," Smith said. "The Jenkins' have CCTV, and they caught Frankie in the act."

"Where exactly do you come into this equation?" DI Smyth said.

Smith told him. He explained about the visit to the Jenkins' and the threat of the underage purchase of fireworks.

"I was bluffing," Smith said. "And they called my bluff. Now I'm in a bit of shit. Baldwin told me they're not only going ahead with the charges against Frankie, they're going to lodge a formal complaint against me too. They have me on CCTV going inside their house, and I don't have any explanation for why I was there."

"You are an idiot," DI Smyth said.

"I'm aware of that, boss," Smith said. "What do you suggest I do?"

"You say the damage to the fireworks was caught on camera?"

"That's right."

"As was your presence at their property."

Smith confirmed this too.

"So," DI Smyth said. "From a legal perspective, their entire case rests on that footage."

"According to Baldwin, they'll be bringing the CCTV footage to our attention when they lodge the formal complaint. I can't see a way out of this."

"You do realise," DI Smyth said. "The very fact that I'm now privy to this information puts me in a delicate position. You attempted to pervert the course of justice and that is grounds for instant suspension. You could lose your job over this."

"What do you suggest I do?"

"I think I may have a solution."

"I'm all ears," Smith said.

"I need some time to think about it."

"I appreciate it, boss."

"Why do you do this to me?"

"Why do I do what?"

"Why do you persist in making my life hell? If you weren't the best detective I've ever worked alongside, I would wash my hands of you and let you take your chances, but you're needed right now. Especially in light of this Preacher maniac. Leave it with me. Now, I'd appreciate it if you would fuck off before I change my mind."

Smith got the hint.

"I'll get cracking on finding out who our mystery freezer man is then. Thanks again, boss."

CHAPTER TWENTY SEVEN

Whitton had given DC King a few snippets of information about Kelly Banks, but the young DC from Bradford still thought she was going in blind when she knocked on the door of the house where Jane Banks had spent the majority of her life.

Kelly opened the door and DC King explained that she needed to ask her a few questions.

"What possible questions could you want to ask?" Kelly said. "And since when did the police get involved in a teenage suicide?"

"Please," DC King said. "Can I come inside?"

"I suppose so."

Kelly told her to take a seat in the living room. The house smelled strongly of cigarette smoke and DC King was sure she could smell alcohol too.

"Do you want something to drink?" Kelly asked.

"No thanks," DC King said.

"What exactly do you want to know? My daughter ended her own life, and I really don't know what I can tell you about that."

"I'm going to say some things now that you might find hard to hear," DC King said.

"I'm listening. Are you sure you don't want some coffee? I'm going to make one for myself anyway."

"Only if it's not too much trouble."

Kelly left and returned with two cups of coffee. She handed one to DC King. "It's got milk and sugar. I didn't think to ask."

"It's fine," DC King said.

"Go on then. What did you want to tell me?"

"We have reason to believe that Jane was coerced into taking her own life."

DC King wasn't sure what kind of reaction Kelly would have to this information, but she certainly wasn't expecting what she said next.

"I half suspected it."

"Can you explain what you mean by that?" DC King urged.

"I should have seen the signs. I knew something wasn't right."

"Was Jane acting out of character?"

"I put it down to teenage stuff," Kelly said. "Kids can be so evil these days, can't they? The venom that's spouted on social media has become the norm, and we don't realise how dangerous it can actually be."

"Did Jane mention something to you about this?"

"She didn't have to," Kelly said. "In hindsight it was pretty clear. She would disappear to her room with her phone for hours and when she did show her face again she, would be different. Are you telling me that this is all about some hate campaign on social media?"

"That's not what I'm telling you at all, Mrs Banks."

There was a knock on the door and Kelly got up to answer it.

She came back a couple of minutes later.

"It was Mrs Howe from next door. I sent her away. I know she means well, but she'd stay for hours if I let her in. Where were we?"

"Like I said, we believe that Jane's suicide wasn't her own doing. There have been other suicides recently that bear striking similarities to Jane's. One of them brought some disturbing facts to our attention."

"What facts?"

"I'm afraid I can't go into the details," DC King said. "But it's quite clear that the suicides are connected. Jane cut her own throat. Can you think of any reason why she would choose to end her life in that way?"

"What the hell? What kind of question is that?"

"I apologise," DC King said. "It was not an easy question to ask, and I'm sorry for that. Let me put it another way, and I would appreciate it if this went no further."

"You have my word."

"It's looking like people are being targeted," DC King said. "By an extremely dangerous individual. This person believes himself to be an all-seeing, all-knowing entity, and he also believes he has the authority to play God. He's clearly delusional, and he's hell bent on doling out his delusional form of justice. He's punishing people he believes to have sinned by making those closest to them kill themselves in specific ways. The methods he chooses are relevant to the crimes he believes have been committed."

Kelly picked up her coffee cup and raised it to her mouth. She stopped halfway and focused her eyes on DC King.

"This is my fault, isn't it?"

"Why would you think that?" DC King said.

"I want you to answer a question of mine first."

"If I can."

"These other suicide attempts," Kelly said. "How were they carried out?"

"I can't go into the details."

"I've already given you my word that whatever you tell me will go no further. You owe me this at least."

"I really can't discuss the details of an ongoing investigation."

"Don't give me that detective series bullshit," Kelly said. "Do you want some answers or not?"

DC King thought for a moment. She decided that the press would cotton on to Sarah Peters' past sooner or later anyway, so she didn't think she was breaking any rules by telling Kelly Peters the truth.

"Yesterday afternoon," she said. "A man tried to kill himself by throwing himself in front of a bus. He's still alive, but he's in a critical condition. We found his mobile phone and on it were detailed instructions of where and when and how he was to end his own life. We've later learned that his sister was the driver of a bus that was involved in a terrible accident. A young boy was killed, but she was exonerated of all blame. The threats that were issued were sufficient to force the man to jump in front of the bus yesterday, and that's why I'm here. I'll ask you again – can you think of any reason why Jane would choose to end her life the way she did?"

Kelly nodded. "This is all my fault."

"Talk to me, Kelly," DC King said.

"It was a long time ago."

She stopped there, and DC King didn't press further. She waited for her to continue.

"It was an accident. A terrible accident. Jane had just started school and it meant I could work a few extra hours at the warehouse where I was temping. It was a place at the industrial park over in Woodthorpe. They built custom made furniture and I worked as a packer. One morning the power tripped in the warehouse, and nobody knew what had caused it. One of the technical blokes was an electrician, and he narrowed it down to a short on one of the industrial saws and set about fixing it. We were all told to take a break while the fault was being repaired, and we were called back to our stations after about an hour. The technician who was servicing the saw was still busy when we got there, and the power was still off. He was using a battery-powered drill to fix whatever he needed to fix, and it was really loud. He saw me and asked me to flip the mains switch back up."

She stopped again.

This time DC King did say something.

"What happened then? After he told you to switch the power back on?"

"That's what I thought he'd asked me," Kelly said. "But the drill was loud and that wasn't what he said at all."

"Go on."

"I did what I thought he'd asked, there was a scream as the industrial saw came to life and the blade shot across the room. I'll never forget the look on the man's face just before it cut through his neck and almost decapitated him."

"Oh my God."

"He was killed instantly," Kelly said. "And the worst thing is – I'll never know what he was really trying to tell me."

CHAPTER TWENTY EIGHT

"It's been an extremely productive morning," DI Smyth told the team in the small conference room. "We have confirmation that three of the attempted suicides are connected to past events. Bridge, do you want to fill us in on what you gleaned from Vincent Allen?"

"It wasn't easy getting him to talk about it," Bridge said. "And we had to divulge more than we wanted to about the investigation, but we got some answers in the end."

"Vincent killed his mother," DC Moore said.

"It's a bit more complicated than that," Bridge said. "Mrs Allen had terminal cancer. She'd gone through months of treatment and it hadn't worked. She was given painkillers and six months to live."

"Tops," DC Moore said.

"You could see it was painful for him to talk about it," Bridge said. "Especially so soon after his wife's suicide, but after breaking down in tears a couple of times he calmed down enough to explain what happened. Mrs Allen refused to die in a hospital. She wanted to live out whatever time she had left in the house she'd spent fifty years in. Vincent's father passed away when he was a teenager, and his mother never remarried."

"What did he do to her?" DC King said.

"He ended her suffering," Smith replied for Bridge. "He dosed her with pills and booze, didn't he?"

Bridge nodded. "A mercy killing, some might say."

"It's still murder," DC Moore said.

"That's irrelevant, Harry," Smith said.

"The painkillers she'd been given weren't working," Bridge said. "And Vincent couldn't stand to see his mother suffering like that. According to him, she was fully aware of what he was doing in the final hours of her life. It was even her idea to breathe her last breath in a warm bath. She won't have felt a thing."

"Euthanasia," Whitton said. "It's a grey area."

"Not according to the law it isn't," DC Moore said. "Assisting someone in their death is considered to be murder in this country."

"Harry," Smith said. "Shut up. We're not interested prosecuting a son for putting his mother out of her misery years ago. It's not important now. What is important is the fact that somehow The Preacher found out about what he did. That's what we ought to be discussing. How did he know?"

"According to Vincent," Bridge said. "There was no post-mortem. Mrs Allen was terminally ill, and there was no reason to suspect foul play. The cause of death on the death certificate was natural causes."

"How did he get wind of it?" Smith said. "How did The Preacher come to hear about it? The accident with the bus where the young boy died was in the papers. There was an enquiry and that will have left a paper trail, but Vincent's Mother's death wouldn't have. How did the bastard find out what he'd done?"

"We didn't ask Vincent about that?" DC Moore said.

"Did you at least ask him how many people he mentioned it to?" Smith said.

"We didn't."

"Well you should have. It wasn't in the papers, so it must have come from someone Vincent talked to about it."

"Perhaps Maggie Allen knew about it," DC King suggested.

"It's a bit late to ask her," Smith said.

"What about Robert?" Whitton said. "It's possible that Vincent's son somehow heard about it."

"It's not exactly a topic to bring up with a teenager," Bridge said.

"He could have heard them discussing it without them realising," Whitton said. "It's worth checking out."

"It is," Smith agreed. "That teenager wasn't telling us everything when we last spoke to him, and I've got a feeling he knows more than he's letting on."

"We'll come back to that," DI Smyth decided. "Kerry, could you bring the rest of us up to date with what Jane Banks' mother revealed to you?"

"Kelly was also partly responsible for someone losing their life," DC King said. "She was working in a warehouse, and she was involved in a terrible accident one day."

She elaborated. She told them about the power cut and the gruesome death of the technician.

"Bloody hell," Bridge said. "What a way to go."

"She must have felt terrible," Whitton said.

"I managed to get hold of the accident report," DC King said. "According to the investigation into the man's death, it really was just an accident. The technician had removed the circular saw blade to get to the cause of the short but, because of the power cut he hadn't realised that the machine was still switched on. He didn't manage to reattach the blade properly, and when Kelly Banks misheard him and flicked the switch back up, the saw came to life again and the blade was flung across the room."

"And she wasn't charged with anything?" DC Moore said.

"She was cleared of all culpability," DC King said.

"And there's our common denominator," Smith said. "We have three people who were all involved in people dying, but none of them were punished for this involvement. And that's because these people didn't do anything wrong."

"Not according to The Preacher," DC Moore said. "He obviously can't sit back and let them get away with it."

"It's all in his head," Bridge said.

"Be that as it may," DI Smyth said. "He needs to be stopped."

"Me and Whitton couldn't find out much about freezer man," Smith said. "We trawled the net," Whitton said. "And we looked for reports of people who have died inside chest freezers, and there were very few. The Refrigerator Safety Act was set in place in America in the fifties, and similar legislation came here a decade later, and the act stipulated that any chest freezer has to be easily opened from the inside and the outside. Also, disposal of refrigerators and freezers has been carefully controlled for years. Gone are the days where a freezer could be left on a piece of waste ground for a kid to stumble across and get stuck inside."

"You said there were very few incidents," DI Smyth said. "But you did find some."

"We did," Smith said. "Both of them were similar in that the freezers involved were old models – manufactured before the legislation came into effect, and both incidents occurred in the home."

"A seven-year-old girl and a teenage boy," Whitton said. "Both of them climbed inside the freezer and suffocated before anyone realised what had happened."

"Where and when was this?" Bridge said.

"The boy perished in a house in Bradford in 2000," Smith said. "And the girl died in Cornwall four years later."

"What do we know about the parents?" DI Smyth said.

"I've asked Baldwin to try and track them down. We're going back almost twenty years here."

"It doesn't matter," DI Smyth said. "It could still be relevant. It's very possible that The Preacher found out about it and is now punishing the people he believes were responsible."

"Do you think he's getting his info from the Internet?" DC Moore said.

"Why not?" Smith said. "It's where we get the majority of our information from these days. It's the best place to look if you want to find anything out.

How old would you say freezer man was?"

"It was difficult to tell," Bridge said. "He didn't look too pretty, but I'd say he was late-thirties, maybe early-forties."

"A bit young to be the father of either of the kids who died twenty years ago then," DC King calculated.

"He could be the brother of one of them," DC Moore suggested.

"It's possible," DI Smyth said. "But we won't spend time on speculation. We'll wait and see what Baldwin can come up with first."

Smith's phone beeped to tell him he'd received a message. He swiped the screen and glanced at the message. Then he read it again and his heart stopped beating for a few seconds. When he was finally able to breathe again, he stood up.

"What now?" DI Smyth said.

"I have to go," Smith said. "Something's come up."

"You're really starting to piss me off with your cryptic crap," Bridge said.

Smith nodded. "I'm sorry, but there's something I really need to sort out."

CHAPTER TWENTY NINE

The identity of the man the team had colourfully dubbed *freezer man* came later that afternoon. It hadn't taken PC Baldwin long to track him down. Dennis Bright was thirty-four years old, and he was the brother of the girl who had died in a freezer in Penzance in 2004. Dennis was seventeen at the time.

The newspaper article on the Internet didn't mention Dennis by name but there was something about a brother who was supposed to be looking after seven-year-old Fiona when the tragedy occurred. According to the piece in the *Penzance Herald*, Dennis raised the alarm after he hadn't seen his sister for an hour or two. He and his girlfriend at the time were upstairs and he assumed that Fiona was watching television as he'd instructed her. It was nine hours later when her frozen body was finally found inside the freezer. The incident was ruled an accident.

Baldwin managed to ascertain that Dennis had moved to York five years ago. He was an insurance salesman, and he lived with his wife and two children not far from where Smith lived. A photograph on his LinkedIn profile page confirmed it – Dennis Bright was indeed *freezer man*.

Smith still hadn't returned and nobody knew where he was. He wasn't answering his phone and his car was gone from the car park. DI Smyth was justifiably annoyed, but he decided to carry on without him.
"There's one thing that strikes me as odd about this whole *freezer man* business," he said.
"If The Preacher believes Dennis to be responsible for the death of his sister," DC King said. "Why was he the one who killed himself?"
"Precisely, Kerry," DI Smyth said. "It's at odds with the series of events we've seen thus far in the investigation. In The Preacher's mind, Dennis

needs to be punished for Fiona's death, but why didn't he make someone close to Dennis commit suicide?"

"Has his wife been informed?" Bridge said.

"A couple of uniforms have been tasked with that unfortunate job," DI Smyth said. "Does anybody have any thoughts on how we can move forwards? I'm running out of ideas."

"If we're assuming that he's getting his information off the Internet," DC King said. "We can probably rule out a connection between the victims. These people have been chosen at random because of what The Preacher believes they've done. They haven't been suitably punished, and he's taken on that responsibility. Perhaps we ought to get the opinion of a psychologist."

"A profile?" Bridge said.

"It might be worth a shot," DI Smyth said. "He's clearly delusional and he definitely has a twisted system of morals, but a professional might be able to give us some more insight than that."

"It's possible he's a victim of a crime himself," Bridge said. "Perhaps some kind of abuse where the abuser wasn't punished for it. There are many documented cases of serial killers who suffered abuse early on in their lives."

"I'll give it some thought," DI Smyth said. "I suggest we take a break, and if anyone hears from Smith I want to be the first to know."

* * *

Smith read the message for the tenth time, even though he'd memorised every word. There were only eight of them:

I know what you did on the viaduct.

He didn't know how to interpret it. What was the purpose behind the message? The threat was implied, but there was no indication of what that threat actually was, and this made the eight words even more sinister.

Smith had tried calling the number the message had been sent from but the voice telling him that the number he was trying to dial did not exist indicated that the number was no longer in service. He didn't know what to do. He silently cursed the invention of unregistered phones, or *burners* as DC Moore was so fond of referring to them. Smith wondered why these phones hadn't been outlawed. They really did make the job he did a whole lot more difficult.

He thought hard about that night up on the viaduct. It was still very clear in his head. He'd done something terrible, but it was absolutely necessary. The alternative didn't bear thinking about, but what he'd done was something that would destroy his life if the truth ever saw the light of day. His thoughts turned to the people who were there with him when he overstepped the mark by a mile. The only people who knew about it were Lucy and Darren and the people on the team, and Smith didn't think any of them would mention it to anyone.

Was there someone else there that night? Someone he wasn't aware of. Smith didn't think so.

He was parked outside his house, debating whether to get out of the car and ring the bell of the house next door. He'd only spoken to Lucy that morning, but he really needed to speak to her again. He had to ask her whether she or Darren had mentioned the night at the viaduct to anyone. The message left little doubt that someone else was privy to the events of that night, and it made Smith sick to the stomach.

He got out of the car and walked up the path to number 18. A firework exploded somewhere in the distance and a dog barked. This was followed by a more familiar bark. Theakston rarely barked – it was a Bull Terrier thing, and Smith took it as a sign. He walked away from number 18 and headed for the house next door. He would spend some time with the dogs. It was just what the doctor ordered right now. He took out his keys, inserted one in the lock and went inside the house.

CHAPTER THIRTY

The Preacher was baffled. He'd watched from a distance as Detective Sergeant Jason Smith walked up the path to number 18 Greenway Avenue. Someone had let off a firework and Smith had gone next door instead. The Preacher knew that this was where Smith lived, and he also knew that Smith owned the house next door too. That was where his adopted daughter lived with her boyfriend and baby boy. The Preacher made sure he knew things like this.

He wondered if Smith's irrational behaviour was connected in any way to the message he'd sent earlier. He hoped that it was – it would make the next part of his plan much less tricky. Smith wasn't going to be as easy as the others to manipulate but if he was unnerved it would make things go a lot more smoothly. The others had been weak – that's why he'd chosen them, and The Preacher wondered if Smith and his team had figured this out yet. Were they aware that all four victims were vulnerable and easily manipulated? This wouldn't have worked otherwise.

In truth, The Preacher had no idea what happened up on the viaduct. He'd read every news article he could find on the topic, but he could only speculate on what actually went on that night. He had his suspicions but what he lacked was proof. He hoped that Smith wouldn't be able to figure this out.

He would play the long game with DS Smith. He wouldn't receive any more messages for a day or two, and even then, there would be no hint of what was to come. Smith was going to be a hard man to break, and it wouldn't happen overnight. It would take time for his own demons to work their magic, and The Preacher had every confidence that they would do just that. He just needed to be patient.

The door to number 16 opened and Smith reappeared. He didn't go next door. Instead, he got into his car and drove off down the street. A dog barked again, and the sound gave The Preacher an idea. Playing the long game was all very well, but in order to win that game every preceding move had to be beneficial to the victory in some way. He knew that Smith owned two dogs – he loved those dogs, and this was something The Preacher could exploit.

He stepped out from behind the van and started to walk up the street. He took the first left and the next left again. He made his way down the access road that ran past the back of Smith's house, and he stopped by the fence in Smith's back garden. The portly Bull Terrier and the gruesome Pug were asleep on the grass. The Preacher took out his phone and took a few photographs of them. Neither dog woke up. He headed back in the direction he'd come from, turned the corner and watched as a police car approached. There were two men in the front, and The Preacher recognised one of them. It was a shifty-eyed PC with an unfortunate nose. The car passed by, and The Preacher turned to watch it drive away.

* * *

"Smith lives around here somewhere, doesn't he?" PC Miller said. He indicated and took the next left.
"Who cares?" PC Griffin said.
"You and he really don't get on, do you?"
"He's a fossil," PC Griffin said. "A fossil from a bygone age that has no business in modern law enforcement."
"He gets results."
"That's precisely the kind of hero-worshipping attitude that's allowed Smith to get away with so much over the years. His time is coming, you mark my words."
"I like him," PC Miller said. "I've always found him to be a decent bloke."

"He's a thug and he's not far off being a criminal himself. You'll see – Smith will get what's coming to him one day."

PC Miller was glad when the Satnav informed him that they had reached their destination. Even though they were here to inform a woman that her husband was never coming home, that task was infinitely preferable to listening to PC Griffin babble on about DS Smith's inadequacies.

"This has to be the worst part of the job," PC Miller said. "It never gets any easier."

PC Griffin didn't comment.

"I'll do most of the talking if that's OK with you," PC Miller said.

"I'm quite capable of being compassionate," PC Griffin said.

"If you say so."

Rita Bright was a short woman with black hair. The expression on her face when she saw two uniformed officers on her doorstep suggested that she knew exactly what they were doing there. Her eyes darted from PC Miller to PC Griffin and her mouth opened wide.

"No," she said. "Please no."

"Mrs Bright?" PC Miller said. "Can we come inside?"

"Please no," she said once more.

They managed to persuade her to let them in, and the PCs Miller and Griffin sat with her in the living room.

"We're very sorry, Mrs Bright," PC Miller said.

"I knew something was wrong," she said.

"How did you know that?" PC Griffin said.

PC Miller glared at him.

"He didn't come home last night," Rita said. "And he wasn't answering his phone."

"We really are sorry," PC Miller said. "Is there anyone I can call for you?"

Rita skirted the question. "What am I going to tell the children?"

"We can arrange for a family liaison officer to pop round," PC Miller said.

Rita stood up and walked to the window. "He was supposed to fix the fence this weekend."

PC Griffin gave PC Miller a puzzled look.

"Can I call someone for you?" PC Miller offered again.

Rita turned around. There were tears in her eyes.

"What happened to him?"

"We're not sure yet."

"You're not sure?"

"I'm afraid your husband was murdered," PC Griffin said.

"Murdered? That's not possible."

"We're very sorry, Mrs Bright," PC Miller said.

"We've been together for nearly twenty years you know," Rita said. "Childhood sweethearts. We've been together since we were sixteen."

CHAPTER THIRTY ONE

"The picture of Dennis Bright's suicide has become a whole lot clearer," DI Smyth said to Bridge in the canteen. "The uniforms who went to inform the wife found out something that may explain why Dennis killed himself in that freezer. PC Miller told me that Rita Bright said she and Dennis had been together since they were sixteen. I think it was Rita who was with Dennis the day his sister died, and I also believe The Preacher blames her entirely."

"Makes sense," Bridge said. "The man has a twisted sense of logic, and he probably believes that Dennis's little sister wouldn't have died if Rita hadn't been there with him. He threatens Dennis with unspeakable violence towards his wife, and makes him take his own life the same way his sister died."

Smith came into the canteen and made a beeline for the coffee machine without acknowledging DI Smyth or Bridge.

"The prodigal son returns," DI Smyth said. "The prodigal son is treading on thin ice."

Smith joined them at the table. "Sorry, boss. It couldn't be helped. Did I miss much?"

"This kind of behaviour will not be tolerated much longer."

"Point taken."

"I mean it," DI Smyth said.

He filled Smith in on everything they'd discussed in his absence.

"This just gets more and more bizarre," Smith said. "What exactly are we dealing with here? A deranged psychopath who thinks he can play God? He's punishing people who he believes have sinned by manipulating the people closest to them to commit suicide. It's like the *Flytrap*, *Viaduct* and *Demons* investigations all rolled into one. Speaking of which..."

He took a look around the canteen. A PC he vaguely recognised was engrossed in something on his phone in the far corner of the room, but apart from him they were the only people there.

"Is there something on your mind?" DI Smyth said.

"I got to thinking about the viaduct earlier," Smith said.

"What brought that on?" Bridge said.

"I have no idea," Smith lied. "What happened that night could ruin a lot of lives if the truth ever came out, couldn't it?"

"That's why it's never going to be spoken of again," DI Smyth said. "And I don't think it's a good idea to be discussing it in here."

He nodded to the PC across the room. He was still tapping away on the screen of his phone.

"He can't hear us," Smith said. "I was wondering if there was anyone else there that night."

"It was just you, me, Kerry and Harry," Bridge reminded him. "And you know who of course, but he's hardly likely to blab, is he? Unless he happens to rise from the grave."

"Why are you asking about this?" DI Smyth said. "Is there something I need to be aware of?"

"Forget I said anything," Smith said. "What's the plan of action?"

"You're going to hate me for this, but I believe we need to go back to the beginning. There are a number of things we've yet to look at."

"I agree."

DI Smyth observed him as though he'd sprouted horns.

"I'm serious, boss," Smith said. "Too many aspects of this case are bugging me, and it's time I did something about that. I've got a feeling in my gut about Robert Allen and it's not a pleasant feeling. I want to speak to him again. We also need to look more closely at Sarah Peters. She knew the person who killed her, and we haven't followed that up yet."

"We're considering getting the help of a shrink," Bridge said. "I think we need to compile a profile of this psycho."

"Who did you have in mind?" Smith said. "I'm not in the mood for Dr Vennell."

"Have you two had a falling out?" DI Smyth said.

"It's not that. Every time she's involved in a case, it creates a bad atmosphere between me and Whitton. I could do without that right now."

"Are you telling us that you're putting your family before an investigation?" DI Smyth said.

"I reckon I am. And you're not going to change my mind."

"I'm not even going to try to change your mind," DI Smyth said. "I think it's admirable, and long overdue."

"How many times do I have to tell you?" Smith said. "You're looking at the new, improved Smith."

"I'll have a chat with Porter," DI Smyth said.

"How are things going with you two?"

"That's none of your business. Now, if you don't mind, there's something I need to discuss with DS Bridge. In private, if you don't mind."

Smith smiled. He finished his coffee and stood up.

"Touche. I'm going to go out for a quick smoke, and then I'm going to pay young Robert Allen a visit. There's something not right about that kid. I'll take Kerry with me. Where is she?"

"She's doing a bit of research," DI Smyth said. "She has a theory that she's working on."

"What theory?"

"She didn't elaborate," Bridge said. "She wanted to get a few things confirmed first."

"Sounds promising." Smith said and left them to it.

"Have you heard anything from your IT man?" DI Smyth asked when Smith was gone.

"Porter's troll is using a VPN to send the emails," Bridge said. "But it's an old version, and Barry thinks he'll be able to bypass it via some kind of backdoor. He did explain it to me, but you know what tech geeks are like."

"It's a foreign language to me," DI Smyth said.

"Barry has some kind of program that he can implant into the network the troll is using," Bridge said. "But we have to hope that the venomous emails keep coming."

"He received another one just last night."

"Do you know if he replied to it?" Bridge said.

"Not yet."

"Make sure he doesn't. Not until he's spoken to Barry first. He can stick some kind of spy bot in the body of the reply email. The bot will infiltrate the VPN and bypass the protection."

"Are you saying we'll be able to identify the sender?"

"Apparently, we will. Once the bot has done its thing, Barry will be able to get the IP address hiding behind the VPN, and once that's done, we'll have the identity of your hypnotist's troll."

"Your friend sounds like he knows what he's doing," DI Smyth said.

"What Barry Stone doesn't know about IT isn't worth knowing," Bridge said.

"There might be something else he may be able to do for me."

"If it's IT related, I'm sure he can help. What do you need?"

"It's not actually for me," DI Smyth said. "Smith has run into a bit of trouble, and I think Barry may be able to help him out."

He told him all about it.

CHAPTER THIRTY TWO

"What's this theory of yours?" Smith asked DC King.

They were in his car on their way to Robert Allen's girlfriend's house. The teenager was refusing to go home, and he was still staying with the Illman family.

"Sarge?" DC King said.

"The boss said you were doing some research on a theory," Smith said.

"Something occurred to me. I was struggling to comprehend how someone could make someone else end their own life."

"The threat The Preacher issued to Keith Peter's sister was pretty nasty," Smith said.

"Just hear me out. I thought about that, and I tried to put myself in the same position as Keith. If that was me, I would do everything I could to make sure the threats couldn't be carried out. I would go to the police, and I would make sure my sister was protected. I would definitely not kill myself because some maniac told me to."

"But that's you, Kerry," Smith said. "You're someone who is not to be fucked with. Keith Peters clearly isn't."

"And that's precisely my point, Sarge," DC King said. "That's what I was looking into earlier. I spoke to some friends of Keith's. By all accounts he was a mild-mannered man. He was a yes-man, and he always shied away from confrontation. I think he was extremely easy to manipulate."

The car in front slammed on brakes for no apparent reason and Smith had no choice but to do the same. His car came to a stop, inches from the other car.

"That was close," he said. "I hear what you're saying, but what about the other victims?"

"I didn't just check out Keith Peters," DC King said. "Maggie Allen's sister told me something very similar. The words she used to describe Maggie were *soft as shite*. Maggie saw the good in everybody, no matter how bad they actually were. She was gullible, and she too would always back down in an argument. Dennis Bright too. According to his co-workers he was a terrible insurance salesman. He was far too honest to be in that line of work, and he was on the verge of being sacked because of it. I tracked down one of his friends, and he confirmed it too. Dennis was what he termed *nice but naive*. All of these people will have been easy targets. I think The Preacher chose them because of this."

The car in front now seemed to be debating whether to turn left or right. The indicators seemed to have a mind of their own. Eventually, the driver settled on turning right and Smith increased his speed.
"You could be onto something there."
"I didn't get much info about Jane Banks," DC King said. "But she was a teenager, and the mind of someone that age is much easier to manipulate than a mature adult."
"Lucy told me that she and Jane haven't been close since Andrew was born, so she couldn't say if anything had been troubling her."
"Jane's mother said she'd been acting strange for a while. She would disappear to her room with her phone for hours, and when she came out, she would be morose and irritable. I think this is how he's choosing them, Sarge. It wasn't that long ago that we had to deal with something similar."
"The *Creed* investigation," Smith remembered. "This bastard has done a lot of research, hasn't he?"
"He has. And I think he's been planning this for a very long time. We still don't know why he's doing it, but I'm convinced that he's choosing them because they have weak personalities and they're easy to manipulate. This is the house here, isn't it?"

It was Brian Illman who answered the door. Today, he was dressed in a pair of black jeans and a black T-Shirt with the logo of a band Smith would prefer to forget on it.

"Wishbone," he said.

"Cool band," Brian grinned, and revealed his pointy teeth. "Cool band back in the day. They've broken up now, but then you'll know all about that, won't you?"

Smith wasn't in the mood for a cocky creature of the night.

"Is Robert here?" he asked.

"Looks like he thinks he's moved in for good," Brian said. "Shelly will kick him out sooner or later – he's being such a downer."

"Shelly?"

"Mother dearest. *Mum* is so not cool."

"I think you need to reconsider what passes for cool these days, Brian," Smith said. "And perhaps Robert is being a *downer* because his mother has just died. Could you please stop being a prick and let us come inside."

Brian held up his hands. "Whoa. Chill, Sergeant Dibble. I'm just messing with you."

Robert Allen looked slightly more human than he had done the last time Smith spoke to him. They were sitting in the living room. Once again, his girlfriend Emma insisted on joining them. Smith wasn't fazed. He had a few questions for her too.

"How are you feeling?" he asked Robert.

"A bit better," the teenager said. "I think the shock is wearing off."

"Why did you come back?" Emma said.

She was wearing a long-sleeved shirt with a print of some kind of ghoul on the front. Smith thought it was slightly at odds with her cherubic features, and he wondered if that was the whole point.

"Robert," he said. "The last time we spoke you were rather vague in your replies. I understand that shock affects people in many ways, and I'll put it down to that. I want you to be honest with me now, can you do that?"

"I don't know what you want me to tell you," Robert said.

"Some new information has come to our attention. Did your parents ever talk about your dad's mother – your grandmother?"

"I never met her," Robert said. "She died before I was born."

"That wasn't what DS Smith asked," DC King said.

"What was the question again?"

"Did your parents ever speak about your dad's mother?" Smith repeated.

"Sometimes."

"Did they mention how she died?" DC King said.

"Not really."

"Either they did, or they didn't," Smith said.

"I can't remember," Robert said. "Probably."

"She had cancer," Smith said.

"Why ask if you already know?"

Smith's phone started to ring. The ringtone told him it was a call he should really take but he let it go to voicemail anyway.

"Robert," Smith said. "You're doing it again. You're being deliberately vague, and that tends to get my goat."

"Get your what?" It was Emma.

"Could you please keep quiet," Smith said. "Robert, did you ever hear your parents talk about how your grandmother died?"

"She died of cancer," Robert said. "Like you just said. What's that got to do with what happened to my mum?"

"More than you think. OK, can you tell me why you're so reluctant to go home?"

"His mum died there," Emma said. "Can't you understand that?"

"And that's the only reason?" Smith said. "You're afraid to go back because of what happened to your mum? Aren't you concerned about your father? I

would imagine he would prefer to have you home at a time like this."
"You don't know anything," Robert said.
"Then help me. Do you and your father not get along?"
"He's a loser."
"All teenagers think their parents are losers," Smith said. "But that doesn't excuse what you're doing. Is there another reason why you're refusing to go back home?"

Robert didn't get the chance to answer. Brian came into the room and made himself comfortable on the single seater. It was like déjà vu, only this time he was holding something in his hands. When Smith looked more closely, he saw that it was a black rat. It wasn't moving, and Smith wondered if it was dead. He wouldn't be surprised with Brian Illman.
"Can I go?" Robert said. "I don't know anything."
"So I'm starting to understand," Smith said. "You can go. I just want to have a quick chat with Emma."
"What for?" she said.
Smith looked at Robert. "You can go."

"What have I done?" Emma asked when her boyfriend had left the room.
"Look," Smith said. "I appreciate that these are tragic circumstances, and it must be a difficult time for you, but we're trying to get to the bottom of what happened to Robert's mother."
"She killed herself," Emma said. "What else do you need to know?"
"Did Robert ever talk to you about his grandmother?"
"The one he never met?" Emma said. "Why would he talk about someone he didn't even know?"
"I never met my grandmother," DC King said. "On my mum's side, but I was still curious about her. I asked my mum about her a lot. Do you know if Robert spoke to his parents about his grandmother?"
"How should I know?" Emma said. "It's not really something you talk to your

boyfriend about, is it?"

"How long have you and Robert been together?" Smith said.

"Just over a year. We're going to get engaged when we finish school – get a place together."

"Give me a break." It was Brian.

Smith had forgotten he was even there.

"I need the loo," Emma said.

"I think that's all for now," Smith said.

He watched her walk out of the room. She looked like a little girl pretending to be an adult, and it made Smith feel a bit sad. His phone started to ring again. It was the same ringtone. The intro of *Oliver's Army* told him it was the boss.

"Cool ringtone," Brian commented.

Smith nodded.

"For a seventies throwback," Brian added. "Will there be anything else, Sergeant?"

"Detective Sergeant." Smith couldn't help correcting him. "There's a big difference. You were at the Halloween party, weren't you?"

"Guilty as charged."

"What do you remember about that night?"

"Apart from a girl ripping her throat open?"

"Where were you when she did that?" Smith said.

"I was on the other side of the dancefloor. I saw the whole thing."

"Could you talk us through what happened in the moments before?"

"I was sitting on one of the chairs against the wall."

"You weren't dancing?" DC King said.

"It was a Bruno Mars song," Brian said. "What do you think?"

"Go on," Smith said.

"The song ended," Brian said. "Thank God, but the DJ didn't play another one."

"Why do you think that is?" Smith said.

"How should I know? Perhaps the sound system gave up the ghost after having to endure Bruno Mars. You're not a fan, are you?"

Smith didn't reply. The ringtone sounded once more.

"Perhaps you should answer that," Brian said.

Smith handed the phone to DC King. "Could you see what the boss wants? I won't be much longer."

She left the room to take the call.

"You're clearly a smart kid," Smith said.

"I've been called worse," Brian said.

Smith's attention was caught by the rat.

"Is that thing dead?"

"She's sleeping," Brian said. "She's a deep sleeper. Her name is Selene, after the Roman goddess of the moon. She's a night owl like me. Do you want to hold her? Or do black rats scare you?"

"I want you to cut the crap now. This attitude of yours is starting to seriously piss me off. What do you remember about the time just before the music stopped?"

"I wasn't really paying much attention."

"Were most of the kids on the dancefloor?"

"I suppose so."

"What about the teachers?" Smith said. "It was Mrs Newton and the Head of Maths, wasn't it?"

"Mr Grigg," Brian said. "Mrs Newton was there by the drinks table I think, but I don't know where old Grigg was."

"You can't recall him being in the hall at the time?"

"I don't think so. You'd be better off asking my mate, Dean."

"Why's that?"

"Because he was the one who kept an eye on old Grigg all night."

"Why would he do that?" Smith said.

"We'd smuggled some booze in," Brian explained. "To make the night a bit more interesting. Vodka in a few coke bottles, but Grigg has eyes like a hawk and Dean was supposed to keep watch. If anyone can tell you where the old fucker was when the music stopped it'll be Dean."

"Do you have his contact details?" Smith said.

"He lives in Woodthorpe. Real fancy place."

Brian gave him the address.

Smith thanked him and got to his feet.

"You really don't have to put on this smart-arse act all the time," he said in the doorway. "You're obviously not stupid, so why would you choose to put on an act that makes you come across as a total dickhead?"

For once, Brian was speechless. The wannabe vampire had no comeback for this.

DC King was waiting by Smith's car outside. She handed his phone back to him.

"What did the boss want?" Smith asked.

"Keith Peters has regained consciousness," DC King said. "The DI got a call from the hospital. He's awake, but the doctors aren't sure how long that will be the case. We need to get to the hospital now."

CHAPTER THIRTY THREE

The Preacher checked his watch. It was three-thirty and the traffic on the way to the school had been a nightmare. He knew it would be. This wasn't the first time he'd parked outside. School pickup was always a busy time here, and he wondered why these children couldn't walk to and from school like he used to when he was a child. Parents were just lazy these days. Most of the kids probably only lived five-minutes away.

The disguise he'd chosen meant that none of the parents paid him much attention. He doubted if they would even look twice at him if he wasn't disguised to look like an old man – a grandfather of one of the pupils, perhaps. But even though these people were so wrapped up in their own lives and paid little attention to anything else, he couldn't take any chances. He took out his phone and pretended to be looking at something on the screen. He did this with the phone held out in front of him and he allowed himself a chuckle.
"I'm just a myopic old fool," he told himself. "A harmless grandfather who can't read the shit on the screen."
Another chuckle followed.

The two children he'd come to see rarely got picked up in a car. The Preacher knew this. At 15:40 the two eight-year-old girls would exit the school gate and be greeted by a teenage boy. Sometimes he would have his teenage girlfriend with him, but The Preacher doubted she would be there today. She had other things on her mind. The clock on the phone told him it was almost time.

Regular as clockwork, the boy arrived, and The Preacher grinned a smug grin when he realised that he was alone. The teenage mother was home alone with her baby. The two girls came out together – they usually did, and The Preacher activated the camera on his phone. After zooming in, he took a number of photographs in quick succession. He wasn't sure if all of them would be usable, but he only needed one. He closed the phone, put it back in his pocket and turned the key in the ignition. After checking the road, he pulled out and drove away from the school, confident that none of the parents would remember he was ever there.

* * *

Smith got out of the car in the hospital car park. DC King got out of the passenger side. According to the doctors treating Keith Peters he was not out of the woods yet. He'd sustained a number of injuries – his right femur was broken, as were his collarbone and right arm. The bus had hit him side-on which meant that his right shoulder took the brunt of the initial impact. There was some swelling to the brain caused by his head hitting the road, but it wasn't as bad as they initially feared. It could have been a lot worse. If the driver hadn't reacted as quickly as he did, Keith could easily have been killed. And his sister would still be alive.

DI Smyth had suggested they keep this piece of information to themselves for now and Smith had agreed. He knew that they would get much more out of Keith if he still believed his sister was alive. As far as he was aware, the medical staff hadn't informed Keith of his sister's demise, and Smith wanted to keep it like that for as long as possible.

After announcing their presence at the reception desk, Smith and DC King were told to take a seat and wait for a Doctor Williams. Smith remained standing. DC King did too.

"We need to see him now," Smith said. "What if he loses consciousness again?"

"Do you think he's going to be able to tell us anything?" DC King said.

"Sarah Peters knew the person who killed her, Kerry," Smith said. "Everything at the scene suggests this. She let him in, they drank coffee, and he killed her. She knew this bastard, and it's possible that Keith knows him too."

"If that's the case, surely it would have been much harder to make him kill himself."

"I'm not saying that Keith was aware of who was sending him the messages," Smith said. "He used a voice synthesiser and that also suggests that they were acquainted. Those messages were sent by someone known to both Sarah and Keith. The Preacher is somebody they know."

Dr Williams was a tall, thin man with a full beard. After introducing himself he told Smith and DC King what to expect.

"Mr Peters is extremely lucky. He's sustained numerous injuries but most of them are not life-threatening. We were concerned about the swelling on his brain, but it seems to be abating and it's possible that he'll make a full recovery."

"Is he lucid?" Smith said. "Do you think he's up to answering some questions?"

"I wouldn't have informed your DI if I didn't think so. I appreciate how important it is that you question him, but I'll ask you to please keep it brief, and I'll also ask you not to ask him anything that might put him under any stress."

"He doesn't know that his sister was murdered, does he?" Smith said.

"He does not. We thought it best not to tell him about it just yet."

"And we're not going to mention it either," Smith said. "Not right now, anyway."

"I appreciate that. I have rounds to attend to. I'll get one of the nurses to escort you to Mr Peters' room."

Keith Peters looked much better than Smith had anticipated, and he reckoned it boded well. His obvious injuries aside – he wore a neck brace, and his right leg had been elevated, but he was wide awake, and his eyes seemed bright.

Smith told him who they were and Keith's eyes opened wider.

"Sarah. I need to warn Sarah."

"Sarah is fine," Smith lied. "We recovered your phone, and we listened to the messages. Uniformed officers were despatched straight away, and she's perfectly safe."

He could sense that DC King was finding his lies uncomfortable. She was refusing to make eye contact with Keith, and she was picking at the cuticles on her nails. Smith didn't like lying but it was necessary right now.

"How are you feeling?" he asked.

"Like I've been hit by a bus," Keith said. "I can actually say that, can't I?" The nervous laugh that followed was clearly very painful. Keith winced and his right hand reached for the brace on his neck. The other hand had been rendered immobile by the splint on the arm.

"Are you up to answering a few questions?" Smith said.

"If I can."

"We've listened to the messages," Smith said. "So there's no need for you to explain why you jumped in front of the bus. What we need to know is whether you might know the person who made you do that."

"Of course not," Keith said.

"I want you to think hard. We have reason to believe that you've crossed paths with him."

"What makes you think that?"

Because your sister invited him into your house and made him coffee, minutes before he bashed her brains in.

Obviously, Smith didn't voice this thought.

"He seemed to know a lot about your life," he said instead. "The content of the messages implies that he is not a stranger to you."

"The voice was disguised," Keith said.

"We're aware of that," Smith said. "He used a voice synthesiser, but contrary to popular belief those devices are far from foolproof. Even when a voice is disguised there will be certain aspects of speech that might reveal a person's identity – personal nuances and the like. Did you recognise anything like that in the messages?"

"They're all a bit of a blur to be honest. You're not going to make me listen to them again, are you?"

"That may be necessary," Smith said. "But not now."

"Is Sarah going to be alright?" Keith said. "Does she know what happened?"

"She does," Smith lied again.

"Why hasn't she come to see me?"

Smith was sure his nose was growing as he came up with the next lie inside his head. It was a real whopper.

"Sarah has been advised not to do that. We don't know if this person is watching the hospital, but we have to work on the assumption that he is, and we can't take that risk."

"I understand," Keith said.

The resignation in his voice made Smith feel depressed. This poor man had almost been killed by a bus, his sister had been brutally murdered, and now he was being fed blatant lies by a police detective. Smith decided that he was going to catch this bastard. He was going to find The Preacher if it was the last thing he did.

"We won't keep you much longer," he said. "You need to get some rest. Could you do me a favour?"

"If I can," Keith said.

"I'm going to leave one of my cards here. If you think of anything that was said in those messages that seemed familiar to you, I want you to give me a call. Day or night."

He took out a card and put it on the table next to the bed.

"Are you going to find out who did this to me?" Keith said.

"I am," Smith promised. "Get some rest, and call me if you think of anything."

They said their goodbyes and Smith and DC King left him alone with his broken bones and painkillers.

"The deception made you a bit uncomfortable back there, didn't it?" Smith asked DC King by the reception area. "You didn't say a word."

"It wasn't that, Sarge," she said. "Something occurred to me when we were in there, but it was something I couldn't go into with Keith in the room. I was going over the timeline. He jumped in front of the bus at about quarter to two. The ambulance arrived soon afterwards, and he was taken to hospital."

"Shit." Smith knew exactly what she was going to say next. "We went to Sarah Peters' house later that afternoon, and we were just too late. How did he find out that Keith's suicide attempt was unsuccessful?"

"How did he find out so soon you mean? If Sarah had been murdered a day or two later, it could be explained. The failed suicide attempt would probably have made the papers by then, but he knew straight away."

"Which means either, he was there when Keith jumped in front of the bus," Smith said. "Or he came to the hospital. I don't think he was at the scene of the attempted suicide. With all the commotion and the paramedics, and the flashing lights, there's no way he would be able to know if Keith was dead or not."

"He was here, wasn't he?" DC King said.

"I think he was. I think The Preacher followed the ambulance to the hospital to find out what his next move was going to be. And if that's the case, we have a pretty accurate time to look at."

"Are you thinking CCTV?"

"What else, Kerry?" Smith said. "Best thing that's ever been invented."

CHAPTER THIRTY FOUR

Lenny Jenkins opened the door and looked the man on the doorstep up and down. His clothes and his shaggy hair made him wonder if he was a beggar looking for help. Perhaps he was a homeless man, but if he was after money he'd come to the wrong house. Lenny decided to find out what this human scarecrow wanted and send him on his way.

"Mr Jenkins?" the scarecrow said.
Lenny wasn't expecting this. How did he know his name?
"Who wants to know?"
The man produced a card. "Mike Phillips. I'm a technician with I Spy."
"I Spy?" Lenny repeated.
"It wouldn't have been my choice for a company name either," Mike said.
"You're using our system for your CCTV cameras."
"What do you want?" Lenny said. "If you're selling something you've come to the wrong house."
"I'm not selling anything. You pay a monthly subscription, and according to what I've seen on my side you're not using the service to its full potential. Perhaps I could come in and explain in more detail. You'll have to excuse my appearance – I rarely leave the house, and this is how I normally dress. I can do most of my work remotely you see."
"Hold on," Lenny said. "I Spy you say?"
"That's correct."
He left Mike on the doorstep and returned a minute later with a woman dressed in an identical tracksuit to her husband's.
"Invite him in then," she said.
She told Mike that her name was Sheila and asked him to take a seat in the living room.

"Our Lenny says you're here about the cameras."

"As I explained to your husband," Mike said. "The subscription you took out is not being used properly. You're not getting everything that you're paying for."

"I didn't know that," Lenny said.

"The cameras you've installed are top of the range," Mike said. "Packed with features. The sensors are designed to detect movement, even in the middle of the night."

"We know that," Lenny said. "We get a notification on our phones as soon as the sensors are activated."

"But are you aware that you can extend those notification alerts to additional devices?"

"What do you mean?" Sheila said.

"At present, you're only able to view the camera footage on your mobile phones. Do you have a laptop or a tablet perhaps?"

"We've got a laptop each," Lenny said. "And Sheila has a tablet."

"Is that a smart TV?" Mike pointed to the massive screen on the wall.

Lenny grinned. "Best there is."

Mike stood up and walked over to inspect it. "Just imagine what the camera footage will look like on this thing."

"Are you saying we can watch whatever the cameras pick up on the television?" Sheila said.

"You can."

"How much is that going to cost us?" Lenny said. "What's the catch?"

"No catch. As I've explained, you're already paying for it – you're just not utilising the full package. That's why I'm here."

"Can you set it up for us?"

Mike grinned and scratched his two-day growth of beard. "That's why I'm here."

He opened up his bag and took out a laptop.

"Give me two tics."

"Do you need us to do anything?" Lenny asked.

"I'm going to need admin access in a minute, but right now I'm just bringing up the right program. Here we go. I'll need your password."

"Password?" Sheila said.

"The password you chose when you did the initial set-up."

"Lenny did that."

"If you're concerned about divulging it," Mike said. "You can type it in for me."

"No need for that," Lenny said. "You're doing us a favour – it's not like you're here to rip us off. It's *Loadsofdosh1*. All one word with a capital *L*."

"Loads of dosh?" Sheila said.

"It was all I could think of at the time," Lenny said.

"OK," Mike said. "This might take a while. Could I possibly trouble you for a cup of coffee? I work faster with a bit of caffeine in my system."

"I'll make it," Sheila offered.

"And if you could retrieve your laptops and that tablet, please."

"I'll get them," Lenny said.

Mike got to work. His fingers tapped the keypad at lightning speed.

Mr and Mrs Jenkins came back together. Sheila handed Mike his coffee and Lenny placed the laptops and tablet on the table.

"I'll just link them up," Mike said. "Could you turn on the TV for me. Put it on AV. That will be the default setting for the CCTV."

The screen came to life and shortly afterwards it was filled with a view of the back garden. The shed was clearly visible at the end of the garden, as was the outside tap. There was no hosepipe in the shot.

"What do you think?" Mike asked.

"That's amazing," Lenny said.

"So, we can watch the camera footage on the big screen."
"Correct," Mike said. "And you can even control it from your mobile phones. You can split the screen so you can view all four cameras at once. You're all set."
"What about the laptops and the tablet?" Lenny asked.
"Already set up," Mike said. "I connected them via Bluetooth. And I've fixed the minor glitches with the back garden camera and the one looking out onto the front."
"Glitches?" Lenny said.
"You probably weren't aware of it, but it appeared that the cameras weren't operational at certain times in the past few days."
"We didn't notice it," Sheila said.
"No harm done," Mike said. "You're all set."
He downed the coffee in one go and packed up his laptop.
   "Thanks for this," Lenny said on the doorstep. "We really appreciate it."
"Just doing my job," Mike said.
"No," Lenny said. "You did us a big favour there. Not many employees these days would go the extra mile. Let me give you something extra for your trouble."
"There's no need for that."
"We're not short of a few quid."
"No," Mike said. "The pleasure really was all mine."

CHAPTER THIRTY FIVE

It was late by the time Smith and DC King finished up at the hospital. DI Smyth called to inform them that he was calling it a day. Smith dropped DC King off at the station and headed home. He needed a night in with the girls and the dogs. The message about the viaduct was niggling away at him but he chose not to dwell on it. He would sleep on it and come up with a plan of action tomorrow.

He'd managed to get a copy of the CCTV footage from the entrance of the hospital where Keith Peters was being treated, and he'd decided to leave that for tomorrow too. He also wanted to speak to the friend of Brian Illman's in the morning. Something about the Head of Maths' behaviour at the Halloween party was sounding some warning bells and Smith needed to silence them.

He was surprised when he went inside his house to find Lucy and Darren in the kitchen. Andrew was also there. The baby was feeding himself some kind of green mush and he wasn't doing a very good job of it. Most of it was plastered around his mouth and on his cheeks.

"What on earth is that shit he's painting his face with?" Smith asked Lucy.

"Mashed potato and spinach," she said. "He loves it."

"So I see. How are you feeling?"

"A bit better," Lucy said. "Still numb, but better. I can't get what Jane did out of my mind. It doesn't feel real."

"I hear what you're saying. It wasn't her fault. She was targeted by a very dangerous man, and she didn't have a choice."

"I don't think this is the time or the place," Whitton said.

"Lucy already knows about The Preacher," Smith told her.

"Andrew can hear you."

"Andrew is a year old," Smith said. "I doubt he's going to blab."

"I know, but can we talk about something else?"

"No worries. I really feel like pizza."

"I thought you hated pizza," Darren said.

"People can change. Do you want to join us?"

"Free pizza?" Darren said. "What do you think?"

"Who said it was going to be free?" Smith said.

"I'll order it on the app," Lucy said. "I've still got your credit card details on my phone."

Smith was on the verge of commenting on this, but he opted to keep quiet. Lucy hadn't been this upbeat since Jane's suicide and he wanted to keep it that way.

The pizza was delivered thirty minutes later, and twenty minutes after that all that remained was one slice of ham and pineapple. Smith let Fran and Laura share it.

"I'm going outside for a smoke," he said.

He opened the back door and went out to the garden. The dogs followed him out. Theakston and Fred were a bit put out that all they'd managed to beg from the table was a few dry pizza crusts. Smith didn't care – they were both getting a bit porky and needed to lose a bit of weight.

He'd no sooner lit the cigarette when the sound of his phone caused him to curse out loud. It wasn't so much the phone as the ringtone. *Oliver's Army* meant it was the boss. Smith fetched the phone, came back outside and lit a cigarette.

"Boss," he answered it. "Please tell me there hasn't been another one."

DI Smyth humoured him. "There hasn't been another one. That's not why I'm phoning. I thought I'd let you know that your problems with Mr and Mrs Walmart have been sorted out."

Smith had actually forgotten all about that.

"How did you manage that? Did you go and speak to them?"

"That wasn't necessary. Let's just say the evidence they had against you and Frankie Lewis has conveniently disappeared. That's all I'm going to say on the matter."

"Come on, boss," Smith said. "You're killing me here."

"OK," DI Smyth said. "I asked Bridge to put me in touch with his IT expert friend."

"The fat bloke? Barry Stone?"

"That's him, although he's lot quite a bit of weight. Porter had some unpleasant business he needed help with, and I wondered if Barry could help you with yours too. You owe him, Smith."

"You're going to have to give me a bit more than that."

"Mr Stone paid the Jenkins' a visit," DI Smyth said. "He posed as a technician for the company they use for their CCTV cameras. He managed to get admin access, and he deleted the relevant footage."

"Won't they smell a rat?" Smith said.

"He told them he'd noticed a few glitches with two of the cameras, but he assured them the problem was fixed. There's no way they'll be able to connect Barry to you. He went there dressed like a hobo."

"You're right," Smith said. "I owe him."

"They no longer have a case," DI Smyth said. "Without that CCTV footage, all they have is their word that Frankie flooded the shed, and you subsequently tried to cover it up."

"I'd love to see their faces when they figure that out," Smith said. "This is brilliant. What was it that Barry did for Porter? What was his unpleasant business?"

"That's not your concern. Oh, and I spoke to him about coming up with some kind of profile on our preacher and he's more than happy to help."

"Glad to hear it. I'll let you get on with your evening. Thanks for letting me know."

The cigarette had gone out, so he relit it, took a long drag and grinned like a village idiot. The business with Mr and Mrs *Mullet* was a headache he didn't need right now, and it was now ancient history. For the first time that week Smith felt like things were going his way for once, and he let that feeling linger.

It didn't last long. His phone started to ring again, and the screen told him it was a number he didn't recognise. And when he answered the call, all he could hear was something that sounded like a piece of industrial machinery turning over. Then there was another noise – the sound of metal scraping over something solid. The high-pitched screech was difficult to listen to.

"Who the hell is this?" Smith said.

Then everything went silent.

"If this is your idea of a joke," Smith said. "You have a lot to learn about humour."

He hung up after this.

Soon afterwards the phone beeped twice to tell him he'd received two messages. There was no text to the messages – just two attachments. He tapped the screen to open them.

The first photo had been taken in his garden. Theakston and Fred were asleep on the lawn. Smith wondered why someone would send him a photograph of his dogs.

The second image caused him to open his mouth wide, losing the cigarette in the process. Smith recognised the location immediately. It had been taken in front of Laura and Fran's school. The two girls were standing with Darren Lewis. Possibly the most disturbing aspect of the photograph was the jumper Laura was wearing, more specifically, it was how she wore it. For a long time, she'd gone through a phase where she preferred to wear her school jumper inside out or back to front. Of course, the teachers would always make her put it on correctly when she arrived at school, but she always changed it to the way she preferred it as soon as she left the school building. But today she'd somehow grown out of that phase, and she'd come downstairs that morning wearing it how it was supposed to be worn.

    That's what Smith found the most unsettling. This photograph had been taken that afternoon.

CHAPTER THIRTY SIX

The Preacher stared at the screen of his phone for quite some time. The sound of a firework exploding somewhere close by woke him sufficiently to realise he'd lingered too long. He removed the back cover, took out the battery and the sim and put the phone on the table. With a practiced action he snapped the sim card in half and then into quarters. He opened one of the prepaid phone starter packs and inserted another sim card. After replacing the battery, he clipped the cover back on and started up the phone.

He wondered if he'd made a blunder. He'd changed the plan of action, and he didn't know if it had been a mistake. The Preacher had never been impulsive, and he wasn't sure what had brought on this sudden impatience. He would have to be more careful in future.

He'd memorised the number he was now keying into the phone. He pushed all thoughts of DS Jason Smith from his mind and focused on the task at hand. After activating the voice synthesiser and reciting a brief but detailed message, he put the phone down, closed his eyes and waited. Another firework lit up the sky outside the window for a moment and The Preacher opened the curtains wider to get a better look. The window was open and there was a whiff of sulphur in the air. It wasn't an entirely unpleasant smell, and The Preacher breathed it in.

The firework odour brought back a memory from a distant age. It was the November of The Preacher's first year at secondary school and he and his brother had gone to the firework display in the local park. His brother was two years older, and The Preacher worshipped the ground he walked on. He'd been born with albinism, a rare condition that causes a lack of melanin in the skin, hair and eyes. His white hair, alabaster skin and pale blue eyes caused people to look twice, and he was often the butt of cruel jokes.

There were a group of boys at the firework display. The Preacher can't recall their names, but they were all a few years older than him. It started with a cruel jibe here and a mean word there, but it soon escalated to something much more sinister. There was a huge bonfire in the middle of the park and the flames were in full swing. The wooden effigy that had been placed on the fire earlier had been consumed by the flames and the gang of boys decided it would be a good idea to sacrifice another, very different kind of *Guy*.

"Burn the freak. Fry the albino oddball. Boil his skin off."
The boys were getting really worked up. The Preacher recalled that the adults who were present that evening didn't step in and put a stop to the cruelty, and he didn't understand why, even many years later.

He was shorter and weaker than all of the boys, but what he lacked in strength he more than made up for in determination and the sheer will to fight, and when two of them grabbed his brother and started to drag him towards the bonfire, he was consumed by a rage like no other. His vision was blurred by a red mist, and he was no longer in control of himself.

One of the boys suffered a broken arm in the struggle. Another would live out the rest of his life with half an ear. A third would have a permanent half-moon shaped scar on his cheek. The adults stepped in this time. The Preacher and his brother moved away soon after the bonfire incident, but the cruelty followed them. His love for his brother only got stronger, and he made a vow that he would always look out for him.

And he did just that. Until an unfortunate series of events meant his brother's welfare ended up out of his control. The prison sentence and the subsequent torture were something The Preacher had no say in, and when he received the news from the prison earlier in the year, it set off a chain of events that had already resulted in the deaths of three people. His brother had gouged his wrists open with the sharpened pieces of a broken mobile phone casing. His cellmate didn't do anything to stop him, and he died before help could arrive.

The Preacher's reverie was cut short by the sound of the message notification of his phone. A glance at the screen told him that this one was going to be easier than he'd anticipated. Tomorrow morning, a woman was going to jump into a swimming pool, chain herself to the pump outlet and perish in the most horrible manner imaginable.

* * *

"Penny for them."

Whitton had come into the kitchen without Smith realising it.

"Excuse me?" he said.

"Penny for your thoughts."

"I was miles away there," Smith said.

"So I saw. Something's bothering you."

"What's new?"

"No," Whitton said. "You've got something on your mind – I know you too well."

"It's nothing that can't wait until tomorrow," Smith lied.

In truth, he knew he wasn't going to be able to sleep tonight. The photographs he'd received were going to keep him up, and the coffee on the table in front of him probably wasn't the greatest of ideas either.

"Are you coming to bed?" Whitton asked.

"In a bit," Smith said. "I just want to check something out on my laptop before I come up."

"Work?"

"Sort of. Lucy seemed a bit better tonight."

"It's going to take time," Whitton said. "But I think my mum was right – she'll bounce back eventually. I'm going to bed."

She kissed him on the cheek and left him alone.

Smith switched on his laptop and waited for it to boot up. When it was ready he keyed the name of Lucy's sixth-form college into the task bar. As he'd expected, the college had its own website. He found the list of teachers and clicked on the one he wanted. Tony Grigg was one of the longest serving staff members. He'd taught Maths at the college for almost twenty years. There was a photograph of him on the page and Smith studied it. He seemed vaguely familiar, but Smith decided that it was possible he'd seen him at one of the college open nights. He was an average looking man with thinning hair and large spectacles. He looked like an archetypal Maths teacher – he certainly didn't strike Smith as a psychotic serial killer.

He took a drink of coffee and winced – it had gone cold. He was ready to close down his laptop when something occurred to him. He'd managed to get the CCTV footage from the hospital for the time when Keith Peters was brought in. Smith was convinced that The Preacher had followed the ambulance there and if that was the case he would probably have been caught on camera. He inserted the memory stick and clicked the keypad to view the footage. It was supposed to be a task for tomorrow, but Smith was wide awake so he might as well get it done tonight.

Keith Peters had arrived at the hospital forty-five minutes after being hit by the bus, so Smith started the footage from then. The entrance was busier than Smith expected it to be. He counted more than fifty people coming and going in the first fifteen minutes alone. He paused the footage and went through the sequence of events once more in his head. Keith had jumped in front of the bus at roughly 13:45. The ambulance had arrived quickly, and after being attended to at the scene, Keith was driven to hospital. He arrived there at around half-two. Smith recalled that he and DC King had gone to speak to Keith's sister an hour later.

"The fucker went straight there," he told the screen of his laptop. "He found out that Keith was still alive, drove straight to Sarah's house and killed her."

The coffee in the mugs in her kitchen was still warm, and Smith cursed himself again for not paying Sarah a visit earlier. If they'd been ten minutes earlier it was possible that she might still be alive.

He resumed the footage. He calculated the distance from the hospital to Sarah Peters' house to be roughly seven miles. It was early Sunday afternoon so the traffic wouldn't have been too bad, but it would have still taken at least fifteen minutes to get to Sarah's house. Add on at least another ten minutes for her to make the coffee and for The Preacher to kill her, and that left a window of less than thirty minutes. Smith carried on watching. If The Preacher was somewhere on the CCTV footage it would be between 14:30 and 15:00.

Nothing jumped out at him for the first ten minutes, and Smith wondered if he was barking up the wrong tree. Perhaps The Preacher had been at the scene of the bus accident after all. He could have been watching from a distance, and it was possible that he would realise that Keith was still alive from the actions of the paramedics. Hell, it was also possible that he spoke to one of them and asked if the man was going to be alright. A paramedic wouldn't think it suspicious. Smith cursed himself for not even thinking about talking to the people at the scene of the accident.

At 14:52 something caught his attention on the screen. It was actually two things – two identical tracksuits, and two unmistakable *mullet* hairstyles. Smith rewound the footage, started it again and paused it when the Walmart couple entered the hospital. There was no doubt about it – Lenny and Sheila Jenkins were at City Hospital shortly after Keith Peters was brought in.

CHAPTER THIRTY SEVEN

Wendy London was well on her way to becoming intoxicated. It was just before seven on a cold November morning and the sun was yet to wake up over the city of York, but Wendy had already finished three quarters of the bottle of wine she'd brought with her to the leisure complex in Heslington. There were a few cars in the car park, but Wendy knew that these would belong to the members of the gym on the opposite side of the complex to the swimming pool. She knew this because she'd worked at the swimming pool for more than five years.

The wine hadn't been part of the plan. It hadn't been mentioned in the instructions, but Wendy thought it was a good idea. It would make what she was about to do a lot easier. She was starting to feel slightly ill, but she didn't want to be sick – she needed as much alcohol in her system as she could get. She forced down the remaining wine and swallowed a handful of painkillers for good measure. These too were deviations from the original plan.

She got out of the car and looked inside her handbag. The chain and the thin padlocks were still there. The locks were open, and Wendy made sure not to push the shanks into the locking bars. She didn't have the keys. This part *was* in the instructions. She didn't bother to lock the car door. It would be pointless.

Her head was spinning as she made her way to the staff entrance of the swimming pool, and it took three goes to eventually get the key in the lock and open the door. A few deep breaths didn't help. Wendy wondered if the painkillers were kicking in. She headed for the pool and unlocked that door without too much trouble.

The outlet for the filter pump was located halfway down the pool wall in the deep end. The depth was twelve feet here. Wendy knew there was a protective grate covering the water blower. It was a safety measure, and it was this safety precaution that would enable her to carry out the instructions to the letter. Wendy wondered if the people who came up with the health and safety regulations would rethink its effectiveness after this.

After smashing the brand-new phone and leaving it by the edge of the pool, as per the instructions, she took out the chain and wrapped it around her neck. She used one of the padlocks to secure it around her throat, but she'd made it too tight. It was too late – she didn't have the key for the padlock. She felt constricted and her gag reflex kicked in. She couldn't stop it – her throat lurched, and she vomited red wine and half-digested painkillers into the deep end of the pool. The result resembled the scene of a murder, and Wendy's final thought before she jumped into the pool, fully clothed was that it was soon to become one.

* * *

"A woman has tried to kill herself at the leisure complex in Heslington." Smith had only just walked through the doors of the station when Baldwin pounced on him with this information.

"What happened?" he asked her.

"She was found in the swimming pool," Baldwin said. "By the caretaker. He'd arrived earlier than he usually did, and he spotted her floating in the deep end. She had a chain around her neck."

"What makes you think it was suicide?"

"Because she told the paramedics it was. We don't have any more details than that, but it seems she went there to commit suicide, but she passed out before she could carry it out. The caretaker got her out just in time."

It didn't take Smith long to jump to the only conclusion he could. "Someone close to her is in danger."

"The DI is already aware of it, Sarge," Baldwin said. "We got the details of her family from the leisure complex and uniforms have been sent out."

"This bastard is exceptional," Smith said. "Let's hope we're in time."

Bridge and DC Moore were already seated in the canteen. Smith joined them at their table.

"No coffee this morning?" Bridge said.

"I'm trying to cut down. Did you hear about the woman in the swimming pool?"

"Of course," DC Moore said. "The DI is at the hospital with her now."

"That was quick."

"He was here when the call came in," Bridge said. "I don't think he slept much last night."

"There must be something in the air," Smith said.

"Where's Whitton?" DC Moore asked.

"School run," Smith said.

"I thought you had a slave living next door for stuff like that," Bridge said.

"We thought we'd give Darren the morning off."

This was a lie. In fact, Smith suggested exactly that to Whitton. He used the excuse that it would do Darren good to have a lie in for a change, but really, he wanted the girls to be taken to school by someone more equipped to take care of them should the need arise. The photograph of Laura and Fran he'd been sent was still troubling him, and he didn't want to take any chances. He'd offered to pick the girls up after school.

DCI Chalmers came into the canteen and walked up to their table.

"Don't you lot have work to do?"

"Just refuelling on coffee before we get stuck into the day, boss," Smith said.

Chalmers noted the lack of coffee in front of Smith, but he didn't comment on it.

"Fill me in on the developments in this Preacher case."
Smith told him everything that had happened so far, including the incident at the swimming pool earlier that morning.

"Any decent leads?" Chalmers said.
"We've hit dead end after dead end," Smith said. "I thought I'd got a break with the CCTV footage of the hospital one of the victims was taken to, but once again it was a dead end."

The footage of Lenny and Sheila Jenkins was a shaky lead at best, and Smith couldn't believe they could be involved in something as complex as this. He'd checked out their story, nevertheless and it was confirmed by someone at the hospital that the Walmart couple were regulars there. Visiting time was from three until four on the weekends, and they were there on Sunday to visit Lenny's mother. She had bowel cancer, and she was in the final stages. This information made Smith feel slightly guilty for suspecting them, but when he thought about it, it was an extremely long shot anyway. The Preacher was an incredibly ruthless, sophisticated killer and the Jenkins' were merely *Chavs* with matching *mullets*.

"The DI has asked Porter Klaus to see if he can come up with a profile on this maniac," Smith said.
"A profile?" Chalmers said. "Are you going all American on us now?"
"It might help," Bridge said.
"And we need all the help we can get at the moment," Smith added. "We've got pretty much fuck all to look at. There's a teacher at the college where the girl killed herself on Saturday that I'm interested in, but I've got a feeling that he'll be yet another name to be ticked off a list."
"Exactly how long is this list?" Chalmers said.
"About as long as the names of people in Uncle Jeremy's fan club."
"That long? Speaking of which – the Super is hinting about a press conference."

"Of course he is," Smith said. "And what exactly is he planning on telling the people of this good city? We have a rather dangerous man who is going around telling people to kill themselves. If they don't comply, someone close to them will be slaughtered in an unimaginable way. This person is not to be approached. A press conference is a terrible idea right now, boss."

"I'm on the same page as you, Smith," Chalmers said. "I'm just telling you what the public-school amoeba told me. Catch this bastard before the Super gets the chance to hold his press conference."

With that, Chalmers left the canteen.

CHAPTER THIRTY EIGHT

"The woman from the swimming pool is going to be alright," DI Smyth said. "According to the instructions she received, she had to commit suicide by chaining herself to the grate that covers the water pump outlet. It's six feet below the surface of the water."

"What a horrible way to end it all," DC Moore said.

"She was reluctant to talk at first," DI Smyth said. "But once I'd convinced her that her loved ones were safe, she opened up. It appears that The Preacher's target was her husband. Apparently, Neil – that's the husband was unable to save a man who got into difficulty in the sea off Scarbrough. Neil was working as a lifeguard one summer - the swimmer swam too far out and couldn't make it back. Neil went in after him, but the man drowned before he could get to him."

"It wasn't his fault then?" DC Moore said.

"Of course it wasn't his fault, Harry," Smith said. "The Preacher has the most twisted sense of logic of any lunatic I've ever come across. What did he threaten to do to Wendy's husband?"

This question was posed to DI Smyth.

"Unspeakable torture," the DI said. "Wendy didn't elaborate, but she's given us the location of her mobile phone, so we'll be able to retrieve the messages The Preacher sent to her."

"Was there a broken phone at the scene?" Smith said out of the blue.

"Next to the pool," DI Smyth confirmed. "Smashed to pieces."

"Why get them to smash up brand new phones?"

"To distract us from the stuff that's on their real phones," Bridge said. "I thought we'd already established that."

"No," Smith said. "I'm starting to have doubts about that theory. This one is not stupid, and he knows that we're not either. Destroying the new phones serves no purpose whatsoever. Any teenager would see straight away that the phones haven't even been used, so there has to be another explanation for them."

"Such as?" It was DC Moore.

"I don't know yet," Smith said. "But those phones are important to him. They're significant somehow."

"Do you think the husband is still in danger?" DC King said.

"He is," Smith said without hesitation. "Until this maniac is caught, Wendy London's husband is at risk. Hold on…"

"You've got that look on your face again," Bridge said. "That *lightbulb moment* look."

"He killed Keith Peters' sister very soon after he realised that Keith wasn't dead," Smith said. "Why was Wendy's husband spared?"

"Luck was on Neil London's side," DI Smyth said. "If the caretaker hadn't come to work early, Wendy would be dead. She was lucid enough to alert the paramedics of the danger to her husband and the police were called. Uniforms were sent out to their house within the hour."

"He messed up," Smith said. "This is going to piss him off."

"What difference does it make?" DC Moore said.

"It makes a hell of a lot of difference. This is his first mistake, and past experience has taught me that often, one mistake leads to many more."

"Like a domino effect?" DC King said.

Smith nodded. "Something like that.

The door opened and Whitton came inside the small conference room. She wasn't alone.

"Look who I found, lingering by the front desk."

It was Porter Klaus. Smith thought the German hypnotist looked somewhat troubled and then he remembered what DI Smyth had told him about some problems he was experiencing.

"Good to see you again," Smith said.

"You're not here to hypnotise us, are you?" DC Moore said.

"Only if you want to be hypnotised," Porter said.

"Porter was up half the night," DI Smyth said. "I asked him to compile a profile of sorts on The Preacher."

"It can't hurt," Bridge said.

"This is by no means conclusive," Porter said. "And I could be way off the mark, but from what I've learnt about this case, I can say with ninety percent certainty that the man you're seeking is suffering from some kind of God complex. He has delusions of grandeur, and he truly believes that what he's doing is for the greater good. You'll have already gathered that he is of above average intelligence, and he is technologically adept. I would hazard a guess to say that something happened recently to trigger a change in him – some life-altering event, perhaps."

"Where do we start looking for him?" Bridge asked.

"I'm afraid I can't give you an answer to that. But I would suggest you begin by looking at suicides – recent ones in particular."

"Suicide is important to him, isn't it?" Smith said.

"I wouldn't use the term important," Porter said. "But it is definitely a significant factor in his life. It's possible that somebody close to him has committed suicide. I could be wrong."

"I don't think you are," Smith said. "Self-termination is a prominent feature in the instructions he gives to his victims. He wants them to kill themselves to punish the people closest to them."

"Continuing on with the suicide aspect," Porter said. "If we're to consider a suicide as the trigger to his recent actions, it's likely to be the suicide of a loved one, and it's also likely that the suicide was the result of something unjust. That is a key element in this."

"Someone close to him killed themselves," Smith said. "And The Preacher is finding people to blame for it?"

"Something like that. He needs to reset the balance somehow. In his mind, justice wasn't served, and he believes he has been appointed to rectify that."

"The methods he's coming up with are not important, are they?"

"I'm not sure I understand what you mean," Porter said.

"He's clearly delusional. His logic is more twisted than a box of corkscrews, and what he's making people do is absolute madness. What I mean is the methods he comes up with are not important to *us*. We shouldn't waste time analysing them because they're not going to help us find him."

"Possibly. What is of tantamount importance is the catalyst to his actions. What prompted him to set off on this journey?"

"We get closer to that," Smith said. "We get closer to the man himself."

"We need to take a look at recent suicides," DI Smyth said.

Smith disagreed. "Not necessarily recent. What he's managed to carry out does not happen on the spur of the moment. He's spent a lot of time on this. It's clear that the suicides had to happen in quick succession and to manage that takes a lot of forward planning."

"He will have done a lot of research before choosing his victims," DC King said. "You don't just key *deaths where the person responsible is cleared of culpability* into the task bar and hope to get a ready-made list. He will have spent months picking out his victims."

"Do we know how many suicides occur each year?" DC King said.

DC Moore took out his phone and brought it to life.

"Just over five thousand," he said a short while later. "Approximately ten per hundred thousand people."

"Five thousand?" Bridge said. "Seriously?"

"We can probably narrow it down," Smith said. "It's clear from the local knowledge he's displayed so far that he's from York."

"Just because he's a local," DC Moore said. "Doesn't mean the suicide we're looking for happened in the city."

"No," Smith said. "It doesn't, but it's as good a place as any to start. And then we look for possible connections between suicides and York. We look at relatives and friends of local people who have ended their lives."

"It sounds like a lot of work," DC Moore said.

"What's your point, Harry?"

"Nothing."

"We'll get onto it after the briefing," DI Smyth said. "I'll ask Baldwin and PC Griffin to give us a hand."

"Is there anything else you can tell us about this psychopath?" Smith asked Porter Klaus.

"I can tell you without a shadow of a doubt that he isn't a psychopath," the giant German said.

"Sociopath then," Bridge said. "It's quite clear that he suffers from a lack of empathy."

"Wrong again," Porter said. "This man does feel empathy. It's that empathy that drives him."

"With respect, Doc," DC Moore said. "He's making people top themselves for his own twisted pleasure."

"That's not why he's doing this at all. In his mind, everything he's done thus far can be justified. He truly believes that what he's doing is right."

"He's delusional," Whitton said.

"He is definitely delusional," Porter agreed.

"Do you think he might have spent some time in a nuthouse at one stage?" DC Moore said.

"Your terminology leaves a lot to be desired. Terms like *top themselves* and *nuthouse* wouldn't be my choices, but the answer to your question is, no. I don't believe he's ever sought treatment because he genuinely does not believe himself to be ill."

    Smith's phone started to ring. He let it go to voicemail. Soon afterwards the sound of Whitton's ringtone could be heard. Smith knew instantly that something was wrong.

CHAPTER THIRTY NINE

The person who had phoned Smith and Whitton was the deputy head of the school that Laura and Fran attended. Laura had told her teacher that a strange man had waved at her from behind the fence. It had happened during the morning break. Laura and Fran were in the playground and the man walked past and waved. When the teacher was alerted, he went to take a look, but the man had gone.

Whitton didn't think it was anything to be concerned about. She told Smith as much.

"There's something I haven't told you," he said.

He took out his phone and showed her the photographs. He also told her about the veiled threat about the viaduct.

"Why am I only finding out about this now?" she said.

"I didn't want to worry you," Smith said. "I reckoned it was just some nutjob who gets a kick out of shit like this."

"Someone took a photograph of the girls, Jason. And now a strange man is waving at our daughter, and you didn't want to worry me. He's been to our house. The photo of the dogs mean he knows where we live."

"What are we supposed to do about it?" Smith said. "We have no idea who this bloke is."

Whitton rubbed her eyes.

She looked at Smith. "That's why you wanted me to take the girls to school this morning. That's why you offered to pick them up. Who is this person?"

"I have no idea," Smith said. "When I tried to call him back the number no longer existed."

"What if it's The Preacher?"

"Why would you think that?" Smith asked, even though it was the first thing he'd considered.

"We need to go and fetch the girls."

"And take them where?" Smith said. "Think about it – they're much safer at school. The grounds are locked, and nobody can get in. If it is The Preacher, and I very much doubt it is, he's hardly likely to try anything at a school."

"I want to know about any future messages," Whitton said.

"OK," Smith said.

"And what did he mean when he said he knows what happened on the viaduct?"

"I don't know, Erica," Smith said. "The only people who know about that are Lucy, Darren and the people on the team. None of them would ever tell anybody else."

"If what happened that night ever comes out, our lives will be destroyed."

"Do you think I don't know that?" Smith said. "I was the one who…"

"I'm sorry. What now?"

"We get on with what they pay us for," Smith said. "We've got plenty of people sifting through the suicides - I want to speak to the Maths teacher, but I need to pay a visit to a kid called Dean before I do that."

They were in his car, heading west five minutes later. Smith had explained to Whitton what Brian Illman had told him about the Halloween party. The creature of the night had mentioned something about his friend Dean keeping an eye on the Head of Maths during the party.

"They smuggled vodka into the party?" Whitton said.

"They're seventeen," Smith said. "We were that age once."

"I didn't drink when I was seventeen."

"You're not like everyone else," Smith said. "Anyway, according to Brian it was Dean who was keeping an eye on Mr Grigg. I want to know where he was just before Jane killed herself."

"Wasn't he sorting out some kind of fight in the toilets?"
"That's what he claimed," Smith said. "But he could have been lying."
"Why are you so interested in an old Maths teacher?"
"I don't know. He needs to be ruled out."

Dean Underwood lived in an attractive detached house in Woodthorpe. The property was situated a stones' throw away from the small stretch of water that had the strange name of Hogg's Pond, and Smith sensed that this was an affluent neighbourhood. The stands that houses stood on were well above average size and most of them had large gardens.

"Expensive places," Whitton said.
"They're houses," Smith said. "Brian told me that Dean lives at number 4."
They got out of the car - Smith opened the gate and they walked up the path to the front door. As they got closer Smith could hear music playing inside the house. It was a familiar song, but something didn't sound right about it. He realised what it was – someone was playing along to the track on an electric guitar, and they weren't doing a very good job of it.
"They're murdering that song," Smith said.
He remembered what it was. It was an old one by Deep Purple – *Sweet Child in Time*.
"Are we allowed to arrest someone for being tone deaf?"
Whitton laughed. "I don't think that's actually against the law yet."

The music stopped and Smith took the opportunity to ring the doorbell. It was a loud one and he could hear its chimes from outside. Soon afterwards the door opened and a teenager in a plain black T-Shirt looked them up and down.
"Dean Underwood?" Smith said.
"That's right. Who are you?"
Smith took out his ID and explained why they were there, and he was surprised when Dean invited them in without any questions.

They sat in what he described as the sitting room and Smith wondered why anyone would want two living rooms.

"Was that you playing along to the Deep Purple track?" he asked.

"It was my brother Dan," Dean said. "He's just started playing and he's got terrible taste in music."

"The song is a classic," Smith said. "So, I'll give him a break for ruining it. Why isn't your brother at school?"

"He goes to the same sixth-form as me. He's my twin brother."

And Smith knew that the college was closed until tomorrow.

"Brian Illman told me about the vodka you smuggled in to the Halloween party," he said.

"I don't know what you're talking about," Dean said.

"I'm not interested in the booze. I'd be concerned if alcohol wasn't smuggled into a college party. Brian also mentioned something about you being in charge of keeping an eye on the Maths teacher."

"Old Grigg," Dean said. "He's a relic from the Victorian age."

"What do you mean by that?" Whitton said.

"He'd still beat the kids for misbehaving if he was allowed."

"A bit of a stickler for the rules, is he?" Smith said.

"A bit?" Dean said.

"And that's why you had to make sure he didn't catch you with the vodka?"

"He would have gone ballistic."

"Can you remember where Mr Grigg was just before Jane Banks did what she did?"

"He wasn't in the hall," Dean said.

"He claimed that he had to deal with some problems in the Gents toilets," Smith said.

"That's bullshit," Dean said and looked at Whitton. "Sorry."

"It's fine," she said. "I've heard worse. Why did you say that?"

"The toilets are through a door at the back of the school hall. I would have seen him go that way."

"Where exactly did he go?" Smith asked.

"The last time I saw him he was heading for the door that leads out to where the caretaker's workshop is."

"Are you sure?" Smith said.

"I was watching him all night."

"And that was definitely the last time you saw him?" Whitton said.

"I remember we all downed some vodka straight away afterwards. That was where he went."

    Smith thanked Dean for his time and told him there were no more questions. He'd got enough answers from the teenage boy. The caretaker's workshop was directly next door to the shed that housed the distribution board.

CHAPTER FORTY

"We managed to access Wendy London's phone without too much problem," DI Smyth told Smith.
He and Whitton were on their way to Tony Grigg's place in Heworth.
"Did you find any messages?" Smith asked.
"The entire thread. And it makes for stomach churning listening. The messages started over a month ago. It appears that Wendy London wasn't an easy woman to manipulate."
"He misjudged her there, didn't he?" Smith said. "All of the previous victims were chosen for their pliability. You mentioned something earlier about The Preacher threatening to torture Wendy's husband."
"It's all in the message thread. The Preacher told Wendy that if she didn't go through with the suicide, Neil would suffer. He would be tied up and tortured in ways that would make the most seasoned torturer flinch. He was aware of Neil's schedule, and he knew things that didn't seem possible."
"He's done his homework," Smith said. "I don't suppose there's any way we can trace the caller from the messages."
"What do you think? He wouldn't be that stupid. Every message was sent from a different number. He's running the show and some of the messages suggest he knew exactly where Wendy and Neil were at all times."
"How is that possible?"
"Your guess is as good as mine. Have you spoken to the Maths teacher yet?"
"We're on our way there now," Smith said. "One of the kids who was at the party claims that Mr Grigg was nowhere near the toilets at the time of Jane Banks' suicide. He lied to us about it."
"Is the kid's version reliable?"
"I got the impression he was telling the truth," Smith said. "He said the last time he saw Mr Grigg was by the door that leads out to the caretaker's

workshop. The distribution board is located in a shed right next door. The timing fits – the Maths teacher was by the distribution board at the same time the power to the DJ's decks was cut off."

"A Maths teacher?" DI Smyth said. "I think I've seen everything now."

"Stranger things have happened," Smith said.

"Do you believe backup is necessary?"

"No," Smith said. "If the Maths teacher is The Preacher, and I reckon it's very doubtful that he is, he's not your average killer. He only kills according to his delusional logic. Neither me nor Whitton are on his radar, so I don't believe we're in any danger."

Smith didn't know then how very wrong he was. He and Whitton were definitely on that radar. They were two dots right in the centre and those dots were getting bigger every day.

The house that Tony Grigg lived in wasn't what Smith expected at all. He assumed a Maths teacher would be meticulous in the upkeep of a property, but number 32 Leyland Road looked like nobody lived there. The exterior brickwork was crumbling away in places, and the paint on the window frames and door was peeling off. The front garden was overgrown and riddled with dead weeds.

"Are you sure this is the address?" Whitton said.

"According to the college records," Smith said. "This is where the Maths teacher lives."

"He could have given a false address."

"He's worked at the sixth-form for two decades," Smith said. "I doubt they'd have the wrong address in their files. There's only one way to find out. The college is closed until tomorrow, so he won't be at work."

After ringing the bell and getting no response, Smith opened the letterbox and peered inside the house.

He took a step back. "God, it stinks in there."

"I think we've got the wrong place," Whitton said. "It doesn't look like anybody has lived here in months."

Smith looked up and down the street. The house next door was in much better shape, and the flickering of a television set in the living room told him that someone was home.

"Let's ask the neighbours if anyone lives here," he said.

He tried the door of number 32 but it was locked.

"Nobody lives here," Whitton insisted. "This place has been abandoned."

The door to number 30 was opened by an elderly couple. Smith thought they looked to be in their seventies and the man was at least a foot taller than the woman.

"We're not interested," he said.

"Whatever it is you're selling," his wife added. "We don't want it."

"We're not selling anything," Whitton said. "DS Whitton and this is DS Smith. We were told that Tony Grigg lives next door."

"Do you have any identification?" the man asked. "You don't look like coppers, especially him."

He nodded to Smith. He was dressed in a pair of black jeans and a checked shirt that wasn't tucked in.

They produced their IDs and the couple seemed satisfied enough. The man introduced himself as Bob and his wife was Glenda.

"Why are you interested in Grigg?" he said. "I would have thought the squalor he lives in would be a council matter."

"The place should be condemned," Glenda said. "It's bringing down the neighbourhood."

"The house hasn't always looked like that," Bob said. "He used to be so proud of keeping it well maintained, but he's really let the place go in the past month or so."

"Perhaps he's had something else on his mind," Smith said. "Have you noticed a change in him recently?"

"A what?"

"Has he been acting out of character at all?"

"What do I look like," Bob said. "A bloody psychologist?"

"Do you know if Mr Grigg is at home?" Whitton said.

"How should we know?" Bob said.

"When was the last time you saw him?" Smith said.

"Sunday," Glenda said. "He stuck his wheelie bin out for Monday's collection. That's not allowed either."

"What time was this?"

"Early afternoon," Glenda said. "You're only supposed to put the bins out on Monday morning. Some people think they're exempt to the rules."

"Have you seen him since then?" Whitton said.

"Can't say we have," Bob said.

Smith realised they were wasting their time. He thanked them and went back next door. He lost his footing on a loose paving stone as he walked and if Whitton wasn't there to hold onto, he would have taken a tumble.

"What's wrong with you?" she said.

"I have no idea," Smith said. "I'm usually quite steady on my feet. I think I might have a stone in my shoe."

He made it next door without further incident and stopped outside Tony Grigg's house.

"Something doesn't feel right," he said.

"If I had a quid for every time you've said that," Whitton said. "I wouldn't be standing outside a house that smells like a rubbish dump right now."

Smith didn't give an opinion on this. Instead, he tried the door again and opened the letterbox. The stench that met him really was repulsive. He had a look through the windows into the living room, but the glass hadn't been cleaned for quite some time and it was impossible to see anything clearly.

"Something is definitely not right," he said.

"He's probably out," Whitton said. "Perhaps he went shopping. Maybe he's out stocking up on cleaning products."

"I think he's inside," Smith said. "I'm going to see if I can break in."

"What for? You're going to break the law so you can speak to a suspect you suspect isn't really a suspect at all."

"I didn't understand a word of that," Smith said. "This window has almost no putty around it."

He gave the pane a tentative shove and the glass gave way. Another harder push and the window came loose and fell forwards into the house.

"You shouldn't have done that," Whitton said.

"It was an accident," Smith said. "I didn't know it would give so easily. I'm going in."

He climbed through the frame and stood up inside the living room. The first thing that struck him was the filth. It was everywhere. The carpet looked like it had never seen a vacuum cleaner in its life. Dust covered every possible surface, and Smith didn't want to think about the origin of the stains on the walls. The reek he'd got a taste of through the letterbox was much worse inside the house. It was a sour, pungent funk that caught in the nose and throat. Smith lifted up the bottom of his shirt and covered his nose and mouth.

He left the living room and opened the door to the next room. Inside was a table with two chairs and nothing else. As dining rooms went, this one was as minimalistic as it was possible to get. The kitchen was at the end of the hallway and there was another door before you got to it. Later Smith would curse himself for opening it. He would regret letting his curiosity control his actions. He would also later describe the reek that exploded from the small home office as something akin to a biological weapon. The material of the shirt did very little to mask the lethal gases that assaulted his senses. The heat that accompanied the stench caused Smith's eyes to water and he would subsequently explain that this blurred vison was welcome. He wasn't fully able to comprehend what had been done to the man on the floor in the home office.

CHAPTER FORTY ONE

"Tony Grigg's injuries were extensive," DI Smyth began the afternoon briefing.

Smith hadn't stuck around inside number 32 Leyland Road. He'd left the house the same way he came in and told Whitton to call it in. He wasn't capable of making the call himself. After filling his lungs with clean air he'd lit a cigarette and even that didn't get rid of the reek that had settled inside his nose and mouth.

"Mr Grigg suffered numerous stab wounds," DI Smyth said. "To his chest, stomach and neck, and initial reports suggest that he was also disembowelled."

"According to Webber," Smith said. "That was the cause of the ungodly stench. The heating inside the room had been turned up to the maximum, and that will have expedited the decaying process further. It's going to take a long time to get that reek out of my system."

"The injuries Mr Grigg sustained were definitely not self-inflicted," DI Smyth carried on. "And there was no weapon found at the scene."

"The Head of Maths was murdered," Smith said.

"According to the next-door-neighbours," Whitton said. "The last time they saw Mr Grigg was early Sunday afternoon. He put his wheelie bin out, and they haven't seen him since."

"He was killed soon after that," Smith said. "The decomposition on display in that home office was something else. The neighbours told us something that might be worth looking at. The house was in a real state – it had been seriously neglected, but it hasn't always looked like that."

"It's possible that something was troubling Mr Grigg," Whitton said.

"Something recent," Smith said.

"We spoke to the bloke," Bridge said. "After the Halloween party, and I did think it was odd that he insisted we speak to him away from his house."

"What impression did you get of him?" Smith said.

"There was definitely something not right with him," DC Moore said. "I just put it down to the shock of the events of the Halloween party."

"Do you think he'd been threatened by The Preacher too?" DC King said.

"I don't know," Smith said. "As far as we're aware, the only part the Maths teacher played was in turning off the power to the music at the party. Why was he killed?"

"Did Forensics find a phone at the house?" Bridge said.

"Not as far as I'm aware," Smith said. "If Webber does find a phone, we'll soon find out."

"A door-to-door is underway," DI Smyth said. "So hopefully that will give us something."

"Are we definitely treating this as part of The Preacher investigation?" DC King asked.

"It's too early to determine whether Mr Grigg's murder is connected to that," DI Smyth said.

"It's connected," Smith decided. "The Maths teacher was at the Halloween party where Jane Banks committed suicide. It's…"

"Too much of a coincidence," Bridge finished the sentence.

Smith grinned and nodded.

"Am I that predictable?"

"You need to think of some new catchphrases."

"You're making me feel old," Smith said. "Although I'm sure those noxious gases I inhaled have added a decade to my life."

"Moving on," DI Smyth said. "After a morning of dredging through suicides connected to the city this year, we've come up empty handed. We've still got a lot more to look at, but nothing so far has sounded any warning bells. Porter has made another observation after sifting through the case files on The Preacher."

"Is a civilian actually allowed access to our files?" DC Moore said.

"Shut up, Harry," Smith said. "Who cares?"

"It's an observation that is actually rather obvious," DI Smyth said. "In retrospect we ought to have picked up on it too. The Preacher needs his work recognised. All of his victims were instructed to acknowledge him before they killed themselves."

"What does that tell us?" Bridge said.

"He's not only delusional," Smith said. "He's also an egotist."

"A megalomaniac even," DC King said.

"Porter believes that this is par for the course in patients suffering from a God complex. And he also thinks that these traits are usually difficult to keep hidden. The person we're looking for will have an inflated sense of their own self-importance. It will be someone who believes themself to be far superior to others, and that will be hard to keep under wraps."

"So, we're looking for a big-headed psycho," DC Moore said. "I don't mean to put a downer on things, but most of the nutjobs I've come across fit that profile."

Smith's phone beeped and when he looked at the photograph he'd been sent, he could feel the bile rising in his throat. It was tinged with the stink from earlier and he had to use every inch of self-control to prevent himself from losing the breakfast he'd eaten that morning. Whitton noticed his discomfort.

"Can I have a quick word outside?" she said.

"I need a drink of water anyway," Smith said.

"Is there something I need to know?" DI Smyth said.

"No, boss," Smith said. "My throat is as dry as hell and I need to fix that."

"What is it?" Whitton said outside in the corridor.

Smith showed her. The photograph was of a very familiar building. It was the house where Lucy, Darren and Andrew lived – the house next door to Smith's.

"We need to tell someone about this," Whitton said.

"What would be the point?" Smith argued. "The sender is anonymous. The number the photo was sent from no longer exists. I don't want anyone else involved."

"We need help, Jason."

"Are you not listening to me? You can't get help from people who can't help you."

"This is The Preacher, isn't it?"

"I think it is," Smith admitted. "But I can't figure out what he wants. The photographs and the thing about the viaduct are nothing like the messages he sent to the other victims. I don't know how to interpret it, putting The Preacher in the picture. This isn't his usual MO."

"Killers change their MOs all the time," Whitton said. "You of all people ought to know that. We really need to share this with the rest of the team."

"No," Smith said. "Until we have confirmation that this is actually the handiwork of The Preacher, we keep it to ourselves. We'd better get back in."

Another message notification prevented them from going back to the small conference room. Smith opened it and showed it to Whitton.

"We need to share this with the team," she said.

It was a photograph of her parents' house.

"He knows far too much about us," she said.

"We still don't know that it is The Preacher," Smith said.

A message arrived from the same number soon afterwards. This one contained text. Smith read it out.

"I see you've found the maths teacher. Did it disgust you? I hope so, because what I did to him does not compare to what I will do to everybody you love if you don't do what I tell you."

If they needed confirmation, this was it – Smith had been targeted by The Preacher.

CHAPTER FORTY TWO

Smith persuaded Whitton to give him some time before they got the rest of the team involved in their predicament. He needed to process it in his own way to see if he could come up with a solution. In the meantime, they tried to distract themselves by getting stuck into the records of suicides since the beginning of the year. Smith wasn't entirely convinced that the answers they sought would be there, but they didn't have much else to look at.

"There must be some way to narrow down the search," DC King said.
"What have you been focusing on so far?" Smith said.
"Suicides in the past twelve months with a connection to the city. It's taking time because it's possible that the person who killed themselves has family in York even if they ended their life elsewhere."
"They have computer programs to do this kind of grunt work in America," DC Moore said. "You feed the info into the system, and it does all this for you."
"You watch too many dodgy detective films, Harry," Bridge said. "No computer program will ever replace the human mind."
"It's coming though," DC Moore said. "AI is going to take over the world before we know it."
"Stop whinging," Smith said. "And keep looking."

Two hours later they were no further ahead. Whitton thought she'd got lucky with the suicide of a man in Leeds. He was a York local and he was studying at the university in Leeds. He'd taken his own life by knocking back a cocktail of drugs and alcohol, and all of his family still lived in York. What had caught Whitton's attention was the fact that the family were devoutly religious. According to an article containing an interview with the father of the man, he didn't believe that his son could have committed suicide. It went against everything he'd been brought up to believe in, and the father was convinced his son had been murdered. The police in Leeds never bothered to follow up this claim, and the father was quoted as saying that the Lord would punish the people responsible, regardless. There would be retribution, and that retribution would come quickly.

After making a number of phone calls, Whitton realised that she was on the wrong track. The entire family of the dead man had been out of the country for three weeks. They were at a religious retreat in France, and they weren't in the city when the recent suicides had been carried out. As alibis went, theirs was as solid as they came.

Smith hadn't been able to focus. He'd left the small conference room no fewer than five times since they started. He'd had four cups of coffee, and he'd smoked a dozen cigarettes in that time. His mind was elsewhere. The photographs and the message he'd received were all he could think about. He was standing in front of the coffee machine in the canteen, debating whether to have a fifth coffee when DI Smyth came in.

"Something's bothering you."

Smith turned around. "Is it that obvious?"

"You're an open book, Smith. Talk to me."

Smith took out his phone and found the photographs. He handed the phone to DI Smyth.

"When were these sent?" the DI asked.

"I got the photos of the dogs and the girls' school yesterday," Smith said. "And the ones of Lucy's house and Whitton's parents' place came earlier today. The text message came just afterwards."

"What do you think it means?"

"There's only one explanation," Smith said. "I'm being targeted by The Preacher, but I have no idea why."

DI Smyth studied the photographs and the message again.

"OK," He said. "This is good."

"I'm glad you think so," Smith said. "Did you not read what he threated to do to everybody I care about?"

"That's not what I'm talking about. He's taking a huge risk in threatening a police detective. This could be how we're going to catch him."

"I don't mean to burst your bubble of optimism, boss," Smith said. "But how do you plan to do that? The photos were sent from different numbers, and those phone numbers no longer exist. He's got the upper hand here – he knows a hell of a lot more about me than I know about him. And I refuse to use my family as pawns in a deadly game of chess. The bastard has threatened my dogs, for fuck's sake."

"How did he know you'd found Tony Grigg?" DI Smyth said.

"What?"

"He mentioned the Maths teacher. How did he know you were the one to find him?"

"Shit," Smith said. "I'm losing my touch. I should have smelled a rat straight away. He's watching me, isn't he?"

"I don't think that's even possible. How was he to know you and Whitton would pay Mr Grigg a visit? It wasn't a logical conclusion to come to. You were the one who decided that the Maths teacher was worth speaking to, nobody else."

"Do you think he's tracking my movements in some way?"

"It's a farfetched idea," DI Smyth said. "But it needs to be considered."

"We had something similar with the *Hitchhiker* investigation, didn't we?" Smith said. "He was using some kind of tracking device to keep an eye on his victims."

"If that's the case," DI Smyth said. "It means that you've crossed paths with him at some time during the course of the investigation."

Smith turned back to face the coffee machine. He decided not to drink any more coffee. He would be awake for days if he did.
He looked at DI Smyth again. "He could have put a tracker in my car."
"How would he even know what car you drive?" DI Smyth said.
"He knows everything about me, boss. He knows about the viaduct – he knows where I live, and he knows where everyone in my family lives. The Sierra isn't parked in a garage, so it would be relatively easy to sneak up in the dead of night and attach a tracking device."
"If that's the case," DI Smyth said. "We'll find it."

Smith suddenly thought of something. "He hasn't issued any demands. The photos and the message left no doubt about his intentions, but he hasn't explained what he wants from me yet."
"This is part of his plan of execution," DI Smyth said. "He doesn't threaten and strike with his demands straight away. He leaves his victims to stew for a while. The threats he issues are designed to consume his targets. He gives them time to process the implications, and he lets nature take its course. Take the Maths teacher for example. Tony Grigg fell apart. We still don't know what he was threatened with, but it resulted in him letting himself go. He neglected his house, and I think he was consumed by fear. The Preacher is patient – he observes his victims carefully and only moves in for the kill when he knows the time is right. We can use that to our advantage."
"How do you figure that out?"
"It gives us time to come up with a suitable counterattack move."

"I'm still trying to work out his motive," Smith said. "Adding me to the mix, I mean. If we follow his logic, he's got me on his list because of something the person closest to me has done."
"I assume that would be Whitton," DI Smyth said,
"That's right. All of the other victims have been close to someone who was responsible for somebody dying. That bit doesn't fit with Whitton. If it was

the other way round and he was targeting her because of people I've helped on their way to the other side, it's plausible, but Whitton hasn't done that."

"I suppose we'll cross that bridge when we come to it," DI Smyth said. "We'll only know what he wants from you when he contacts you again. In the meantime, I suggest we get someone to take a look at your car."

"I wouldn't even know what to look for," Smith said. "I wouldn't know what's supposed to be attached to a car and what isn't."

"Then we'll find someone who does."

Smith smiled. "I know just the person."

CHAPTER FORTY THREE

The inspection of Smith's Ford Sierra yielded nothing. He'd called Gary Lewis on the off chance that he had a spare hour or two, and Darren's brother had got there in ten minutes. Smith reckoned that if there was anyone who knew his car better than anyone else it was Gary. He'd brought the car back to life earlier in the year, and he knew the vehicle inside out.

"Don't we have access to tracker scanners?" It was DC Moore.
The inspection of Smith's car had attracted an audience, and everyone on the team was outside in the car park.
"You really need to stop watching CSI," Bridge said. "This is York, and this is real life. We're not the FBI."
"Are you sure he knows what he's looking for?" DC Moore nodded to Gary Lewis.
The mechanic was giving the undercarriage of the car a quick once over again.
"He knows what he's doing," Smith said. "Gary is familiar with that car. What he couldn't fix, he replaced with new parts."
"I still think it's a bit of a long shot," Bridge said. "It's possible he hasn't even been tracking your movements."
"He knows too much," Smith said. "He knew it was me who found the Maths teacher and there's only one explanation for that. It was hardly broadcast."

A familiar car drove into the car park. The black Land Rover parked horizontally across three parking bays, and a man and a woman got out.
"What do they want now?" Smith said.
Lenny and Sheila Jenkins made their way to the small crowd of people standing by Smith's car. They were dressed in identical pink tracksuits today, and Smith wondered if they had a different one for every day of the week.

"I thought you said their evidence had disappeared," Smith said to DI Smyth.

"It has," the DI confirmed. "And keep your voice down. If anyone finds out about that CCTV footage, there could be trouble."

"What's going on?" Lenny asked.

"Nothing for you to be concerned about," DI Smyth told him.

"Are you looking for a bomb?" Sheila said.

"Of course not."

"Is there something we can help you with?" Smith said.

"If there's a bomb in there," Lenny said. "We have a right to know about it."

"We're not quite sure yet," Smith said. "But it might be an idea to stand back, just in case."

"You think you're clever, don't you?" Lenny said.

"I'm just thinking about your safety," Smith said.

"I'm talking about our cameras. We know what you did."

"Glad to hear it," Smith said. "What did I do?"

"You know very well," Sheila said.

"We're a bit busy here." Whitton joined in. "Is there something we can assist you with?"

"We've been forced to drop the charges against Frankie Lewis," Lenny said. "And we have no choice but to drop the complaint against you too, but you haven't won – not by a long shot. Lady luck will run out for you one day."

"Luck never gives," Sheila added. "It only lends. You think about that."

Smith wondered if she'd got that from a fortune cookie, but he couldn't be bothered to ask her about it.

"I'll give it some serious consideration," he said. "If there's nothing else, I'm sure you have better things to do. I imagine there's some paperwork you need to complete to get the ball rolling with dropping those charges."

He watched them as they marched towards the entrance of the station.

"You're terrible," Whitton said.

"They deserved it," Smith said. "There should be laws about allowing people like them into society – strict curfews and other preventative measures."

"I think we can call it a day," DI Smyth said.

It was starting to get dark, and even though they were still only halfway through the list of recent suicides, it had been a frustrating day and everyone on the team needed a break.

"Do you feel like a meal at the Hog's Head tonight?" Smith asked Whitton.

"Where did that come from?" she said. "I thought you were boycotting the place until they reverted back to the old steak and ale pie recipes."

"They do have other options on the menu."

"And in the fifteen-odd years you've been going there," Whitton said. "I've never seen you order anything else. You've always been a creature of habit."

"A bloke can change."

"You have an ulterior motive, don't you?"

"What makes you say that?"

"I know you, Jason," Whitton said. "You're planning something – it's written all over your face. You're an open book."

"Funny," Smith said. "The boss said something similar. And you're right – I might have an ulterior motive for going to the Hog's Head."

"Could you say that again," Whitton said. "I don't think I heard properly."

"I may have an ulterior motive."

"Not that part," Whitton said. "The bit about me being right."

"You were right, OK?" Smith said. "Happy now? The pub has rooms to rent upstairs. I think you and the girls should stay there for a bit."

"Are you serious?"

"I am. The Preacher knows where we live – he knows where Lucy, Darren and Andrew live, but he won't know about the rooms at the Hogs Head."

"I think it's a ridiculous idea," Whitton said. "Lucy has college. Laura and Fran have school. And what about the dogs?"

"Fuck."

"What now?"

"I was supposed to pick Laura and Fran up from school," Smith said.

"Relax," Whitton said. "My dad went to fetch them. They're at my parents' house."

"It's not safe there. I think your mum and dad should stay at the Hogs Head for a bit too. I'll look after the dogs. This maniac doesn't want to hurt me – he wants to hurt the people I love. I'll be fine at home. Just promise me that you'll think about it."

"I'll think about it," Whitton humoured him.

Smith took out his cigarettes and dropped them on the ground in the process. As he was bending down to pick them up he felt something rub against his right big toe, and he remembered the stone from earlier. He removed the shoe and rummaged around, looking for the offensive stone.

It wasn't like any stone he'd ever seen before. This stone was flat shaped, and it was roughly the size of a pound coin. It was metallic and when Smith looked more closely, he saw that there was writing on it. He held it up for Whitton to see.

"What is that?" she said.

"I have no idea," Smith said. "It somehow managed to get inside my shoe."

DC Moore walked past. "You were right then."

"Right about what?" Smith said.

"The tracking device. That looks like quite a fancy one."

Smith looked at the small device. "How the hell did this thing get into my shoe?"

"God knows," DC Moore said. "At least you've figured out how he's been able to monitor your movements."

"Can we get any info from it?"

"We've been here before, Sarge," DC Moore said. "It'll probably be linked up to a mobile phone. The phone picks up the signal, but the tracker can't give us any idea where the phone is. It's a one-way technical conversation, if you like."

"So, it's useless as evidence?"

"Pretty much. I doubt we'll be able to pull any prints from it either, especially if it's been squashed by your stinky foot all day. At least whoever planted it there will no longer be able to track your movements."

"But they'll know that I've found it," Smith said.

"Why does that matter?"

"I don't want them to be aware of it."

He glanced around the car park, and an idea began to form in his head. The black Land Rover was the first thing that caught his attention. It was hard to miss, parked badly across three parking bays. The second thing that Smith noticed was the back right hand window had a gap in it. It was no wider than a man's thumb, but it was wide enough. Smith walked over to the Land Rover and slotted the tracking device through the gap. He watched as it slid down the inside of the window and landed somewhere in the back of the car. Smith walked back with a grin on his face. Mr and Mrs *Mullet* were about to be under surveillance.

CHAPTER FORTY FOUR

Smith and Whitton arrived at the Hog's Head together. After a lengthy discussion she'd agreed to stay at the pub for a few days. Smith was convinced that The Preacher's implied threats were genuine, and he wasn't going to take any chances. They'd agreed that she and the rest of the Smith clan would wait it out at Smith's favourite pub. Lucy was up to date with her college work and she could easily catch up on any work she missed. She and Darren Lewis would share a room with Andrew. Whitton would occupy another room with Laura and Fran. The girls were justifiably excited. This was a great adventure for them. Both of them were blissfully unaware of the reason behind the impromptu holiday. Whitton's parents had point blank refused to leave their house. Smith still recalled Harold Whitton's precise words when he'd brought it up.

Anyone who thinks he can come into my house and hurt me or my wife, is going to wish they hadn't.

Smith couldn't argue with that. There was no changing the mind of a Yorkshireman.

They piled into the pub. Smith had booked two rooms and that's where Whitton and the others went first. Smith waited by the bar while they were busy putting their things in the rooms. Marge was there for once. She'd been taking a back seat since she'd hired a manager, but this evening she was in her usual place behind the bar. She spotted Smith and walked over.

"It's lovely to see you again."

"You too, Marge," Smith said.

"Pint?"

"I'd love one, thanks."

Marge took a glass out and set about pouring the Theakston.

"Is everything OK?"

"Not really," Smith admitted.

"I must admit I was taken by surprise when you booked the rooms. Are your family in danger?"

"Is it that obvious?"

"It is. Is there anything I should know?"

"I can't talk about it," Smith said.

Marge handed him his beer. "I'm sure everything will work out in the end. It usually does with you."

Smith realised something. He hadn't seen Pete the manager since he'd arrived. He'd got an instant bad vibe from the man when he met him, and they'd had a number of disagreements since. He asked Marge about him.

"He doesn't work here anymore," she said.

"You fired him?" Smith said.

"He resigned. We had a bit of drama in here a week or so ago."

"What happened?"

"A group of the regulars got together and launched a campaign to protest about the way things were heading at the pub. I'm all for change, but when that change results in upsetting my loyal customers, it's not worth it. Anyway, I explained these concerns to Pete and I told him he either leaves things how they are, or he leaves, full stop. He opted for the latter."

"Good riddance to him," Smith said. "This is one of the few traditional pubs left in the city and I happen to like it how it is. Please tell me that you're making the steak and ale pies again."

"I am," Marge confirmed. "I should have never agreed to let Pete change the recipe. You know, we had a table of eight in at the weekend. All of them ordered the pies and all eight were returned."

"They were terrible pies," Smith said. "You've made my day."

"Happy to hear it. I'd better get back to the kitchen. Looks like we've got a busy night on our hands."

Smith downed half of his pint in one go. The news about the steak and ale pies was the best news he'd had in weeks. He didn't realise how much he'd missed them, and he was suddenly very hungry. He finished his beer and ordered another. Whitton and the rest of the family still hadn't come down from their rooms, and Smith wondered what they were doing up there. He reckoned the girls were probably inspecting every inch of the room.

He raised the glass to take a drink and froze halfway when the message tone on his phone sounded inside his pocket. He was starting to really hate that sound. He put down the beer and took out his phone. It was a WhatsApp voice message. The pub was busy and the volume inside was loud, so he made his way to the exit and went outside.

He'd drunk the beer quickly and it had gone straight to his head, but he was wide awake after hearing the first few words of the voice message. The synthesiser that had been used only served to lend the message a more sinister tone, and Smith had to stop the message and listen to it from the beginning again so he could concentrate on the words.

That was a nice touch. But it served no purpose other than to delay the inevitable.

Smith had no idea what this meant. It became apparent shortly afterwards. *I did debate whether to invite them to the party – the trailer trash with the cash. I wondered if it would be fun for you to have their suffering on your conscience, but it's debatable whether you would even care. And I think the world is more colourful with people like them in it, wouldn't you agree?*

That was it. Smith wondered what the point of the message was. It was clear that The Preacher had cottoned on to the tracking device in the *Mullets'* Land Rover, but the message made no sense whatsoever. Smith lit a cigarette and gave it some more thought but nothing came to him. It really was a pointless message.

The phone started to ring, and he answered it straight away.

"Are you paying attention?"

It was the same synthesiser disguised voice.

"What do you want?" Smith asked.

"There's an abandoned house in Osbaldwick. The doors and windows are boarded up, but there's a loose board over the window at the back."

The phone went silent, and Smith wondered if the caller had hung up.

He hadn't. "Are you listening?"

"I'm listening," Smith said.

"There's a cellar in the house."

Great, Smith thought. *Just what I need – another fucking cellar.*

"The door to the cellar is unlocked. Inside, you'll find everything you need to do what I tell you to do."

"Fuck you," Smith said.

"Your family isn't home at the moment. But that doesn't concern me."

"You're threatening the wrong bloke, Mr Preacher," Smith said.

"Good. That's good. Your canine friends really need to get more exercise. I can see they like their food. Do you think they'd like me to feed them now? I've prepared a rather special treat for them. They'll experience immense agony as their internal organs fail, one by one. I'll get it on camera. Give me the word and I'll put them out of their misery right now. I'd have to wake them first – they seem to like their sleep."

"Fuck you," Smith said once more, and hung up.

He finished the cigarette and went back inside the pub.

CHAPTER FORTY FIVE

Whitton and the rest of the family were sitting at one of the bigger tables when Smith went back inside the Hog's Head. Smith joined them.

"Where have you been?" Whitton asked.

"I went outside for a smoke," he said.

He decided not to mention the phone call and the voice message just yet. There wasn't much he could do about it. He wasn't concerned about Theakston and Fred. He knew for a fact that The Preacher had been bluffing. He wasn't anywhere near the dogs. Smith had asked Frankie Lewis if he would take care of them for a few days and Darren's dad had been happy to oblige. He was so grateful that the business with the fireworks was ancient history that Smith thought he could have asked him to give the dogs a bath too and he would have done it.

"Guess what?" Smith said to Whitton.

"The steak and ale pie police have sorted out your problem," she said.

"How did you know that?"

"Marge told me," Whitton said. "Are you happy now?"

"You don't know the half of it."

"Why are you so obsessed with those pies?" Lucy said.

"They're not just pies," Smith explained.

Whitton let out a huge sigh. "Here we go."

Smith was unfazed. "They're an integral part of this place. Without those pies, the Hog's Head might just as well be any old pub in the city."

"You're weird," Darren dared.

"And you're renting my house," Smith reminded him. "The revival of those pies has shown that good always prevails."

The steak and ale pie discussion was cut short by the arrival of Marge at the table. She rubbed Andrew's head.

"Look at you. How old is he now?"

"Just over a year," Lucy said.

"He looks just like his mother."

"Thank God," Smith said.

"Are you ready to order?" Marge said.

"I am," Smith told her.

"I think I'll have the pie too," Whitton said.

"Me too," Darren joined in.

The order was taken and only Laura opted not to have the steak and ale pie.

"Five pies then," Marge said. "And a chicken burger. It's going to take a while – there's a bit of a backlog in the kitchen."

"No worries, Marge. The best things in life are worth waiting for. Is there somewhere the girls can go and play? There's a few things we need to discuss and I don't want them to listen in."

"I'll tell you what," Marge said to Laura. "How about you give me a hand in the kitchen. I could do with the help."

Laura didn't have to be asked twice. She was on her feet in an instant.

"Good Lord," Marge said. "Look how much you've grown. I remember you when you were knee high to a grasshopper."

The puzzled expression on Laura's face told her she had no idea what she was talking about.

"Come on then," Marge said and turned to Fran. "You too, love."

"How long do we have to stay here?" Lucy said.

"I don't know," Smith said. "To be honest, I have no idea what to do next. We're no closer to discovering the identity of The Preacher than we were at the start of the investigation, but I'm going to do everything I can to catch him. That's a promise."

"Has he threatened you?" Darren said.

"He has," Smith said. "But I don't have a clue why I'm on his list."

"Has it got something to do with the viaduct?" Lucy said.

"Possibly, but I don't think so. It doesn't fit with his logic, however twisted that logic may be."

"I don't understand," Lucy said.

"So far, all of his victims are people who were close to someone involved in the death of someone else. The Preacher makes them kill themselves because he wants their loved ones to suffer."

"But if that's the case," Lucy said. "It means that it's Mum who was involved in the death of someone."

"Exactly," Smith said. "And I can't figure that part out."

"I don't really think we should be having this discussion now," Whitton said.

"Lucy and Darren need to know what we're up against. Whether we like it or not, this affects all of us. The Preacher has made that quite clear."

Laura and Fran came back, and the food arrived soon afterwards. Smith looked at the steak and ale pie and sighed deeply. A huge grin spread across his face.

"You look like someone whose been reacquainted with an old friend," Whitton said.

"That's exactly what this is. Would you look at that pie. That is heaven on a plate."

"Perhaps you should eat it then," Whitton said. "Instead of talking about it. You'll be taking a photo next."

"Rubbish. I'm going in."

With that he picked up his knife and fork and tucked in.

Fifteen minutes later, all that was left on the plate was a solitary pea. Smith stretched his arms and smiled.

"That was spectacular."

"I cracked the eggs for the top of the pastry," Laura told him.

"I helped," Fran said.

"That's why it tasted so great," Smith said. "I'm going to the Gents."

He finished what he needed to do, and he was halfway to the door when his phone told him his evening was about to take a turn for the worse. He didn't know why he was so sure of this, but he was certain, nevertheless.

The message was short, and it was a text message this time.
Inside the cellar is a table and on the table, you'll find a surgical scalpel. You will pierce your heart with it. One well-aimed stab ought to be enough.

Smith read the words once more and he realised that he still had no idea what this was all about.

CHAPTER FORTY SIX

Smith received thirteen more messages during the night. He wasn't aware of them when they arrived – he'd purposefully left his phone downstairs, and he'd switched it to silent, but when he looked at the screen the following morning, there was little doubt that this nightmare was still very, very real.

All of the messages were voice messages and once again the voice was disguised. All thirteen had been sent from different phone numbers. Smith didn't listen to all of them. The first three were enough. The content was extremely unpleasant, and even though Smith knew he'd have to listen to all of the messages later, now wasn't the time.

The house was too quiet, and Smith didn't like it one little bit. He wondered how Whitton and the rest of the family had slept at the Hog's Head. He imagined that Laura and Fran were having the time of their lives. No school, and a pub to play in all day. Smith envied them. His thoughts turned to the dogs. He hoped that Theakston and Fred were behaving themselves at Frankie Lewis's house.

He was halfway through his second cup of coffee when he decided to face the baker's dozen of voice messages that had arrived during the night. He needed to listen to them at some stage and he thought it might as well be now. He knew that he needed to share these with the team, but this was personal, and he wanted to have some privacy to hear what was said for the first listen.

The initial voice message was simply a prequel to the following ones and Smith deduced that The Preacher was a big fan of drama. He liked a suspenseful build up, and this made Smith's blood boil. He sensed that the man who called himself The Preacher was enjoying this.

The next couple of messages were reminding him about the cellar in Osbaldwick. Smith didn't know the area very well, but he recalled there were very few houses in that part of town. This was probably why The Preacher had chosen it as the location for Smith's *suicide*.

The first threats to his family arrived with the fifth message. He spoke at length of the torture he would inflict on everybody that Smith loved. It made him feel sick to the stomach, but it also spurred him on. This was as personal as it was possible to get and after hearing what The Preacher planned to do to Laura, Smith was ready to kill. He knew he probably would if it became necessary. Somebody was talking about his baby girl as if she were a pawn in a sick game of chess – someone who could be sacrificed at the drop of a hat, and Smith's fists clenched without him realising it.

He went outside and smoked two cigarettes, one after the other. It was still early, and he wasn't due at work for another hour, but he needed to do something. He needed a task to occupy his mind. He went back inside and booted up his laptop.

According to Google Maps, Osbaldwick was situated in the far east of the city, not far from the ring road. To the east was nothing but fields. There was a substation there and not much else. Smith didn't know the location of the house with the cellar, but he half-expected to get the address very soon. He closed down Google Maps and rubbed his eyes. It was pointless speculating about where The Preacher wanted him to go, without an exact location.

The screensaver on the laptop was a photograph that was taken a few years ago. Smith didn't know why he'd chosen this particular photo as his screensaver – it had been taken shortly before the worst week of his life, and it depicted Whitton, Laura and him standing in front of a road sign for York, Western Australia. They were happy in the photo and then everything went wrong. Smith really didn't know why this image was the one he'd chosen to look at every time he booted up his laptop.

The phone next to him started to ring, and Smith looked at it as though it was a snake getting ready to strike. The ringtone told him it wasn't a venomous asp – it was the tone he'd assigned for Whitton. Even though he despised Meatloaf, the sound of *Bat out of Hell* made him smile now.

"Are you OK?" he answered it.

"I slept like the dead," Whitton said. "The beds in those rooms are amazing. The girls went out like a light too. I think Marge worked them a bit too hard in the kitchen yesterday."

"What about Lucy?" Smith said. "Have you checked on her?"

"Relax, Jason," Whitton said. "We're all fine. The DI called and told me to stay put. Was that down to you?"

Smith paused for a second. "It might have been."

He'd phoned DI Smyth as soon as he got back from the Hog's Head and told him in no uncertain terms that Whitton was not to venture out of the pub.

"What about the investigation?" she said. "I'm needed at work."

"Until I have this bastard where I want him," Smith said. "It's not safe for you or the girls. Please, Erica just do this for me."

"And how long are we going to be holed up in a pub?"

"I don't know. But I do know I'm going to do everything I can to catch this fucker. I promise. He's extremely dangerous and he's resourceful too. It's too risky for you to be out on the streets."

"I'm scared."

"Me too," Smith admitted. "But I intend to do something about that. Promise me you won't leave the Hog's Head."

Whitton promised.

"I will find this monster," Smith said.

"I know you will. I love you."

"I love you too. Can you do me a favour?"

"Of course," Whitton said.

"See if you can get the recipe for Marge's steak and ale pies out of her. I've been trying for years, and she's always refused to divulge it. It's top secret, apparently."

"Not going to happen," Whitton said. "Get some work done."

Smith shut down his laptop and made sure the back door was locked. He grabbed his car keys, phone and laptop, and left the house, making sure to lock the front door too.

CHAPTER FORTY SEVEN

Smith was the last one to arrive at the station. Even though he was thirty minutes early the rest of the team had beaten him there. After grabbing a coffee from the canteen Smith had headed straight for DI Smyth's office to find Bridge and the DCs King and Moore inside.

"Is there something I've missed?" he said.
"Missed?" DI Smyth said.
"I wasn't aware about the earlier start," Smith said.
"It appears we're all on the same page today."
"I couldn't sleep," Bridge said. "The DI told me about the threats to Whitton and the rest of your family, and I laid awake all night dreaming up ways to make this bastard pay. I came up with some real beauties, and all of them involved extreme torture."
"I appreciate it, mate," Smith said.

"We've managed to locate Tony Grigg's mobile phone," DI Smyth said. "And it was relatively easy to access the recent history. It appears that the only part the Maths teacher played in all of this was his presence at the Halloween party. He was approached by The Preacher and ordered to cut the power to the music."
"I don't get it," Smith said. "Why was he killed?"
"Because he didn't do what he was told," DC King said.
"And The Preacher slaughtered him for that? I still don't buy it."
"The threats that were issued were not pretty," DI Smyth said. "All he had to do was trip the power to the music decks at a precise time, but he chose not to, and we all know what happened next."
"What else was on the phone?" Smith said.
"A clear indication that Mr Grigg refused to carry out The Preacher's instructions."

"Why didn't he come to us about it? We spoke to him the day after the party, so why didn't he mention it?"

"He was probably terrified," DC Moore said.

"Hold on," Smith said. "If the Maths teacher didn't trip the power, who did?"

"Who indeed?" DI Smyth said. "It appears that The Preacher had someone keeping any eye on the proceedings at the Halloween party. Someone who would make sure the power went out, Maths teacher or no Maths teacher."

"I still can't understand why the music had to stop," DC Moore said. "The girl would have killed herself anyway. The ending was still the same."

"No," Smith said. "No, it wasn't. The Preacher needs his efforts recognised. He feeds off this recognition and it was imperative that everybody who was there could hear him being acknowledged. Jane spoke about him before she did what she did. Her words wouldn't have been heard if the music was still playing. But that's not important. This is another lead. Who turned off the power?"

"I don't think it's worth bothering with, Sarge," DC Moore said. "We've spoken to everyone who was there, and nothing jumped out at us."

"I suppose you're right. I'm running out of ideas."

"We'll persevere with the suicide records," DI Smyth said. "I'm still convinced that a suicide is the catalyst for The Preacher's actions."

"I agree," Smith said. "Someone close to him ended their life and it pushed him over the edge. The answer will be in those records somewhere."

"I have a meeting in half an hour," DI Smyth. "But you can crack on in my absence."

"What kind of meeting?" Smith said.

"That's not your concern. Get to work."

* * *

"I'm bored."

Laura threw her tablet on the bed in front of her.

"Why don't you watch some TV?" Whitton suggested.

"There are only, like three channels," Laura said. "How can a hotel only have three channels on the television?"

"I don't think the people who stay here come for the TV," Whitton said.

"How long are we going to be stuck in here?" Fran said.

"Not long. I thought you were having fun."

"For, like ten minutes," Laura said.

"It can't be helped," Whitton said. "We have to stay here. And since when did every sentence you speak have to include at least one *like*?"

Laura rolled her eyes. "It's how normal people speak, Mum."

Whitton didn't argue. She wondered if Laura was turning into a teenager, five years before her time. She hoped not.

Her phone started to ring, and she was glad of the distraction, even though it was a number she didn't recognise. She opened the door to the room and went outside into the corridor.

"Whitton," she answered the phone.

There was silence on the other end of the line.

"Who is this?"

"You're not at work today." It was the voice of a robot.

"Who is this?" she asked again.

"The girls are absent from school. I do hope they're not sick."

"What do you want?" Whitton said.

"Your husband is a resourceful man, Erica. Even the dogs have been relocated. I was just there at your house, and there's no sign of them."

"We're going to find you, you bastard."

"We'll see. DS Smith took my threats seriously. I didn't know if he would."

The door to Whitton's room opened and Laura and Fran came out.

"We're going to see if Marge needs help in the kitchen," Laura said.
Whitton put a finger to her mouth to tell Laura to be quiet, but she feared that it was already too late.
"Marge?" the synthesised voice said.
"We're going to catch you," Whitton said. "And you're going to regret ever crossing us. You chose the wrong targets this time."
"Good luck."
The drone on the end of the line told Whitton that the call was over.

CHAPTER FORTY EIGHT

Smith was smoking a cigarette in the car park when Whitton phoned. He answered it straight away.

"He called me."

She didn't bother with any greetings.

"Who called you?" Smith said.

"Who do you think? How did he even get my number?"

"It won't have been hard," Smith said. "What did he say?"

"It was all about us changing our routine. He knew I wasn't at work, and he knew the girls didn't go to school."

"Did he give any indication that he might know where you are?"

"I didn't get that impression."

"That's good," Smith said.

"He's been watching the house, Jason. He knew that the dogs aren't home."

"I know he's been watching the house," Smith said. "That's the reason for the drastic measures. It's clear that he has no idea you're at the Hog's Head, and that's all I care about."

"Laura came out of the room while I was on the phone with him," Whitton said. "She said she was going to see if Marge needed help in the kitchen. What if he heard her?"

"What if he did? It's hardly a clue to your whereabouts. He has no idea where you are and that's going to rattle him. I have to go – we're still no further ahead with the suicide records."

"Will you come here after work?"

"I don't think that's a good idea," Smith said. "It's possible he's going to be watching me. This'll soon be over."

"I don't know whether it will be."

"It will be," Smith said. "I promised, didn't I. Give the girls a hug from me."

He finished the cigarette and turned around when he heard the sound of a car engine. The Ford Focus stopped next to his Sierra and two familiar figures got out. One of them was Porter Klaus. The giant German hypnotist was accompanied by Barry Stone. Bridge's IT friend had definitely lost a lot of weight. He was dwarfed by Porter's huge frame.

They walked over to him.

"What brings you here?" Smith asked.

"We're meeting Oliver," Porter said. "How are you?"

"I've been better. What's the meeting with the boss all about?"

"Something this genius thinks he might have figured out," Porter patted Barry Stone on the shoulder.

"I wouldn't call myself a genius," Barry said.

"I wanted to thank you for your help with my little problem," Smith told him.

"I believe you went there dressed like a tramp."

"I didn't think people like them still existed in the world," Barry said. "Outside of America, I mean. They reminded me of something out of a bad horror film."

"They are an acquired taste," Smith said. "Did they make you take your shoes off too?"

Barry observed him as though he'd grown a second nose.

"We'd better go," he said. "We're already a bit late for the meeting."

Smith followed them in. He went back to the small conference room and woke his laptop back up. DC King was sitting at the table next to him.

"Found anything?" Smith asked her.

"Nothing promising," she said. "Harry thought he might have got a hit with a suicide in a prison in Glasgow."

"Glasgow?" Smith repeated.

"It's a town in Scotland, Sarge," DC Moore said.

"I know where Glasgow is, Harry. What has a suicide in Glasgow got to do with The Preacher?"

"The bloke who killed himself has ties with York, Sarge. I did some checking, and he had a brother in the city. And this is the interesting part – you'll never guess how the bloke topped himself?"

"The suspense is killing me," Smith said.

"He used a piece of a broken phone," DC Moore said. "Somehow, he managed to smuggle in a mobile phone, he smashed the casing and used a sharp piece to slice his wrists open. He bled out before help could get to him."

"The broken phones," Smith said. "It's a connection."

"Exactly."

"But Kerry said you *thought* you might have got a hit," Smith said. "Surely this is being looked into."

"I said he *had* a brother in the city, Sarge," DC Moore said. "As in past tense. Damian Lucas is no longer alive. He was killed at the beginning of the year. Car crash."

"Damn it," Smith said. "That really did look promising. I need to speak to the boss about something."

He left the small conference room without elaborating.

 He didn't bother to knock on DI Smyth's door. Three faces turned to look at him when he went inside the office. DI Smyth, Barry Stone and Porter Klaus looked equally puzzled.

"I'm not interrupting anything, am I?" Smith said.

"We were just finishing up," DI Smyth said.

They were all huddled around a laptop.

"What are you looking at?" Smith said.

"A problem that Barry has all but solved," DI Smyth said.

"What's with the cryptic stuff?"

Smith stepped closer and took a look at the screen of the laptop. "What is this?"

"Someone is intent on making my life pure hell," Porter said. "And I have no idea who it is, nor do I understand why they're doing it. Barry has been assisting me."

"I'm getting close," Barry said. "All I need is for them to reply to the email Herr Klaus has sent and I'll be able to reel them in with a bot that can bypass the VPN, via a backdoor, but as of yet they're not playing ball."

Smith caught a few snippets of the email thread. Something in the message from a week ago caused him to read it twice.

"Hmm," he said.

"What is it?" DI Smyth said.

"Nothing," Smith said. "I'll leave you to it. I'm going out to grab a bite for lunch."

CHAPTER FORTY NINE

Smith wasn't in the least bit hungry. Food was the last thing on his mind as he drove west towards the city centre. He turned onto Foss Islands Road and carried on north. The small section of the email he'd read inside DI Smyth's office wasn't much, but it was enough. He'd recognised the style of writing straight away. He knew exactly who Porter Klaus's troll was but what he couldn't understand was the reason behind the harassment.

He parked in the Monk Bar car park and made his way towards the row of office blocks on Monkgate. He opened the door to one of them and walked past the protesting receptionist to an office he knew well. He went inside without knocking and walked up to the woman sitting behind the desk.
"You can't just barge in here."
Dr Fiona Vennell glared at him with wild eyes.
Smith went behind the desk and when he realised what was on the screen of her laptop, he slammed it shut.
"What on earth has come over you?" Dr Vennell said.
"I'm saving your arse," Smith said. "That's what. You reply to any one of those emails, and some sort of bot will invade your computer and tell the person you're bullying exactly who you are. Why, Fiona – why are you doing this."

She didn't reply immediately. And Smith wasn't expecting the words she spoke when she did eventually reply.
"Say that again."
"Why?" Smith said. "Why are…"
"Not that part," Dr Vennell interrupted. "The way you said *Fiona*. That turned me on a bit."
"Stop it now. What the hell is wrong with you? What has Porter ever done to you?"

"That's not even his real name."

"I'm aware of that," Smith said. "The man is a good bloke. He doesn't deserve this."

"You don't know him. You have no idea."

"I've worked alongside him," Smith said. "I know him."

"He's not who you think he is."

"I'm aware of his background, Fiona. He's been nothing but open about it. He made a big mistake, and he paid for it. Why would you want to try and ruin his life."

"I miss you, Jason."

"What?"

"There was a time when you would come to me for advice about a case," Dr Vennell said.

Smith couldn't believe what he was hearing.

"Are you telling me you went about this hate campaign because you're jealous? That's the most ridiculous thing I've ever heard."

"Just be careful of Porter Klaus," Dr Vennell said. "He's a hypnotist and a charlatan and he's not who you think he is."

"This has to stop," Smith said. "Do you realise what could have happened if I hadn't come here today? You would have been unmasked. The man you've been trolling just happens to be in a relationship with a detective inspector – my boss, and that would not have ended well for you. It needs to stop, for your sake more than anybody else's."

For a moment, the only sound inside the room was the low hum of the laptop.

"I'm sorry," Dr Vennell said eventually.

"It's not me you need to apologise to," Smith said.

"I've really missed you. I've missed working with you. Tell me about the suicides."

"You have got to be kidding me."

"Come on," Dr Vennell said. "I messed up, and I'm sorry, but I might be able to help you."

"How do you know about the suicides?"

"It's been all over the news. A spate of suicides in the city."

"I have to get back to work," Smith said.

"Please," Dr Vennell said. "Tell me about them."

Against his better judgement, Smith filled her in on the recent developments in the investigation. He also told her that he was now on The Preacher's list.

"Why do you think you're on that list?" she said when he'd finished.

"I can't figure it out. If we go according to his twisted logic, the only assumption to make is he wants me to kill myself to punish Whitton for her involvement in someone's death."

"And?"

"And," Smith said. "Nothing springs to mind. As far as I can recall, Whitton has never killed anyone."

"But you have."

"You know I have. Will you promise me you'll cease with this harassment of Porter?"

"On one condition."

"You're not in the position to bargain," Smith said. "If I hadn't warned you about that bot thing, your life could have become extremely unpleasant. Your reputation could have been ruined."

"You haven't heard my terms," Dr Vennell said.

"Go on then."

"Let me back in. I want to help you."

"I don't think you can help me with this one," Smith said. "The Preacher is like no serial killer I've ever come across before."

"You say that about all of them."

Smith had to smile at this. "Do I really?"

"You do," Dr Vennell said. "From what you've told me this one is no more special than any other. He clearly suffers from delusions of grandeur."

"Porter has already compiled a profile for us," Smith said. "I've heard all this before."

"Let me finish. The trigger for his behaviour is something devastating. And the suicide aspect is at the heart of that. Someone close to him killed themselves..."

"That's old news too," Smith cut her short. "We already know that."

"Shut up for a minute. Someone he loved killed themselves and your Preacher blames you and your wife for it."

Smith thought hard about this.

"No," he said. "This has only recently become personal. He's not doing this because of me or Whitton."

"Oh, but he is, Jason," Dr Vennell said. "Everything he's done thus far was leading up to what he plans to do with you. He is a narcissist, and he craves recognition. All of the others have merely been to get your attention. He has your undivided attention, doesn't he?"

"Of course he does. The psycho is threatening everybody I care about."

"This is all about you."

"I still don't buy it."

"He not only wants your attention," Dr Vennell said. "He wants it absolutely. This has been about you all along."

"How? I've already told you – Whitton has never killed anyone."

Dr Vennell looked him right in the eye. Smith maintained eye contact. "You're wrong there," Dr Vennell said. "He wants you to use a scalpel, doesn't he?"

Smith didn't recall mentioning this.

"How did you know that?"

Dr Vennell told him, and in an instant, everything became clear inside his head. Then the lights went out just as quickly.

CHAPTER FIFTY

Smith thought hard on the drive back to the station. Dr Vennell's theory was full of holes. The pretty psychologist had remembered something Smith had told her during their initial sessions. Smith had been referred to her in the wake of the *Electrician* investigation. She'd been tasked with determining whether he was fit for duty after almost losing his life. Smith recalled those early sessions well. He'd been surprised about how easy she was to talk to, and he'd told her things he'd spoken to very few people about.

One of those things was something that happened to him long before he met her. He'd related the time when he'd been seconds away from instant death. A ruthless killer and his sidekick were on the verge of ripping his heart from his chest when Chalmers and Whitton had rushed in. Chalmers had succeeded in putting the sidekick out of action and Whitton had ended the life of Smith's old nemesis. She'd killed him with a scalpel. One stab to the heart had been enough.

But this is where the holes started to appear. The person Whitton had killed was someone who had caused more heartache in Smith's life than any other, but Smith knew he had no family left. There were no loved ones left to seek revenge, and as far as Smith was aware, the sidekick was rotting in jail somewhere, so he couldn't be involved either.

The lights were switched back on when Smith pulled into the car park at the station, and he cursed himself for being so slow off the mark. He got out of the car without bothering to lock it and raced inside the station. He found the team in the canteen.

"You took your time grabbing a bite to eat," DI Smyth said.

"Sorry about that," Smith said. "Harry – that bloke who killed himself in prison up in Scotland. What else do we know about him?"

"It's a dead end, Sarge," DC Moore said. "He sliced his wrists open with a broken phone case. End of story."

"That's not what I asked. What else do we know about him?"

"He was in for life. It's probably why he chose to top himself."

"What was he in for?"

"How should I know?"

"Find out," Smith said.

"What's going on, Smith?" DI Smyth said.

"Pull up the records for the dead prisoner, Harry," Smith said. "Do it now."

DC Moore left the room and returned with his laptop. He booted it up and tapped the keypad.

"The bloke's name was Sebastian Lucas. Forty-six years old. He was inside for murder, and a whole load of other nasty stuff. He wasn't a very nice man. Hold on…"

DC Moore looked Smith in the eye.

"What is it?" Smith said.

"According to the records the arresting officer was someone by the name of McAdams but Chalmers and Whitton are mentioned in the report too. And you, Sarge."

"I almost lost my heart."

Everyone inside the canteen turned to look at him.

"He was the surgeon," Smith said. "He was Victor Boronov's surgeon. He was on the verge of cutting out my heart when Whitton and Chalmers arrived."

"We now have a solid connection," DI Smyth said. "I want to know everything about Sebastian Lucas. I want to know about his family and friends, and the people he was close to while he was inside. Which prison was he sent to?"

"HMP Glasgow, sir," DC Moore said.

"Get hold of someone there," DI Smyth said. "I want a detailed file on this man before the end of the day."

"You said his brother is dead," Smith said. "The one who lived in York?"

"Damian," DC Moore said. "He was killed in a car crash earlier in the year."

"Look into that car crash."

"What for?"

"Because something doesn't feel right here," Smith said. "And I hate it when that happens."

"Did you really almost lose your heart?" DC Moore said.

"No, Harry," Smith said. "I make shit like that up all the time just to get attention."

"Sorry, Sarge. I just thought…"

"What are we waiting for?" DI Smyth said. "I want to know everything about this surgeon psycho before anyone leaves today."

"He was albino," Smith said.

It had just occurred to him.

"Albino?" DI Smyth said.

"I don't remember much about that day, but I do remember him being an albino."

"OK," DI Smyth said. "Get to work."

Everybody but Smith left the canteen.

"Is there something on your mind?" DI Smyth said.

"You can tell Porter that he doesn't have to worry about his troll anymore."

"Go on."

"It's over," Smith said. "He won't be having any more trouble."

"Is that why he or she hasn't replied to the emails?"

"It's over," Smith said. "Let's leave it at that."

"Are you sure? Are you sure this is the end of it?"

"Positive, boss. He can move past it."

"We'll talk about this later," DI Smyth said. "We have more pressing matters to attend to."

"We can talk about it," Smith said. "But I've said all I have to say on the subject."

CHAPTER FIFTY ONE

"The car crash is legit, Sarge," DC Moore said to Smith inside the canteen. He'd found Smith sitting at the table by the window with his eyes closed, and at first he thought that Smith had nodded off. He hadn't – he was trying to make some sense out of everything that had happened recently, and he found it easier to do that with his eyes closed.

"Go on," Smith said, and opened his eyes.

"It's actually a funny story."

"I thought you said a man died in that crash," Smith said. "Do I need to start worrying about you?"

"I don't mean the crash itself," DC Moore said. "Damian Lucas was actually on his way up to Glasgow when it happened. He was driving up to sort some stuff out with the prison after his brother's suicide. The weather was bad – it was raining hard, and he misjudged the distance when he tried to overtake a truck on the A66. He hit another vehicle, head on and he was killed instantly."

"When was this?"

"February," DC Moore said. "A couple of days after his brother Sebastian topped himself."

Smith knew for a fact that this was important.

"What else do we know about the family?" he said.

"I haven't started looking into that," DC Moore said.

"Why the hell not? This is significant. A man dies in a car crash days after his brother commits suicide – we need to look more closely at the family. It's possible that someone from that family is The Preacher. Find out about other siblings. What about the parents? Losing two family members in such a short space of time would give anyone a strong motive to make the people responsible pay. That suicide is the catalyst for all of this. Do it now."

DC Moore left the canteen, passing DC King on the way out. She made a beeline for Smith's table.

"Are you OK, Sarge?"

"I've been better, Kerry," Smith told her.

"Anything I can do to help?"

"There is, actually. I have something I want to run past you – a possible scenario, and I want you to listen to it."

"OK."

"I want you to pick holes in it," Smith said. "Be as honest as you can."

"You know me, Sarge."

Smith did. DC King was one of the most straight-down-the-line people he'd ever met. That's why he enjoyed working with her so much.

"I went to see Dr Vennell earlier," he said. "To discuss something that was totally unrelated to the investigation, but she said something that got me thinking. Dr Vennel believes that this has been all about me from the very beginning."

"Why would she think that?" DC King said.

"I think she might be right. We know very little about The Preacher's other victims, but they all share one thing in common."

"They're all connected to deaths where the person responsible wasn't punished," DC King said.

"That's right," Smith said. "And his MO was the same for all of them. He selects only vulnerable targets – he manipulates them, and he keeps on pushing until they see only one way out. He issues his threats, and he makes it very clear that he knows everything about them. He leaves them little choice."

"He's done a lot of homework."

"He has. But it got me thinking about something you said. You couldn't believe that anyone would kill themselves because someone told them to –

no matter how frightening he is, very few rational people would give in to him."

"I wouldn't," DC King said.

"Me neither, Kerry. And that's why I'm starting to think that Dr Vennell was right. He's picked off the easiest victims first. He knows he'll have my utmost attention and when he has, he begins his campaign against me. He's threatened my wife and kids. He's issued threats against my extended family, and he's even included the dogs in this."

"You know who he is, don't you?" DC King said.

"I think I know who he's trying to avenge, and that's going to lead me to him. I need some more coffee."

He got up and walked over to the coffee machine. He returned with two cups.

"I've pissed a lot of people off during the course of my career. Shit like that seems to gravitate my way, and I've been involved in the deaths of many a scumbag. I won't go into details, but I'll tell you about one of them. I was working on a joint operation with a team from Cornwall. It wasn't unlike the *Workshop* investigation."

"I heard about it," DC King said. "Young people were being lured onto boats, only to have their organs removed."

"The maniac behind it was the most ruthless criminal I've ever met. Viktor Boronov. Him and me shared a very long history. We stopped him, and Whitton ended his life. I know for a fact that this psychopath has nobody left to seek revenge. I know that because I had a hand in killing them too."

"Do I need to be concerned, Sarge?"

Smith laughed. "I don't think so. After reconsidering what Dr Vennell said, I'm now convinced that this has nothing to do with Boronov. But there was someone else there that day. Boronov's surgeon. He was arrested and shipped off to prison."

"He was the one who killed himself with the broken phone."

"He was," Smith confirmed. "And a few days later his brother died in a car crash while he was on his way up to sort some stuff out with the prison. That's two dead brothers in the space of a few days."

"It's a solid motive," DC King said.

"And it's what we need to focus all of our energy on. Whitton and the kids are holed up in a pub because of this bastard. He's not stupid, and I've got a feeling that it's only a matter of time before he figures out where they are."

DC Moore returned with his laptop and a strange smile on his face. Smith couldn't translate it. It wasn't quite a happy smile – it was definitely something else.

"You've found something, haven't you?" Smith said.

"I have, Sarge," DC Moore said. "And I'm finding it hard to digest."

"Spit it out then."

"Damian Lucas wasn't the only Lucas brother. There's another one – and you are not going to believe who it is."

"What part of *spit it out* didn't you understand, Harry?"

"Sorry, Sarge," DC Moore said.

He placed the laptop on the table in front of Smith.

"What am I supposed to be looking at?" Smith said.

DC Moore pointed to the screen. "This is from births and deaths. Sebastian had a younger brother."

Smith looked at the name and he was still none the wiser.

"This doesn't ring any bells."

"I dug deeper," DC Moore said. "The younger brother changed his name by deed poll one week after Sebastian killed himself."

"Interesting," Smith said.

DC Moore tapped the keypad and pointed to the screen again.

"Does this one ring any bells?"

It certainly did. The bells in Smith's head were now so loud he was worried he was about to suffer a migraine attack.

CHAPTER FIFTY TWO

Whitton was frustrated. She shared Smith's concerns, but even though they'd only been confined to the Hog's Head for a relatively short space of time, cabin fever was setting in and it was making her agitated. Laura and Fran were driving her nuts. The initial excitement of staying in a pub had worn off and the girls were starting to get on Whitton's nerves.

Lucy and Darren seemed quite content with the situation. Lucy had brought some college work with her, and she was happy to occupy her time with that, and Darren had his laptop, and he was now abusing the free Wi-Fi at the pub. Andrew was oblivious to their predicament. His was a simple existence. Eat, sleep – repeat, and he wasn't aware of the drama that was unfolding.

"Can we go downstairs?" Laura asked.
"It's better if you stay up here in the room," Whitton said.
"There's nothing to do in here," Fran joined in.
"When is Dad coming?" Laura said.
"He's busy at work, sweetheart," Whitton said.
"He's always busy at work. He spends like, ten minutes a day with us."
"He has an important job."
"You always say that. Why can't he have a normal job like most dads? I wish I had another dad."
"Laura," Whitton said. "Stop being a spoilt brat and shut up."
The words came out a lot louder than she intended and when Laura took a sharp intake of breath and stepped back Whitton was overcome with guilt.

She placed a hand on Laura's shoulder. "Look, none of us want to be here, but it can't be helped. Your dad wouldn't have asked us to stay here if it wasn't necessary."
"Is someone going to hurt us?" It was Fran.

Whitton didn't know how to answer this.

"Nobody is going to hurt you," she said. "Not while you're here at the Hog's Head. Not with me here. I won't let anything happen to you. I tell you what – why don't you go downstairs and see if Marge has some ice cream."

"She does," Laura confirmed. "She has strawberry and chocolate."

"I'm going to have chocolate," Fran said.

"Me too," Laura said.

"Go on then," Whitton said. "Ask Marge to put it on our bill, and don't get in her way."

The girls were out of the room before Whitton had the chance to change her mind.

She left the room and walked down the corridor to Lucy and Darren's room. The door was wide open.

Whitton stuck her head inside. "Can I come in?"

Darren was sitting on the bed with his laptop on his legs. Lucy was nowhere to be seen, but the sound of the shower running in the bathroom explained things.

"How's it going?" Whitton asked.

"I'm actually a bit bored," Darren said. "I've finished all my IT work, and I've resorted to browsing social media."

Whitton laughed. "That bad, is it?"

"I hardly ever look at social media."

"Where's Andrew?"

"Lucy is giving him a bath," Darren said.

"We won't be stuck here for much longer," Whitton said.

"This is serious, isn't it?"

"It is," Whitton said. "But Jason is doing everything he can to find this man, and you know he won't stop looking until he's found him."

Darren nodded.

"I'll leave you to it," Whitton said.

She was halfway to the door when Darren stopped her.

"You need to take a look at this."

Whitton turned around. "What is it?"

Darren positioned his laptop so she could see the screen.

"It's an Instagram page," Whitton said.

"It's Laura's."

Whitton looked more closely. "How did she manage to create an Instagram account?"

Darren held up his hands. "Don't look at me."

"I'm going to have a serious word with that young lady."

"Before you do that, Darren said. "We could have a problem."

He tapped the keypad, and a photograph appeared on the screen. Whitton had seen Laura snapping away on her phone earlier but she didn't think it was anything to worry about. She was very wrong.

"How did an eight-year-old manage to do this?"

There were more photographs on the page. The majority of them were innocuous enough – some of them depicted food, and others were of Laura and Fran but one of them was definitely a cause for concern. It was a photograph of the bar downstairs. It could have been a bar inside any pub in the city if it weren't for the plaque on the wall behind the bar counter.

Hog's Head – traditional Yorkshire pub of the year, 2019.

"It gets worse," Darren said. "She's added text to that one."

We're stuck here for like, forever.

"I didn't think you could do that," Whitton said.

"It's pretty simple. You can customise a photo by tapping the Aa button."

"She's eight," Whitton reminded him.

"That's not the worst of it," Darren said. "Her security is non-existent. Anyone with an Insta account can access this."

"Can you delete it? Can you get rid of it?"

"Get me her phone and I can."

Whitton was out of the room in a flash.

The girls were nowhere to be seen when she got downstairs, and Whitton assumed that she would find them in the kitchen. They were familiar with it now, and Marge didn't seem to mind having them around. The pub was relatively quiet. It was a weekday afternoon, and only a few tables were occupied. Whitton walked up to the bar counter. A solitary barman was cleaning glasses behind it.

"Have you seen two little girls?" Whitton asked him.

"They went into the kitchen I think."

Whitton thanked him and pushed open the door at the side of the bar.

Marge was rolling pastry for a fresh batch of pies. Another woman was stirring something in a pot on the stovetop. Laura and Fran weren't there.

"Where are the girls?" Whitton asked Marge.

"I said they could eat their ice cream in the bar area."

"They're not there."

"Perhaps they went back up to the room," Marge said.

"They didn't," Whitton said. "I've just come from there."

"I'm sure they'll be around somewhere. Have you checked the Ladies?"

"I'll go and have a look."

The girls weren't in the Ladies. Whitton went back to the man behind the bar.

"Did you find them?" he said.

"They're not in the kitchen. Did you see them come out?"

"I'm sorry," he said. "I was busy back here. I'm sure they'll turn up."

"I'm sure they will."

Whitton didn't believe this for a second. Laura's Instagram post left little doubt about where they were, and the sickening feeling in the pit of her stomach told her that something was terribly wrong. The Preacher seemed to know everything about them, and she knew that the innocent post was a serious problem.

She left the pub and went outside. There were very few cars in the car park and all of them appeared to be empty. Whitton scanned the surrounding area. The Hog's Head wasn't exactly on the beaten track and there were hardly any people around. She was ready to go back inside the pub when something caused her to stop in her tracks. She'd spotted movement inside one of the vehicles, and it was a car she recognised. Without thinking, she rushed over to the black Land Rover and banged on the window.

The windows were tinted but she could make out two shapes in the back seat, and the shapes were very familiar. She tried the door handle, but it refused to open. The driver's door opened and a man got out.
Whitton was unable to speak for a moment.
"It's time to choose."
The figure standing in front of Whitton looked like Lenny Jenkins, but the words that came out of his mouth sounded nothing like the voice she remembered.
Whitton found her own voice. "If you hurt one hair on their heads, I will kill you with my bare hands."
"Relax, Erica. Nobody is going to do any hurting. Not if you do as I say."
Whitton opened her mouth to speak but Lenny got there first.
"And don't even think about making a scene. You do anything to attract attention, and your precious girls will die quickly."
He tapped on the window and it opened a fraction. Whitton gasped when she realised that Laura and Fran were both gagged. A woman was sitting between them – it was Sheila Jenkins, and the blade of the scalpel she was holding looked extremely sharp.

"What do you want?" Whitton said.

"It's not what I want," Lenny said. "It's what The Preacher wants."

"You're insane."

"I know everything – I see everything. If that makes me insane then so be it. But I'm not a monster."

Whitton didn't give an opinion about this.

"The little girls will be fine," Lenny said. "The passenger door is unlocked. Get in."

Whitton stared at him. The mullet was gone, and he was dressed in a plain blue shirt and a pair of trousers. She cast a glance at Laura and Fran in the back seat and she was shocked at what she saw. There was no fear in their eyes. If Whitton had to describe their expressions she would use the word *defiance*. Laura and Fran stared directly ahead as though they'd been punished by having their phones taken away from them.

"I'll let them go," The Preacher said. "You have my word that I'll let them go, unharmed. All you have to do is get in the front."

Whitton did as she was asked, and she was somewhat surprised when the back door opened, and Laura and Fran were set free.

"Run as fast as you can back to the pub," she screamed at them.

For once, the girls did exactly as they were told.

The Preacher got into the Land Rover and started the engine. Whitton knew she had to act quickly. She tried the door handle, but it wouldn't open. The Preacher tapped the steering wheel. "This thing is top of the range. Everything can be controlled by the buttons on the wheel, and before you consider your options, I'll make one thing absolutely clear to you. The number 11 surgical scalpel next to your throat is a hundred percent carbon steel. It will slice through everything important without too much effort." Whitton hadn't realised that the woman in the back seat was holding it to her neck, but she felt it now.

"I'd prefer it if we didn't have to go that route," The Preacher added. "It will make such a mess, and I've just had the interior valeted."

Whitton took a deep breath, and the blade of the scalpel became even more apparent.

"What do you want?" she said. "What are you going to do to me?"

The Preacher disengaged the handbrake and drove out of the car park.

"That depends entirely on Detective Sergeant Jason Smith."

CHAPTER FIFTY THREE

"Lenny Jenkins isn't at home," DI Smyth informed Smith.
The more they delved into the life of the man they were now positive was The Preacher the more things began to make sense. Lenny Jenkins changed his name very soon after his brother committed suicide in his cell at HMP Glasgow, and his other brother Sebastian lost his life in the car crash. His real name was Leonard Lucas. Jenkins was his mother's maiden name.

Smith cursed himself for getting taken in by Lenny's trailer-trash act. He'd fallen for it hook, line, and sinker and he felt so foolish. One by one, the pieces of the most baffling puzzle he'd ever seen started to fall into place. Everything that Lenny did was part of an intricate plan, and Smith had to admit that he felt a kind of twisted admiration for the man. He wondered if he'd finally met his match. He hadn't given a second thought to the way Lenny had asked him to remove his shoes before he came inside the house, and he cursed himself for that too. He'd been well and truly blindsided.

"Uniforms went in hard," DI Smyth said. "And they found the son cowering inside the bathroom. The kid had locked himself in. It looks like he played a small part in this."
"Wayne," Smith remembered. "He was at the Halloween party. He goes to the same college as Lucy. It was him who cut the power to the music, wasn't it?"
"It was," DI Smyth said. "He admitted it in the back of the car on the way here. He claims not to have been involved in any other part of it. It looks like he's petrified of his parents – especially his father."

Smith's phone started to ring. The screen told him that it was Lucy.
"Are you still at the pub?" he answered it.

"He's taken Mum."

The three words resulted in Smith's legs almost giving way. He managed to sit down before they did just that.

"Dad," Lucy said. "Are you still there?"

"I'm still here," Smith managed. "What happened?"

DI Smyth told Smith to put the phone on speakerphone. When Smith didn't respond, he took the phone and activated it himself.

"I couldn't get much out of Laura or Fran at first," Lucy said. "They burst into our room and started sobbing. We managed to calm them down, and Laura said Mum had been taken by a man and a woman."

"How the hell did he know?" Smith said. "How did he know where you were?"

"Laura has an Instagram account."

"What the fuck?"

"She posted a photo of the Hog's Head, and Darren thinks that's how he tracked us down."

"We'll find her," DI Smyth said. "What time did this happen?"

"About fifteen minutes ago," Lucy said.

"Why the hell didn't you call me sooner?" Smith said.

"It took a while to get anything out of Laura or Fran."

"They could be anywhere by now," Smith said. "What the fuck was Laura doing on Instagram? She's eight years old for God's sake."

"Calm down," DI Smyth said. "We'll find her."

"And how do you plan on doing that?"

"You let me worry about it."

"Stay exactly where you are," Smith told Lucy. "All of you."

With that, he ended the call.

He rubbed his eyes. His whole body felt numb now. It was as if all the blood had settled in his feet and his energy had been zapped along with it.

"Take a few deep breaths," DI Smyth ordered. "I need to make a few calls." He left Smith alone in the office. He was no sooner out the door when Smith's phone beeped to inform him that he'd received a message.

It was a single photograph, but it spoke to Smith more than any words could. Whitton was tied to a chair. There was a blindfold over her eyes and she had duct tape wrapped around her mouth. More tape secured her to the chair, and her hands were bound together. Smith couldn't see her feet in the shot. The effect was instant. All of the blood that seemed to have drained out of him suddenly flowed again, and his energy levels returned to normal. He expected the call that followed, and he was ready for it.

"The location of the house with the cellar will follow shortly." Lenny Jenkins didn't bother to disguise his voice now – there was little point anymore.

"You're a dead man, Lenny," Smith said. "Or would you prefer Leonard – Leonard Lucas?"

"*The Preacher* will suffice. You will tell nobody where you're going. I will know if you talk to anybody. You'll come alone. If you don't, I'll know. And I will kill her, Jason."

Smith shivered at the mention of his name.

DI Smyth returned. He gave Smith a thumbs up and mouthed two words. *Found her.*

Smith didn't register what he'd said. DI Smyth found a piece of paper and proceeded to write on it. Smith's mouth curled up in a grin that was definitely inappropriate under the circumstances.

"Do you understand?" The Preacher said.

"Whatever happens," Smith said. "You're a dead man. You do understand that, don't you?"

"The location of the house in Osbaldwick is on its way."

The line went dead, and Smith decided to take a chance. He brought up the number of the last caller and tapped dial. He wasn't expecting much and he was surprised when the call was answered.

"I forgot to tell you about your son," he said.

"I'll send the location now," The Preacher said.

"It's Wayne, isn't it?"

"The boy is no longer my concern."

"Thank fuck for that," Smith said. "Because when our officers arrived at your house, they were just too late. They found him in the bathroom. He'd managed to slice his wrists open with a piece from a broken phone. He was still warm, Leonard. Like I said, we were just too late. Sorry about that. It looks like he's with your brother in whatever hell he was sent to, so I suppose that's something at least."

The Preacher's response to this chilled Smith to the bone.

"When a general goes into battle, there will always be collateral damage. I am fighting a war on many fronts – a war that is like no war every fought before."

"You're a bit fucked in the head, aren't you?" Smith said.

"Sending the location now."

CHAPTER FIFTY FOUR

Smith eased his foot off the accelerator when the GPS on the dashboard told him he was four hundred metres from his destination. The Preacher had told him that the house with the cellar was in Osbaldwick, but according to the map it was actually located in Murton Park. The woman's voice told him he was going to turn right in fifty metres.

Smith did what she'd instructed. The gravel road didn't seem to lead anywhere, and he wondered if he'd been given the wrong location. He carried on past a cluster of buildings that looked like they hadn't been used for a while and when he was informed that his destination was on the left, Smith slowed down and stopped. He got out of the car and looked around. The nearest building was a fair distance away and Smith wasn't sure if he was in the right place.

The ringtone of his phone sounded, and he answered the call immediately.

"Follow the path east."

What do I look like? Smith thought. *A human compass.*

He reckoned that he needed to go left. It was the only logical direction to go in.

He looked around again. It was clear that The Preacher was observing him, but he had no idea where he was watching from. The only structure close by was the substation, and Smith didn't think he would be hiding out in there. He crouched down to remove his shoes, but the voice stopped him.

"There are no tracking devices this time. Follow the path east. After a minute or two you'll come to a converted barn. Slight change of plan. Wait there."

Smith took a final look around and did as The Preacher had asked. There was a chill in the air and the wind had picked up and Smith wondered if this was going to make DI Smyth's plan problematic. The DI had convinced him that this was the only way, and Smith had to have faith in him. He didn't have any other option.

His first impression when he arrived at the converted barn was not a positive one. The building was in dire need of repair and Smith wondered what it had actually been converted into. It was obvious that it hadn't been used for anything for a very long time. The roof was falling away in places, and the plasterwork on the exterior looked like it had been carried out by a bored child. There were four windows on the west side of the building and the glass was broken in all of them.

Smith walked up to the stable door at the front and pushed it open. The solution to the puzzle of where The Preacher was watching from was standing in the middle of the barn. He'd been here all along, observing Smith through the windows. There was only one, huge room inside the barn. It didn't look like it had been converted at all. There was nothing inside, but a number of boxes stacked neatly against one of the walls. Smith couldn't figure out where the cellar could be.

"You made it."

Smith looked The Preacher up and down. His face was definitely Lenny Jenkins's face but that was the only thing that resembled the *Walmart* creature Smith had come to know well. Gone was the *mullet* hairstyle – the porn star moustache was no longer there, and the trademark tracksuit was also absent today. If Smith passed this man on the street he wouldn't look twice at him.

"There's no cellar," he said.

"There's no cellar," The Preacher repeated. "You're not here to die in a cellar."

"I'm intrigued. Does that mean you're going to give yourself up?"

"No. You will die today. I imagine you'll have a few questions for me."

"A few," Smith said.

"Then I'll indulge you. Call it a last request for a condemned man."

"Sarah Peters," Smith said. "How do you know Sarah Peters?"

"I'm acquainted with her brother, Keith. I befriended him not long after my brother took his own life. It wasn't difficult to get into the house that day. Anything else?"

"What was the story with the Maths teacher?" Smith said. "Why did you kill Tony Grigg?"

This had been puzzling him ever since he'd found the rotting corpse of Mr Grigg.

"He made my boy's life hell at college. I put a stop to it."

"You killed a man because he was a bit hard on your kid?" Smith said. "You really are insane."

"Madness is a subjective concept. Time's almost up."

"How did you know that Vincent Allen helped his mother to die?" Smith said.

This had also been bugging him.

"Cause of death was ruled to be natural causes. There was nothing suspicious about it."

"I was once friends with Vincent. He confided in me. You were somewhat lacking in your detection, Smith. I really expected more from you."

"You fucked up by taking my wife, you arsehole," Smith said.

"I don't think so."

"I don't suppose you've heard anything from the lovely Sheila, have you?" Smith said.

Silence.

"I didn't think so," Smith said. "And that's because right now, she's being treated like shit in a holding cell. I asked the duty sergeant to offer her our finest hospitality, and that's not a good thing."

"You're lying."

"My boss actually got the idea from you," Smith explained. "The tracker in the shoe was genius. My guys followed the signal in DS Whitton's shoe in the Land Rover, and Sheila wasn't difficult to overpower."

"I don't believe you."

"She was found not too far from here," Smith said.

This got a slight reaction out of the Preacher. His left cheek twitched, and he broke eye contact.

"I forget the name of the lodge," Smith said. "But you rented one of the log cabins there. It wouldn't have been my first choice."

The Preacher didn't speak. His gaze shifted to the stack of boxes.

"Did I mention that you're a dead man?" Smith said after a while.

"We've all got to die sometime. My work is almost done here on earth anyway."

Smith started to laugh. He took out his cigarettes and lighter and held them up.

"Do you mind? I have a sudden craving. You know what? You're like a bad caricature of a bad caricature, if that makes any sense. It's like you've modelled yourself on every cliched bad guy in every movie ever made. You even talk like one."

"I'm your worst nightmare, Jason Smith."

Smith laughed again. "I'd say that proves my point beautifully, wouldn't you? I have to admit, there was a time when I thought I'd finally come up against something really special. I did – I thought this was the time I was going to come out second best. You're good, but now I know you're not that good. You don't mind if I smoke while we carry on this conversation, do you?"

"I wouldn't advise it."

He walked across the room and removed the lid from one of the boxes.

"PE4," he said without turning around.

Smith put the cigarettes and lighter back inside his pocket. He'd seen PE4 before and this looked very similar.

"The other boxes are full of it too," The Preacher said. "Twenty kilogrammes altogether – enough to render you unidentifiable at an autopsy."

"That's probably your best line so far," Smith said. "You're actually starting to grow on me."

The Preacher pulled something from his pocket. It looked like an ordinary key fob for a vehicle.

"One click and it's all over."

"It'll be over for you too," Smith pointed out.

"I told you," The Preacher said. "My work is almost done."

Smith sighed. "I much preferred the autopsy line."

"One click."

"Go for it," Smith said.

He watched as the man who called himself *The Preacher* looked at the key fob. He watched as he breathed in deeply and held the air in his lungs. He closed his eyes and raised his chin to the top of the barn. Then his finger moved towards the button on the key fob.

"It's all over."

Smith raised his hand and scratched his left ear. He hoped that the people watching the proceedings could see him do it.

There was a loud crack, and The Preacher's eyes shot open. He glanced at Smith and then his eyes came to rest on the dark patch that was spreading on his left shoulder. The round from the Parker-Hale M85 had passed through the flesh on the outside of the shoulder, but it was enough to cause the detonator to drop to the ground. Later, Smith would question DI Smyth about the accuracy of the shot, to which the DI would explain that a direct hit from that particular rifle would have probably resulted in the arm being detached from the body.

Smith wasn't concerned about the competency of DI Smyth's sniper right now. He had more pressing matters to attend to. The Preacher was clutching his shoulder, but Smith knew he would soon remember the explosives. He dived to the floor and just managed to grab the remote detonator before The Preacher's hand found it. Smith got to his feet and gave the wounded man a kick under the chin. The Preacher went down. He got to his knees and looked up at Smith.

"I won't stop," he said. "No matter what you do to me, this will not stop." Smith gave him another, harder kick and this time he went down and stayed down.

He went outside and walked in the direction of the substation. He was halfway there when people began to file out and make their way towards him. One of them was DI Smyth. Smith gave him the thumbs up and stopped walking. DI Smyth approached.

"It's over," Smith said.

"Is he dead?"

Smith shook his head. "The shot hit him in the side of the shoulder."

"Brad is one of the best."

"I thought he'd missed," Smith said. "I thought this wind had caused him some problems."

"He's trained to take that into account. We didn't want him dead, did we?" Smith's silence didn't exactly answer the question.

"Smith," DI Smyth said.

"He deserves to die."

"He's not going anywhere. What happened in there?"

"He had no intention of making me kill myself," Smith said. "He was going to blow us both up. There's enough PE4 in there to blow up the Minister. You'd better get everybody back – at least until the bomb team have given it the all clear."

"Come on then," DI Smyth said.

He started to walk back towards the substation.

Smith stayed put. He could feel the key fob device in his hand. He held it up to inspect it. There was only one button.

DI Smyth took a step closer. His eyes and Smith's eyes made contact for a brief moment, then he understood what Smith was about to do.

"Smith. Don't."

Smith wasn't listening.

"Smith. Don't do this. It's not worth it. Come on."

"You might want to get back," Smith said. "I have no idea how big this blast is going to be."

"Put down that detonator," DI Smyth said. "That is a direct order."

"You know me and direct orders, boss. Get the hell back."

DI Smyth hesitated for a second and then he made a hasty retreat.

Smith weighed the remote in his hand. It felt far too light for a device that could cause such destruction. He placed his finger over the button and pressed down.

Nothing happened, and Smith wondered if The Preacher had been bluffing all along. He hadn't. The blast that followed turned the volume off inside Smith's head. The shockwave knocked him to the ground in an instant and he was now able to register sound again. He wished he wasn't – the constant ringing inside his ears made him wonder if his brain was about to explode. He raised his head and looked through the smoke to what was once a barn. The wind was even stronger now and the smoke cleared quickly. Smith's first thought when the result of the blast became apparent, was the barn conversion he'd just carried out wasn't the greatest, but it was probably a vast improvement.

His next thought was a peculiar one. He wondered if Lenny Jenkins regretted playing with fireworks now. That was the last thing that went through his mind before his head hit the dirt and he succumbed to a dreamless sleep.

CHAPTER FIFTY FIVE

"Where is he?" DI Smyth asked.

"Where he's been for the past three days since he was discharged from hospital," Whitton said. "In the bedroom, reading."

Smith had spent just two days in hospital. He'd discharged himself on Bonfire Night, against the doctor's orders. He wasn't able to hear the fireworks going off that night – the bomb blast had affected his hearing, but the doctors had assured him that it was temporary, and it should return to normal soon.

There wasn't much left of Lenny Jenkins inside the barn, and Smith's thoughts often turned to one of the last things the self-proclaimed *Preacher* had spoken before he died.

Enough to render you unidentifiable at an autopsy.

DI Smyth had retrieved the remote detonator before anyone saw it. It was destined to remain at the bottom of the River Ouse forever. As far as everybody else was concerned, The Preacher was the one responsible for detonating the explosives. The officers who searched the bomb site didn't find a detonator, and they didn't expect to. The damage was extensive. Smith had dodged a bullet once again, and once again it was DI Smyth who had saved his skin.

Sheila Jenkins had refused to talk since she was apprehended, but Whitton had given a detailed account of what had happened that day. She'd been taken to a log cabin at a lodge not far from where Smith and The Preacher met up, and she'd been bound and tied to a chair. She was as surprised as Sheila was when the uniformed officers burst in. She wasn't aware of the tracking device in her shoe. DI Smyth had explained to her that it was better that she didn't know. Whitton was a terrible liar, and it was better this way. Whether Sheila decided to talk or not, she was going to spend the rest of her life in prison. Sheila's son Wayne was also keeping quiet, and Smith didn't give a damn. As far as he was concerned, neither of them were his problem anymore. He'd made it quite clear to DI Smyth that his days in York CID were ancient history.

"How are his ears?" DI Smyth said.

"I think he's feigning deafness," Whitton said. "He claims not to be able to hear, but I know him too well. He can hear as well as any of us."

"I'll just pop my head round the door then."

DI Smyth went upstairs to Smith and Whitton's bedroom. Smith was sitting up on the bed with a book in front of him. DI Smyth saw that it was a biography of *Black Sabbath*.

"How are you?" he said.

"Did you know," Smith said. "That Tony Iommi lost the tips of two of his fingers in an accident when he was seventeen?"

"Interesting."

"It was his right hand," Smith said. "And, because he was a left-handed player, it meant that it was his fretboard hand. He was told he would never play again."

"Is there a point to this story?"

"He almost quit," Smith said. "And if he had, we never would have had *Black Sabbath*."

"What made him change his mind?"

"He was a stubborn bastard, I guess."

Smith put the book on the bedside table.

"Is there something I can help you with?"

"I thought you couldn't hear?" DI Smyth said.

"It's called selective deafness. If you're here to convince me to come back to work I may lose the ability to hear again – the docs warned me that it can come and go."

"I figured that your decision to quit was a spur of the moment thing. I expected you to change your mind."

"That's not going to happen. I'm tired, boss. I'm tired of chasing scumbags. I'm sick of waking up every morning wondering if someone in my family is going to be in danger. A bloke can only live like that for so long before he loses his mind."

DI Smyth nodded but remained silent.

"Will there be anything else?" Smith said.

"How did you get Porter's troll to stop harassing him?"

"It's better if you don't know."

"Are you ever going to tell me who it was?"

"Nope," Smith said.

"I'll let you get back to your book," DI Smyth said. "I must admit, I expected more of you. What will you do?"

"I hadn't thought that far ahead. Perhaps I'll become a full-time musician – maybe form a band."

DI Smyth smiled and left the room.

Shortly afterwards Whitton came in. She wasn't alone – Laura, Fran and Lucy were with her. All four of them sat on the bed with Smith.

"We need to talk," Whitton said.

"You're being such a baby." It was Laura.

"I thought you had more balls than this," Lucy joined in.

Smith laughed without meaning to.

"What is this," he said. "A fucking intervention?"

"Dad," Lucy said. "Language. Laura and Fran are in the room."

Smith looked at Fran. "I assume you have an opinion you'd like to share?"

"You need to go back to work," Fran said.

Smith got up from the bed. "It's getting a bit crowded in here. I'm going outside for a smoke."

"So, that's a yes then?" Whitton said.

"You're not going to quit?" Lucy asked.

"I don't want you to do anything else," Laura said. "I want you to be a police detective. I'm sorry for being a…"

She looked at Whitton.

"Spoilt brat," Whitton reminded her.

"One of those," Laura said. "Darren deleted my Instagram account."

"Glad to hear it," Smith said. "You're wasting your time. I've made up my mind."

He was halfway out the door when Laura's voice stopped him.

"Do you know what I thought when that man and woman took me and Fran?"

Smith turned around.

"I wasn't even scared."

"Me neither," Fran seconded.

"I wasn't scared because I knew I would be alright because my dad is a police detective."

Smith could feel tears welling up in his eyes, but he resisted the urge to let them flow. Now wasn't the time.

"Well?" Laura said. "Are you still a police detective?"

Smith smiled at her, turned around and walked out of the room.

"We'll see," he called back. "We'll see."

THE END

Printed in Great Britain
by Amazon